Felicia

HOLDING ON

KIKI MALONE

I truly could not have done this without you. thank you for being so amazing

Love.
KiKi Malone

Kiki Malone

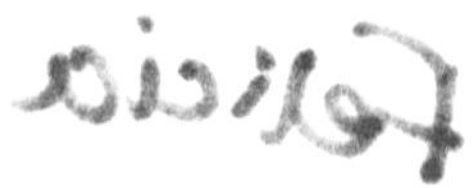

This is a work of fiction. Names, characters, places, and incidents either are the product of the author's imagination or are used fictitiously. Any resemblance to actual persons, living or dead, events, or locales is entirely coincidental.

First paperback Edition August 2019

Ebook Edition August 2019

Cover Design: Just Write Creations

Editor: Miss K Edits

Formatting: Heartstrings Inc

Proofreaders: Melissa Brannon and Michelle Trelford

DEDICATION

Friends are the family we get to choose...
This is for you...

PART ONE

CHAPTER ONE
CARTER

HAPPY SURPRISES?

4 YEARS EARLIER

ON MY WAY home from work, I'm smiling even though I'm not sure why. I know it was a good day in the office, but there's more to it than that. There's no real explanation for this exhilaration. I just wish I knew the reason. Maybe my heart is happy, and my soul is screaming out to celebrate.

Thinking about celebrating, I decide to make a quick stop at the store on the way home. Maggie will be at the house when I get there; she called me earlier and told me we needed to talk. I want to pick up some flowers for her to make her day as bright as mine. I'll probably grab a bottle of that wine she likes so much too. I'm not sure what she wants to talk about, but I have a feeling it's going to be a good chat. I'm even more excited now and I can't wait to get home. When Maggie and I are together, things are great, but after a couple glasses of her favorite wine the temperature rises quickly and it gets steamy. I'm looking forward to us get happier together tonight, if you get my drift.

Walking into the flower shop, I spot a big bouquet of pink lilies and roses. All the flowers are at full bloom, which is unusual for this time of year. They're perfect, and she will love them. After I pay the clerk, I walk next door to the liquor store, to pick up a bottle of Rosé, Maggie's favorite. I'm thankful to buy it pre-chilled because, truthfully, who wants to wait for it to get cold enough to drink? Not me. I want to walk in the house, pop the cork and get on with enjoying the rest of this day with some wine. Delayed gratification is overrated, at least where my beverages are concerned, but there are some other areas where, I enjoy it much more.

When I get back in the car, I take the little key off my keyring before reaching over to open the glovebox. I open the secret compartment and pull out the Tiffany box that has been hidden in there for a few weeks. I think tonight is the night. It's time for Maggie and me to take our relationship to the next level. We've been together for over a year and I'm positive this is where I want our journey to go next. I'm ready to start the family that I've always wanted and know in my heart, that now is the time. There's no doubt in my mind that Maggie will say yes. She loves the life I give her and never having to work. Hell, she's already carrying a black card, but we've been together long enough that I can't see her not being giddy about this.

Pulling into my driveway, I notice Maggie's car parked awkwardly. It's like she rushed in and just didn't care that her front tires were on my lawn. That irks me a little. I like everything well-maintained, and now I'll have tire marks imbedded in my grass. It's not normal for her to be so careless. She likes things as neat and tidy as I do. She may actually be a little pickier than I am when it comes to some things. The flower garden is all her and looks like little flower soldiers all lined up in a row. They're not allowed to grow crooked. If they do, she'll tie them to a stick to train them to grow straight or get angry and yank them out of the dirt to plant something else.

I shake my head to clear it a little and remind myself that I'm still in a great mood. I'm not letting this get in the way. We have celebrating to do this evening. That is, after she hears my proposal and says yes. Maybe she was just in a rush to get into the house to surprise me, like she often likes to do.

There's nothing like walking into my home to find my beautiful girlfriend splayed across the table covered in nothing but a chocolate sundae. Oh, the memories of that day. I licked her clean, only to dirty her up all over again. There were no complaints about the messes that day.

Opening my front door, I hear muffled sounds coming from the kitchen. I'm assuming Maggie is on the phone with one of her girlfriends, so I take off my jacket, hang it in the closet and put my keys and wallet on the table by the door. I note that Maggie's aren't there; she usually leaves everything where I do. Again, we have a routine. She may not live here, but she has the same routines as I do when we walk into each other's homes.

I may just be jumping to conclusions when there may be a reason she didn't notice what she'd done. My mood is quickly shifting and I'm not happy about it.

I enter the kitchen, still hoping to see my girlfriend splayed out on the table again, only to find her sitting in a chair with her head down, her long blonde hair and her hands covering her face. I can hear the low whimpers of her cries. Her shoulders are shaking with her sobs, and now my good mood has shifted into one of deep concern.

I immediately place the flowers and the wine on the counter before dropping to my knees in front of her. I gently grasp her chin and turn her face up to look into mine. What I see in her eyes breaks my heart. Her emerald eyes, usually filled with laughter and light, are red and puffy from crying. This isn't normal for Maggie. As a matter of fact, the entire year and a half we've been together, I've never seen her cry. She's always been so happy and full of light, even though she has moments where she can be aloof. What I'm seeing now is gloom and doom and I'll do anything to make it right for her.

Wiping the tears from her cheeks and under her eyes, I gently lay a kiss to her thin lips.

"What's wrong, love?" I calmly inquire, continuing to wipe her tears.

"I can't believe this happened," she states. "I never planned this; we have to take care of this right away, Carter! This can't happen. Not to me. Never to me." She's sobbing now, her shoulders heaving up and down as she tries to catch her breath.

I don't understand what she's talking about, but still try to assure her that I'll take care of whatever it is that happened to hurt her so deeply. I never want to see her unhappy like this. It's beginning to break my heart.

"Don't you understand, you just can't say you'll take care of it," she cries. "This is your fault, I never planned for this! You did this to me, you have to make it go away!"

She's getting louder now, screaming at me. She's borderline hysterical and I don't understand what I've done to upset her. But you can be damned sure, I'm going to do everything in my power to make it right. I've given this woman everything her heart desires and this is no different.

She should know that by now. Hell, I bought her that lavish apartment she insisted she needed, so that she wouldn't have to worry about rent anymore. I wanted her to just take the leap and move in with me, but she told me that she didn't want to live with someone she wasn't married to. It just wasn't right. The fact that we've been sexually active since the day we met never seemed to be an issue for her, so never understood her issues over cohabitating.

So, I did what I thought was right and bought her a condo. It's a beautiful space, if I'm being honest. If I didn't plan to have a big family one day, I would've bought myself something similar.

However, I decided a while back that I no longer wanted to rent and the time was right for me to purchase a house. I wanted the place that I bought to be more than just a house. I wanted it to be the setting for my future as well.

My house is large, it has five bedrooms and three full baths. The master bedroom alone is five hundred square feet with a full bathroom suite. I love it here and can't wait to start my family with Maggie. There are three bedrooms dedicated to the children I hope to have some day. There's a guest suite complete with its own bathroom where family and friends could stay should they want to spend a night or longer. Hell, I don't care. I love having my friends and family close to me.

Maggie looks at me with something akin to anger in her eyes that tells me somehow I'm the one to blame.

"Tell me, love, what is it that I've done?" I ask, hoping my initial assessment is correct. "I'll do whatever you need, you just have to tell me what I've done to hurt you so deeply."

"How could you not know?" she screams again. Spittle is flying out of her mouth, she's so angry. "You told me we were safe, you always said we were safe, I believed you! I never wanted to believe you'd go behind my back and do this to me! You've always wanted this. I know you did it on purpose! This is all your fault!"

She keeps going on and on about whatever it is that is wrong and how I am the cause and still, I can't figure out what it could be. We do live a safe life. I'm financially secure, I have no known enemies. How can she feel that she's not safe?

Now I'm starting to get frustrated and the concern I felt earlier has escalated into something akin to fear. I can't imagine how Maggie wouldn't feel safe with me. Did something happen where she lives? Something around her apartment building?

"What's happened Maggie?" I ask, again. "Did something happen at your building, is it not safe to be there anymore? Tell me, I need to know. I'll hire a new security team for the building, I'll do anything you need. But you need to tell me what happened first. Let me call Mikael, he'll know what to do."

Mikael Rufus is my longtime best friend and runs a security firm. He'll be able to help with anything safety related. He knows how much Maggie means to me, and he'd do anything to keep her just as safe as I would. Yes, I want Maggie to move here with me, but I wouldn't do anything just to force her hand. I know I said I wanted to propose tonight and was hoping deep down she'd finally decide to move in, but I want her to make that decision on her own, not because she feels forced because she doesn't feel safe in the apartment I purchased just for her.

"Just one phone call and Mikael will make sure you feel safe again," I continue. "I'm just going to need some details to give him. I need you to calm down a little bit, sweetheart and tell me what the issue is."

I get up to grab my phone that I dropped on the counter with the flowers and wine, but Maggie stops me, grabbing my arm with a vise-like grip.

"It's not fucking security or anything to do with my apartment, you asshole!" she screams at me. "You fucking implanted this thing in my stomach, and I want it out! I can't believe I'm pregnant, but you did this! You tricked me into getting pregnant, and now you have to help me get rid of it! You better fix this fast!"

My jaw drops at her statement.

Wait a minute. What is that she just said? Is she having a baby? My baby? Are my ears deceiving me? There's no way she said what I thought she said. Did she really say it? Did she really say we're having a baby?

This is a little sooner than I imagined starting our family, but now I know I was right when I decided to propose tonight. My heart and soul must've known this was coming. This is probably why I felt so elated when I left the office today. This is why, in my heart, I knew today was the day. This is it. The time is now. It's perfect.

I'm grinning from ear to ear as I pull Maggie up to my chest and hold her tightly to me. The happiness I feel so deep down to my soul right now is more than I imagined would happen today. I want some of my happiness to seep out of my pores and straight into Maggie. There's no reason for her to be sad. Maybe she thought I wouldn't be happy and that's why she's upset. But she's wrong, this is a happy occasion. I need to erase her tears and her fears.

"No worries, love," I tell her, holding her tightly to my chest. "I'm ready for this. We're ready for this. We can start our family now. As a matter of fact, there's something I wanted to ask you tonight."

"Family?" she yells as she rips herself out of my arms. "What the fuck are you talking about, Carter? I never wanted to have a family! I knew you did this on purpose. Hell, you probably ripped your condom off in the middle of us fucking just to make sure this happened!"

She begins to pace back and forth in front of me and continues on, "You're so good at fucking that I probably never realized you were pulling out of me to take it off! Now, I'm sure this is all your fault! You always droned on about how you wanted to be a father one day and have a huge family. You never asked me what I wanted. You just assumed."

She's grabbing at her hair, pulling tightly on the strands. "Well, newsflash, Carter, I never, ever want to be a mother," she yells at a pitch I didn't know she could reach. "I thought you knew that since I never put myself in your family scenarios whenever you'd go on and on about those dreams of yours. How could you do this to me?"

All the happiness I felt just a moment ago vanishes with her words. I had no idea she felt this way. What does she mean she never wanted to be a mother? I've always told her my dreams of having a large family. If she's never wanted that, why would she pursue a long-term relationship with me? My heart is breaking and I don't know where I could even start to fix this situation

Somehow, I have to convince her that things will all be okay.

Maybe once she gets used to the idea of being pregnant, she'll start realizing she was meant to be a mother. I have to help her see that this is a blessing and not a curse that we need to get rid of. She can't kill my baby. This baby is a godsend. Whether she sees it now or not, I'm sure she'll see it soon enough. She's just got to give this a chance.

"Maggie, my love, please calm down," I tell her as I guide her back to the chair she was sitting in. "We need to think rationally here. Let's sit down and talk about this. You may be upset right now, but truly this is a blessing. I'd never trick you or remove a condom when we make love. This is a surprise gift for us both. Yeah, maybe it's sooner than we expected, but I've always wanted a family and you knew this. Maybe you wanted the same and that's why you never ran for the hills when I've talked about the family I saw in our future." I tell her as calmly as possible. I feel like I need to tame a rabid animal instead of enjoying this news with the mother of my unborn child. Shit, I'm going to be a father.

"There is no talking, Carter!" she yells again as she stands, knocking the chair to the floor with how abrupt she is. "I'm not ruining my body so that your demon seed can grow inside of me! I definitely DO NOT want children. Which is why I made the appointment with my doctor to ensure I could never get pregnant accidently, but instead she told me it was too late. I am already fucking pregnant. How could you do this to me? I work so hard to keep this perfection, which you so enjoy."

As she goes on, she's pointing to the amazing parts of her body that I do enjoy.

"Look at these boobs, Carter," she says, as she palms each one in her hands. My hands are feeling quite jealous that they are not the ones holding them. Her breasts are perfect, not too large, but not small by any means. "I read that after having kids, they get saggy. I don't want them to sag, I want them to stay perky."

"And look at this waistline," she continues as she puts her hands around her waist. Her waist is a little too slim, in my opinion. I'd like to see her add a few inches there, but now isn't the time to tell her that.

"This ass, can you imagine how fat it's going to get?" she asks as she contorts her body to where she's looking at said ass. That ass is perfect to me, I think to myself as my cock starts to harden.

"Oh no," she says, pointing to the bulge in my pants. "Don't even think about that. How could you even think I'd let that near me after this news?"

"Yes, your body is perfect, Maggie," I reply as I shift my now aching dick. "But it will be more perfect with my baby growing in your belly. To me, there will never be anything more beautiful than you carrying our child. A child we made out of love."

I may be stretching things just a little bit since we've never exchanged 'I love yous', but I know that's where we are headed. There's nothing that tells me we aren't on that path to love. As a matter of fact, knowing she's carrying my baby may have actually escalated my feelings for her.

"I love you, Maggie," I hear myself say before I even realize the words have come out of my mouth. I don't take it back because just at that moment it hits me how true that feeling is. It's why I was so ready to propose tonight.

The look on her face tells me that she definitely didn't see them coming. Hell, I didn't see them coming before I said it, but right now I feel the words and so much more.

"You love me?" she asks, quietly. As if she never imagined it could happen.

"Yes," I reply, realizing that this is an actual truth. I really do love her.

"Then how could you do this to me?" she asks, a little more relaxed this time. "How could you think that ruining my body is a good thing? If you loved me, you never would have done this."

Her voice gets quieter with each statement she makes. I don't understand it.

"Maggie," I say, as I drop to one knee. "I want to marry you." I pull the box out of my pocket and open it.

She puts her hand over her mouth when she sees the size of the ring in front of her. It's a five-carat cushion cut diamond, surrounded by a hidden halo of sparkling round diamonds, with additional diamonds set around the platinum band. I had this ring custom-made for her. I didn't shop around to find something she may or may not like. I know her style, so I had this ring designed to reflect her perfection. My future wife only deserves the best.

"What?" she gasps, not taking her eyes off the ring.

"Marry me, Maggie," I say, as I start to stand. I grab her cheeks and gently lift her face to get her to look into my eyes. "Marry me and have our baby." I place my hand on her stomach. "Make me the happiest man in the world. I'll give you both the best life you can imagine and everything your heart desires if it's the last thing I do, I promise you."

"Everything?" she asks.

"Just say the word, and the world is yours, sweetheart. You just have to say you'll be my wife and have this baby."

"If I do this… after I have this thing, I want plastic surgery to repair any damage to my body. I want a trainer to get me back into my perfect body, I want a new car, mine is dated and I want something nicer, something more expensive and classy. Oh, and while you're at it, I want a new credit card. I'd like to have a variety instead of just using the same one every time I shop. I want to be able to travel wherever and whenever I want. I want it all Carter. Are you really saying you'll give all that to me?" she asks.

"Anything, baby. Just say you'll have my baby and that you'll marry me," I tell her again. Right now, I'll agree to anything. I really want to start my family, and now we've jump started it without even intentionally doing so.

"I don't want to have any more kids after this thing is out of me, you understand that right? This is your one and done. You won't have the huge family you want. I don't want this thing, and you're going to make me do it, but there's no way I'll ever do this again. I want everything taken care of as soon as this demon is out of me to ensure that it can never happen. Do you promise me that, Carter? Are you willing to not have your so-called dream just to have this one creature ruin my body?"

I realize at that moment she really does hate this baby right now, but I don't. I'm already in love with our child she's carrying. I'm sure, in time, she'll love him or her as much as I already do. I'm going to agree to her conditions because as sure as the sky is blue, I'm sure she will grow to love this life we created together. There's no way a mother doesn't grow to love her children. She's just scared, I'm sure of it.

"Anything and everything, my love. Anything," I tell her with newfound confidence.

"Fine, have it your way," she replies. "But remember everything you've promised me. I'm going to hold you to it."

With that, she grabs her coat, keys and purse, and walks to the door. Before she leaves, however, she walks back to me and snatches the ring out of my hand. She looks back to me, then at the ring and says, "I'm sure this cost upwards of ten grand, so I'm sure once the time comes, I can get a pretty penny for it."

What the hell does she mean she'll get a pretty penny for it? I really hope that was an offhanded comment and she didn't realize what she was saying. I paid a small fortune for it and can't imagine she'd ever want to get rid of something so beautiful. Never mind the meaning behind it and the commitment I'm showing her I want to make by giving it to her.

I'll give her time. This has to work out, I think to myself.

CHAPTER TWO
CARTER

THE FIRST APPOINTMENT

THE LAST FEW weeks have been a whirlwind of emotions. I'm elated we're going to be starting our family, however, Maggie has been distant. So distant, that I've only seen her once since she told me about the pregnancy, and I proposed. And when I did see her, it was such a quick visit that I didn't even have time to notice if she was wearing her engagement ring.

She came by my office to pick up the new Centurion Card I got her from American Express. When she found out that she was going to have two cards with unlimited funds, she made it to my office in record time. I don't ever remember her moving that quickly for anything. She's sure made a dent in those two cards in the last few weeks. From spa treatments, to hair appointments, to clothes and shoes. I saw some men's stores on the bill too and wonder if she's bought me somethings to surprise me.

Should it concern me that she's bought nothing for the baby? Or any kind of maternity clothes? Maybe, maybe not. I mean, it's not like the baby is coming tomorrow or that she'll be showing any time soon if the books I've been reading are anything to go by.

Yes, I've been doing a lot of reading. I want to know everything that's going to happen day by day, if not hour by hour. I want to know how much my baby grows daily. I want to know when I'll be able to start to enjoy watching my fiancé's stomach grow. I want to know how to expect her to be feeling, so that I can be there and help her, every step of the way.

But I can't do that right now. She's not allowing me to do so. She hasn't made herself available for more than the five minutes she was here to get that card.

I made her an appointment with one of the top obstetricians in the state and our first appointment is today. Doctor Kristin Hall is the top obstetrician in the state who specializes in high risk pregnancies. While Maggie isn't considered high risk at the moment, I only want the best care for her and my child. I meant it when I told her that I will give her anything and everything her heart desires, and that includes the best maternity care available.

I offered to pick her up and take her to the appointment, but she told me she was busy this morning and would meet me there. That disappointed me a bit because I was looking forward to holding her hand and walking in to the office together. To introduce ourselves to the staff at the facility as Mr. and Mrs. Montgomery.

I know it's not official yet, but it will be next month. We, well she, wanted to get married before she starts showing. She thinks it's important that she looks slim and trim in her wedding photos. She doesn't want to look like 'a fat slob' as she called it. I told her many times, she won't be fat, she'll be even more beautiful than she ever has been in my eyes. To me, there's nothing more beautiful than a woman carrying your child. Yeah, I know I'm acting like a great big sap right now but this is one of my dreams coming true.

Looking at my computer, I notice that it's almost time for our appointment. I stand, grab my jacket off the back of my chair and put it on. I am both excited and worried about this appointment.

I get to the doctor's office and notice that Maggie has yet to arrive. I don't know why it surprises me that she's late, it's normal Maggie behavior. I explained to her on the phone that she needed to make sure she was on time for all of our appointments as this is an esteemed doctor and she doesn't like to wait for anyone. This is unacceptable and I will have a few words with her about it once the appointment is over. I won't react in front of people and embarrass her or I.

I walk up to the reception desk to let them know I'm here but am still waiting for Maggie to arrive.

"Hello, I'm here for the appointment for Mr. and Mrs. Montgomery," I tell her.

"Where is Mrs. Montgomery?" the receptionist asks as she gives me an eye roll.

"She's on her way," I tell her. "She must've hit some traffic as we were coming from two different places." At least I'm hoping she's on her way and that's the case. I intend to find out when she gets here.

"Well, we can't get started without the mother to be, so please have a seat and let me know when she arrives," she tells me without looking at me and continues to look at whatever has her interest on the computer screen.

Fifteen minutes later, Maggie finally strolls into the office, seeming to not have a care in the world. She walks up to reception, not even noticing me sitting here.

"Hi, you have an appointment for Maggie Lucia?" I hear her snidely ask.

"I'm sorry, ma'am," the receptionist replies, "I don't have anyone on the schedule today with that name. Are you sure you have the right place?"

"It's for Mr. and Mrs. Montgomery," I say as I stand and walk back over to the desk. "We're not quite married yet but will be by the time the baby is born. I made the appointment under that name so we don't have to change the records at our next appointment."

"I'm going to have to change it to her legal name," she informs us with a lopsided smile. "I'll change the record and let the doctor know you've both arrived. Please have a seat and wait to be called in."

I'm trying really hard not to let her see how irritated I am with her behavior. I put my arm around Maggie's waist and usher her to a chair and take a seat next to her.

"Hi, love," I greet before I start with the questions. "Did you run into traffic on your way here?"

"No," she answers and pulls her phone out of her purse. She's acting like she doesn't have a care in the world and my temper is starting to ignite once more.

What the fuck?

"You were supposed to be here fifteen minutes ago," I tell her as calmly as I can muster. "Did something happen that made you late?"

"No," she replies once again, completely engrossed in whatever she's doing on her phone.

I'm getting a bit more frustrated now. Why is she acting this way and come to think of it, where the fuck is her ring? She's not wearing anything on her hand, and that angers me.

"Want to explain to me why you were late then? Why you're not wearing your engagement ring?" I ask, pointing to her hand.

She keeps scrolling on her phone and is now completely ignoring me. Why she's acting this way, I don't understand. This appointment is important; she needs to be more in the here and now, not on her fucking phone.

"Maggie, what is up with you?" I ask, snatching her phone out of her hand and making her pay attention to me.

"Nothing," she exclaims, rather roughly. "I'm here, aren't I? I didn't get rid of this thing like you asked and I'm here. Can't you just be happy about that? And I didn't feel like wearing the ring. I don't have to. There's nothing that says I actually have to wear the ring. You didn't say it was a prerequisite, therefore, I made the decision not to wear the ring. If you have a problem with that..." She doesn't continue and just shrugs her shoulders while taking her phone out of my hands.

Nothing is going like I expected it to, nothing at all.

The books I've read, state that there's a possibility of mood swings during pregnancy. It has something to do with hormones going out of whack, so I'm just going to shrug it off as that. She'll come around, I know it.

"Miss Lucia, Mr. Montgomery," a nurse calls from an open door. "If you'll follow me, we'll see you now."

Maggie and I get up and walk through the door to the where the nurse is waiting.

"Please follow me," the nurse says as she walks down the hall, leading the way. "Just in here. Maggie, I'm going to need for you to take all of your clothing off and use the robe there on the table to cover yourself. Mr. Montgomery can either stay in here with you or he can wait in the hall until you are ready."

"He can wait in the hall," Maggie states. I don't understand why she doesn't want me in the room. I've seen her naked millions of times.

"Maggie?" I begin to question, however, with the nasty look on her face, I turn on my heel and walk out of the room to wait until I'm informed it's okay to come back inside.

"You can wait right here until she's ready," the nurse says to me, sympathy in her eyes. It's like she knows something is wrong with us and can see right through how much Maggie's rejection just stung.

Five minutes later, the nurse comes back to the room and notices me still standing outside, she gives me a questioning look and knocks on the door.

"Miss Lucia, are you ready?" she asks through the door.

"Yes, come in," Maggie answers.

The nurse gives me a questioning look once again and opens the door. She allows me to walk in first and I see Maggie sitting on the exam table, crying again. It immediately raises my concern.

Rushing over to the table, I grab her by her face and ask, "What's wrong my love? Why are you crying? Is something wrong with the baby?"

"Nothing is wrong with this thing," she answers. "I just can't believe you're still making me do this."

The nurse looks at us once again and asks, "Do you need a moment?" to which Maggie shakes her head no. "Is it okay to proceed with the examination?"

Maggie nods her head and the nurse gets started. She draws a few vials of blood from Maggie and takes all of her vital statistics. She tells us that everything seems alright so far and lets us know that the doctor will be with us shortly before exiting the room.

I decide to take these few moments and try to cheer up my fiancée.

"Maggie, my love, my beautiful wife to be," I start. "I don't know why you're so upset. Remember, this is a good thing. We're getting married, we're starting a family. Our life from here on out is going to be amazing. You're giving me the most precious gift a woman could ever give a man. I love you and our baby so much. I can't wait for you to see how beautiful this is all going to be."

Maggie looks at me with tears still in her eyes and shrugs her shoulders once again.

"I mean, I will have everything I want, and you get to have this thing, so maybe you're right," she relents.

I'm elated that she actually agrees to the situation. I grab her hand and anxiously wait for the doctor to arrive. Finally, I'm all smiles and feeling so much better about having our baby and getting the family I've always wanted.

When the doctor walks in, Maggie squeezes my hand a little tighter. This makes me smile a bit wider. I feel her being nervous is a good sign.

"Hello, Miss Lucia and Mr. Montgomery, I'm Doctor Hall. I'll be your obstetrician for this pregnancy," she says as she reaches for Maggie's hand.

Maggie shakes her hand daintily and says nothing.

"Hello," I reply. "Please, you're about to be the most important person in our lives until this little one arrives, call me Carter, and this is Maggie. We look forward to seeing you and thank you for taking us in today, even though we were a bit late." I don't want to just say Maggie was late. I'll place the blame on both of us here.

"No problem, my other appointment had to cancel so I had extra time on my schedule today. Shall we get started?" she asks.

"That's fine," Maggie replies snidely.

"Yes, please," I reply and give Maggie a look that I hope conveys to her my disappointment with her attitude.

"Okay, Maggie, looking at your chart, it seems like you are about eight weeks along. I'm going to do a physical examination and feel around your breasts and belly first. Then, since you are only eight weeks, I'm going to take that Doppler over there and insert it into your vagina, so we can get a look at the fetus. I will use a condom on the wand and some gel to make it easier for insertion. Hopefully, we'll be able to see the size of the fetus and hear the heartbeat. Is all of this okay with you?" the doctor asks in a kind and motherly tone.

"That's fine," Maggie says and just waves her hand at the doctor.

"Okay, I need you to lay back first and I'll do the exterior examination now."

Maggie lays back and I watch as the doctor pulls down Maggie's gown and starts to examine her breasts.

I notice a mark on Maggie's breast that resembles a hickey, but we haven't been together since before she found out she was pregnant so that can't be. It's probably just a bruise from her working out so much, so I let it slide.

The doctor notices the bruise and comments, "Okay, you two, I know that things can get heavy during sex, but I highly recommend you refrain from leaving marks behind. Not only during pregnancy, but always. Hickeys, although they seem like a good idea are very bad.

It's essentially causing a blood clot to form at the surface of the skin, and blood clots are never a good thing. So, please, restrain yourself from doing so." The doctor looks pointedly at me, trying not to smirk.

"Oh," Maggie says quickly, "that's not a hickey, I must've, um, bruised myself while, um, working out."

The doctor looks at her quizzically and gets back to her examination.

I'm letting this go for now. If Maggie says it happened during a workout, then that's what happened. The doctor doesn't need to make assumptions. This has happened to Maggie quite a few times since we've been together. So, it's not like I'm not used to finding these types of bruises on her.

"Maggie," I say looking at her, "maybe it's time to reduce your workouts so this doesn't happen anymore. I mean, I know it's pretty common for you to get these bruises, but maybe, at least while you're carrying our baby, you should cut your workouts."

"I'm not going to stop working out, Carter," Maggie answers.

The doctor looks at us again with a strange expression but continues her examination.

When she gets to Maggie's abdomen, she lifts the gown a little, looks at me with an expression I can't decipher, and then puts it back down. She starts feeling around Maggie's stomach without lifting the gown again. Seeming satisfied with everything, she looks at both of us and smiles awkwardly.

"Okay, we're ready for an internal examination," she says. "Maggie, if you'll just put your feet into these slots and shift your bottom to the end of the bed as though you are getting a normal gynecological exam, I will get the ultrasound machine ready to take a look at what's inside."

Maggie shifts to the position the doctor asked her to, and stares at the ceiling.

"Okay, you're going to feel a little pressure when I insert this," the doctor tells her, holding up something that looks like a dildo with a condom on it. Internally, I cringe. I imagine that thing won't be comfortable.

Maggie just shrugs, seeming nonchalant about everything and continues to gaze at the ceiling.

I watch the monitor carefully as the doctor moves the stick around, seemingly taking measurements and jotting down whatever she's seeing. Her face shows concern and I'm wondering if something is wrong, but I don't want to distract her. I notice multiple spots on the monitor and wonder if something is wrong with Maggie or our baby. It's hard for me to sit here in silence while the doctor does whatever it is that she's doing, but I manage to make it through.

Finally, after a few minutes, the doctor turns to look at us while still holding the dildo looking thing inside of Maggie.

"So, I was wondering," she starts.

That immediately raises my interest and I sit up even straighter in my chair. I notice that at this point, even Maggie seems to have stiffened up and is paying attention to the doctor.

"Are there any multiples in either of your families?" the doctor asks looking back and forth between Maggie and me.

"Multiples, what do you mean multiples?" both Maggie and I ask at the same time.

"Multiples, as in multiple baby pregnancies," the doctor answers us. "Twins, triplets, or anything the like?"

I look at Maggie and she looks back at me confused.

"No," I answer. "Not that either one of us is aware of."

Both Maggie and I are only children. Both of our parents were only children. So, nothing we know about our family line would have any multiple children born at the same time.

"Does this mean there's more than one thing inside me?" Maggie screeches.

Wow, that one even hurt my ears.

"Maggie, love, calm down," I tell her and grab her hand again.

"Let's listen to what the doctor has to say before you get yourself worked up."

I'm trying to calm her down but deep inside my heart is racing. I had a hard time convincing her to have one child. If she's having two, I know that will lead to another argument and her possibly not wanting to have our children.

Wow, children, as in two at one time. This makes my heart happier and more fearful all at once.

"I'm not having two things, Carter!" Maggie yells. "I already told you this was a one and done, I refuse to have two! You will have to take them out." Maggie is looking right at the doctor now with a look that screams 'Do what I say'.

"Maggie, look at me," I say in a pacifying tone.

When she turns to look at me, I swear I see murder in her eyes.

"Let's just listen to what the doctor has to say, okay?" I plead. "We don't know what's going on yet and I don't want you to make any rash decisions. Everything will be fine. I promised you, if you had my baby, I would do anything for you. I mean that, love. I love you and my baby, well babies, I'm guessing now, more than anything and I will give you whatever you want. Let's see what's going on before you make a decision you can't take back."

I'm scared and I'm pleading, I know. I'll do anything to have my babies. I'll resort to begging on my hands and knees if that's what it'll take to get Maggie to agree. She can't take my babies from me. I know it's her body and we're not married, so ultimately, it's her decision to make, but I can't let that happen. I'll convince her that this is what she wants, even if it takes my last breath to do so. Before I have a chance to speak any further, the doctor cuts in.

"Maggie, I can't do what you are asking at this time," the doctor explains. "If you are looking to terminate this pregnancy, you would need to make a different appointment. This appointment is only for information and evaluation purposes. For a termination, the procedure takes a lot more time and care and we are not set up for that at the moment. However, if at the end of this appointment, you are resigned to terminate, you can make an appointment with our receptionist for some time next week."

The doctor looks at me with sympathetic eyes and says, "Mr. Montgomery, I'm sorry. I'll step out for a few moments and give you two some time to talk."

She removes the wand from Maggie, cleans it up and goes to step out of the room. Before she leaves, she turns to me and holds up three fingers and points to the screen on the monitor while Maggie isn't looking.

Holy shit. Three babies. There's no way in fucking hell Maggie is getting rid of *three* of my kids. Over my dead body will she do something so egregious. If I have to tie her down and lock her in the basement, I will.

I shift my gaze to the monitor and notice three circles surrounding three little dots on the screen. Tears come to my eyes as I realize that those are *my* babies, right there in front of me. I can't lose those precious babies. With everything in me, I'm going to make this work!

"Maggie, look at me," I start. "I want these babies. I'll do anything you ask if you'll just have these babies for me. You want to have surgery so you can't have any more kids after this, fine, it's done. You want plastic surgery to repair any stretch marks or scars you'll get from having these babies, consider it done. Anything, Mags, anything, and it's yours. You want me to hire a nanny for you, I'll start looking tomorrow. But Maggie, I can't let you terminate this pregnancy, promise me, you won't do this to me, to us, to them."

I finish that last statement while pointing to the screen. Tears are running down my face just imagining not being able to ever hold my children.

Maggie finally looks at the screen and turns white as a ghost. I've heard the expression said millions of times, but actually witnessing it happen is unreal.

"Three?" she whispers. "Three of them. No, no, no. There's no way. Three bowling balls stretching my stomach. Do you know what that'll do to my skin? Oh, no. No way. Nuh-uh, not happening. Oh my God, what have you done? No, I just can't."

She's crying harder now. Pathetically, this actually gives me hope as she stares at the screen crying. I'm sitting here believing with all hope that maybe seeing the babies have her changing her mind.

"I'm making the appointment, Carter, you can't stop me."

I get down on my knees and take both of Maggie's hands into mine. I'm begging now, no doubt about it.

"Please Maggie, the world, baby, don't do this, you can have the world," I sob as the words come out of my mouth. "They mean everything to me, don't do this, please, please, please, Maggie. I'm begging you. I'll give up everything for you to give me those babies."

Maggie looks at me hard. Then, something like resolve comes over her and I see a smile come to her lips.

"Fine, Carter," she relents. "You can have your demons, but I guarantee, you will rue the day you made me do this. Now, get out!"

I get to my feet and got to kiss Maggie on the head. She yanks herself away from me before I even reach her.

"Thank you, Maggie," I cry. "You won't regret this, I promise. I love you."

I turn and grab the door, taking one last peek at the monitor before I walk out. As the door shuts behind me, I hear Maggie say, "Oh, I won't regret this, but you sure will, Carter, I promise *you* that."

CHAPTER THREE
CARTER

TRYING TO HOLD ON

WHEN I LEFT the doctor's office after finding out we were having triplets, I had expected Maggie's attitude toward me to get worse. Especially after I heard her parting words.

As soon as I walked out of the exam room, the doctor was waiting outside the door for me. She handed me a sleeve of pictures she took while doing the examination and I thanked her for them. She informed me that if Maggie was going through with the pregnancy, she would need to be considered high-risk and that she would need to have appointments more often than if this was a single pregnancy. I guess we did need this doctor afterall.

I walked back up front to the reception area and worked with the receptionist on the appointments Maggie would need for the remainder of the pregnancy. After that was all ironed out, I sat in the chair and waited for Maggie to come out.

After waiting for more than 10 minutes, I walked back up to the reception desk. "Excuse me, is there a reason that Maggie hasn't come out yet?" The receptionist gets up from behind the desk and walks to the back to check on Maggie. When she returns, she has a sympathetic look on her face.

"I'm sorry, Mr. Montgomery, it looks like she went out the back door."

"Thank you," I replied, "I'll see you in a month."

I walked out of the office with my head down, staring at the pictures of my babies. This should be a happy time for me, instead I am feeling an overwhelming sadness.

When I get home, I am resolute to spend the day with the photo of my babies alone and in agony. My heart is breaking. My family might not happen, and it hurts like no one could believe.

Next thing I know, Maggie strides into the house with a smile on her face. Surprised, I jump up from the couch and stand there staring at her.

"Well, I'm home," she shrugs. "My shit is in the car. Take it to the master bedroom and then move your shit out of there. You're not staying in my room until we're married, and yes, we are getting married. Exactly one month from today. Make it happen. I will not sign a prenup, you already told me everything is mine. If you change your mind, so do I and goodbye to these things," she says as she points to her stomach.

"Just so we're clear, you're going to plan our wedding, the way I want it. I will have everything I dreamed of. Make it happen," she continues. "Once these are out of me, I'll have a personal trainer of *my* choosing, and that spare room needs to be converted to a workout room."

I look at her, dumbfounded. This is not what I was expecting from her, after I left that office alone. I expected her to be distant, to walk away from everything, for her to hate me and our children. Instead, she's standing in front of me telling me we're actually going to be a family. My heart, I don't know if it can take any more of this up and down, but she's here, in my home, telling me she's giving me everything I want. I'm not going to turn her down.

"Okay," I reply. "I'll do as you ask. I can't wait for you to be my wife. I can't wait for you to have our babies and to be a family."

Before I walk outside to get her things, she starts to walk up to the bedroom. She turns around and calls my name and I look up at her.

"By the way," she says, "you bought me the new Audi Q7 today, thank you."

I don't argue, don't complain. She obviously thought of the babies when she decided I was buying her the car. It's efficient and safe and big enough for three car seats when the babies arrive.

---

1 MONTH later

To say the last four weeks have been a whirlwind is an understatement. Maggie seems to have accepted her pregnancy and has fully moved into the master suite at home. Instead of converting the guest bedroom into a workout room as Maggie suggested, I decided to build an addition onto the house instead. Construction is going fast, and Maggie should be able to use that room soon enough. I've already hired her a personal trainer that she insisted on having right away instead of waiting until the end of her pregnancy. She's been working with him a few times a week while I'm at work and tells me he's exactly what she was looking for. He knows how to handle her body just right, especially since she's pregnant.

Maggie is looking as beautiful as ever but won't let me touch her. She tells me that after I left, the doctor said that because she's carrying triplets, she should be careful having sexual relationships. Because of that, she's asked me to refrain from touching her and I've respected her wishes.

It hasn't been easy, though, I'll tell you that. Having this sexy as fuck woman living in the same house as me, walking around in nothing but tight workout clothes all the time and knowing she's carrying my babies, has been a workout on my libido. My poor hands should be hardened with calluses at this point.

But tonight, tonight will be different.

Tonight, Maggie will be my wife. She will legally be mine, and we can finally share the same bed. She has promised me that tonight, I can make love to her as husband and wife, as long as I'm careful not to hurt her or the babies. She wants to make sure we consummate the marriage right way. The fact that she is actually considering the babies, makes me fall in love with her even more. I will love her easily and happily, and never forget what she's doing for us.

According to the books, Maggie has to be as sexually frustrated as I am. All the specialists claim that pregnancy heightens sexuality, and since it's been months since we've been together, tonight's looking to be epic.

My dick hardens just thinking about being able to have Maggie again. He's suffering, my hand just isn't enough to get the satisfaction he is used to. He's used to long workout sessions, beating the shit out of the pussy he likes to call his home. Oh, fucking hell, guess I'm gonna need another shower to relieve the stress before our wedding tonight.

An hour later, after tugging and working my dick until it is almost raw, I finally get out of the shower, a little more satisfied than when I went in. I'm not completely satisfied, though, but it will have to do for now. If I don't start to get ready, I'm going to miss my own wedding.

Maggie stayed at her apartment last night, insisting that I not see the bride before the ceremony. I don't know why she's being superstitious now, we're going about all of this backwards already.

When I tried to call her last night, she answered the phone all breathy, telling me she was working out and couldn't cut her workout short, so she'd talk to me tomorrow. I hung up, saddened that I couldn't talk to my soon-to-be wife before our wedding day.

She's so hung up on working out, I swear that's all she ever does. Doesn't she realize she's already perfect to me?

A knock sounds on my door, and I know it's Mikael coming to pick me up. He's my best man and has been a good sounding board and my rock since all this transpired. Sometimes, I don't know what I'd do without that man by my side.

Mikael walks straight into my room and looks me up and down. I swear, that man has some gay tendencies sometimes, but hey, I'm not one to judge.

"Looking almost as good as me," Mikael says, grabbing the lapels on his tuxedo jacket.

"Keep telling yourself that, man," I reply. "I'm the one who gets to marry that gorgeous woman who is having my children today. And I'm the one who gets to bring her home afterwards and fuck her all night. Little cockblockers who will cry at the most inopportune time."

Mikael looks at me and starts laughing. "Yeah, you are the lucky one. Shitty diapers for days, months, years to come. Baby puke all over you, the smells, the crying, never mind from one baby, but from three at the same time!" He starts laughing harder now as if it's all a joke.

"I can't wait," I shrug. It's like a dream to me. You'll never find me complaining when it comes to my children. I don't care how bad they may stink or how many sleepless hours I have. These are my kids and I will do anything for them.

"Let's go, Daddy, before you're late," Mikael says, humor still painting his voice.

We walk to the door and I take a moment to look back. When I come back here tonight, I'll have everything I've ever wanted in life —the family I've always dreamed of in one quick shot and a wife I will love and cherish for the rest of my life. My life couldn't be happier or more complete.

STANDING at the altar with Mikael and the minister, I anxiously wait for my bride to walk down the aisle.

"You can still back out," Mikael jokes beside me. Knowing my best friend, he'd get me out of here before anyone could blink.

"Nah, this is what I want," I answer him honestly. And it is. I love my bride and can't wait to show her tonight how much I've missed having her in my arms. Thinking dirty thoughts about what will happen when I get her to the honeymoon suite tonight run through my head. I quickly glance over at the minister and smile. I don't need him to lecture me on having dirty thoughts right now.

"Are you ready, Carter?" the minister asks.

"Yes, sir, I am," I answer him.

I look out at the reception hall we've booked for this occasion. I would have liked to have been married in a church, but Maggie didn't want that. We're getting married in the same place as our reception. I guess it'll be easier to sneak off with her after our vows and hopefully get a quickie in before the actual party starts. Again, there I go with dirty thoughts. That's what happens when you've been waiting to have sex with your soon to be wife.

There aren't too many guests here for the actual ceremony as our family is scarce. Maggie and I both are only children and I lost my parents long ago. Maggie doesn't speak to her parents, so she refused to even tell them we were getting married. We have less than fifty people in attendance for the ceremony and will have about one hundred and fifty for the reception.

The entrance music starts as my eyes immediately go to the door that Maggie will be walking through.

I'm in awe of her beauty as she walks down the aisle in front of all of our family and friends. She's breathtakingly beautiful.

Her gown is a perfect princess gown, tight on the top and flaring out at the waist. The top, a pure perfect white, gradually turning pink until it is a full pink at the bottom. The most beautiful ombre dress I have ever seen, adorning her perfect body. Her beautiful blonde hair is curled to perfection and cascades beautifully over her shoulders and down her back. Her makeup subdued, barely there, giving her natural beauty the chance to shine. I can't believe in just a few moments, this beauty is going to be my wife.

The minister starts his practiced spiel on matrimony and I phase out most of what he has to say. I have no interest in this part. I just want to get to the part where he pronounces us husband and wife. When I'll finally get to kiss my bride.

"No," I suddenly hear and have to shake my head to clear it.

"Excuse me?" the minister asks.

"I said no," Maggie states and looks me in the eye. "I'm not marrying him. I don't want this. I'm leaving." She gives me one last look that conveys she's not even sorry and quickly walks away.

No? She fucking said no?

I spent tens of thousands of dollars making this wedding happen exactly the way she wanted it. The special flowers she wanted flown in, the custom wedding dress, this expensive venue that cost me so much more for booking on short notice. All for her to make a fool out of me and say no. I did everything she asked of me, making all of her dreams come true, giving her everything she asked for to make this day perfect. Yes, the money was a lot but most importantly, we've both been waiting for this day and what it means. At least, I thought we both were.

I rush behind her as she leaves the room, snatching her hand as she tries to run away from me.

"What the fuck, Maggie?" I ask as calmly as I can. "What do you mean no, you can't marry me? Why now, why would you do this?"

"I changed my mind, Carter, I can't have these babies," she says. She points to her non-existent stomach. "Look at what they are doing to me already. I'm so fucking fat! I can't do this. You'll have to find someone else."

I drop to my knees. This *can't* happen. No, no, no.

"Maggie, please, baby, what are you saying?" I ask, hoping that she's not saying what I think she is.

"What I'm saying, Carter," she begins, "is that I will not have these babies you are so desperate for. I will not have these things ruining my body just so you can be happy. That's what I'm saying, Carter."

My world is being ripped from me. I'm running multiple scenarios through my head to try to figure out how to stop this. There's got to be a way. I can't let her take these babies from me. I've already started buying things for their nursery. We decided not to find out what we're having so I'm doing the nursery all in neutral colors. They already own my heart, taking them away will shatter me.

Maggie doesn't know this, but part of the construction to build the workout room was extending out the top floor to make a nursery that connects to the master bedroom. I wanted the nursery to be as close to our room as possible. It was going to be a surprise I gave her tonight as her wedding gift.

I've seen her rub her stomach, I thought she was starting to care for our babies. I've seen her holding her stomach in the mirror when she thinks I'm not looking. She looked like she loves our children. Have I been wrong this last month? Why is she suddenly changing her mind?

"Wait," I say, standing back up and grabbing her wrist again before she walks away. "I'll pay you. Ten thousand dollars a month," I say before I even think it through. I know how much monetary things make her happy and at the moment, it's all I have left to offer.

This makes her pause in her steps.

"Fifty," she replies.

"Done," I exclaim, without even a thought. If this is what it takes to make sure those babies are born, so be it. They are priceless to me. She could've said a million and I would have agreed.

"Fine," she answers. Relief begins to course through me. "And I'm staying in the master bedroom, alone. The moment I have these things, you will pay for me to get my body back. I want to erase any evidence of having them. There won't be a trace of a scar, or you'll pay. Oh, and just to be clear, you will not ever touch me again. You will never have a piece of my body. You'll sleep alone and don't even think about dating or going and fucking someone else. If I even think that you may be with someone else, I'm out. You'll never get these." She waves to her stomach once again.

I don't argue, I don't even answer. I'm just relieved at this point that she agreed to have our children. As I watch her walk away, I drop to my knees and put my hands to the floor in front of me. Crying, sobbing. Letting it all out. If anyone thinks I'm a pussy because I'm sitting here crying, fuck them. My life was just torn apart. I know I should be happy that I will have my babies, but having it happen this way isn't what I was expecting.

Today was supposed to be perfect and now it's all turned to shit. I don't understand how it all went wrong. I was going to have the life I always wanted, the family I always wanted. But now… now, it's not going to be even close to how I imagined. I won't have the loving wife; I won't have the doting mother. I won't have any of that. The only thing that I'll have is my three babies. Three babies that will depend on me. Three children who will have anything and everything if I have any say to it. And, Lord, hear me now, they *will* have everything their hearts desire.

I don't know how much time passes as I pray here on my hands and knees, but, next thing I know, Mikael is putting me in his car. I don't even remember getting up off the floor, never mind being able to walk out of the reception hall and to his car.

I know I must've made a fool out of myself, but I don't care. Mikael tells me he's driving me home, but I can't be there. I tell him to take me to his place instead. He doesn't ask any questions and just heads to his house.

When we arrive at his place, he leaves me alone in the living room and I quickly tear off my tuxedo. This is my best friend, he won't care that I'm practically naked in his living room. I'm going to burn this fucking thing. I don't ever want to see it again.

"Here," he says when he walks back into the room, throwing

some sweats and a t-shirt at me. Guess he knew I was getting out of that suit, as he changed out of his as well.

"Thanks, man," I answer then put on the clothes he gave me.

"We're having bourbon tonight. Plan to get fucked up," he says to me.

I don't argue, I just sit my ass down on his leather sofa and wait for him to return.

When he comes back into the room, he has two bottles of top shelf bourbon in his hands and no glasses. I look at him questioningly.

"No pretenses with glasses, asshole," he says as he shrugs. "We both know we'll finish at least a bottle each before this night is over, so get to chugging," he finishes as he hands me a bottle.

"Wait, what about the guests at the wedding," I ask, finally remembering that there were one hundred and fifty people at the hall waiting for us to get married.

"I took care of all that, man," Mikael answers, his head shaking. "After what I witnessed her saying to you in the hall, I knew there was no way in hell I was letting you get up in front of everyone and try to explain what happened."

I realize then that Mikael is more than a best friend, he's the brother I never had. He's right when he says I couldn't have handled that on my own. He knows me too well.

"Where did I go wrong?" I ask as I take my first sip. That first one burns, but I know that soon I won't feel anything. He knows that was a rhetorical question and doesn't bother answering. We both sit here and stew. I know, being the brother he is, this is tearing him apart as much as it is me. He loved Maggie too, like a sister. He may have teased us about the babies, but he was also excited. He couldn't wait to be the uncle that spoiled the three of them. He wasn't wrong when he said we'd both drink at least a bottle tonight.

That was the last thing I remembered thinking before I woke up the next day with the sun shining in my eyes. I look around the room and notice two empty and two half-full bottles of bourbon.

Mikael must've found his way to his bed last night because he's nowhere in sight.

I get up, clean up the mess, and grab my wadded-up tux. I leave Mikael a note on the table that reads 'Thank you for being the man you are,' and leave. Time to go home and face the music.

CHAPTER FOUR
CARTER

THE BABIES ARE HERE!

6 MONTHS LATER

THE LAST SIX months have gone by with me both brokenhearted and happy at the same time.

Construction on both the workout room and the nursery has been completed. I was going to move the nursery after my fallout with Maggie at our wedding, but she insisted that the nursery stay right next to her. She took over the design and creation. She wouldn't let me help her in any way. Because I made those promises to her on our wedding day, I let her take the reins. I have no idea what the nursery actually looks like, but it's not important right now. What's important is that soon I will have my children.

She's grown to care for the children she's carrying, at least that much has changed. She's always talking to her belly. She's not allowed me to talk to them or touch her stomach. I feel when these babies are born, they're not even going to know who I am. All the experts say talking to the babies in the womb is what helps them recognize you and comfort them when they are born.

Maggie has reluctantly agreed to allow me to be in the birthing room when she delivers our babies. She tells me she is having them for me, after all. All of our doctor's appointments have gone well. The doctor tells us the babies have grown perfectly and on schedule. It's just a matter of time now before they arrive. We are lucky to have made it this far as a high percentage of triplets are delivered very early.

Sitting here in the guest room, I'm trying to focus on work. There's so much to finish before the babies get here and I'm having trouble concentrating.

I've been working from home the last month because I want to be here for Maggie, whatever she needs. She's having a hard time moving around these days with how large her stomach has grown. Sometimes, I truly feel bad about how much her belly has stretched. I can sympathize with her apprehension on having three babies at one time. In all this time, I never imagined she would expand this much.

Not that she's not beautiful, hell, she's the most stunning person I've ever laid my eyes on. Those are my babies she's carrying and nurturing. She's done everything she's supposed to do to ensure they grow healthy while she carries them. She kept up her workout routine until she was about six months along and the doctor warned her that her cervix would need to be sutured because she was doing too much and was afraid if she didn't stop, she would give birth way too early and potentially lose them. At that point, I insisted that she stop and told Marco he would be paid, but he was not to return to the house to train Maggie again until six weeks after the babies were born. He wasn't very happy, but he didn't want to be fired and lose the huge paycheck he was receiving.

I kept my word to Maggie, as well. Every month I deposited fifty thousand dollars into her bank account. I don't know what she's doing with the money, nor do I care, but I can't imagine she's been using it. Everything she's purchased, be for herself or the babies has been on my Centurion and Black Cards.

A lot of changes were happening at the office too. With me owning the accounting firm and the building it's housed in, I have the ability to make any changes I deem necessary. I decided that I'm not going to have Maggie take care of our children alone. Instead, I created a daycare at work. I'll be able to take the children to work with me a few days a week so that she'll have time to rest and heal. I know she will want that plastic surgery for her stretch marks as soon as she can have it and will need a lot of time to recover from that as well. I don't want her to have to worry about the babies while she recovers. It will be too much stress and after carrying them for the last nine months, and what her body will go through to deliver them, I could at least give her as much time as she needs to heal.

Suddenly, I hear a scream coming from upstairs. I jump to my feet and haul ass through the house and up the stairs. These aren't Maggie's normal screams, these are blood-curdling screams and I know something must be wrong. Even though I wouldn't normally enter Maggie's room without her permission, I barrel through the door to see what's the matter.

Maggie is lying on her bed with her face contorted in pain. She's writhing on her bed, screaming and crying.

"Get them out, oh my God, get them out!" she screams, tears running down her face.

She's in labor, that much I can tell, due to all of the videos I've watched preparing for this day. I have to figure out a way to get her to calm down and get dressed. We need to get to the hospital; these babies are coming and we need to make sure they are delivered safely. We don't need to risk any complications.

"Maggie, love, look at me," I say as calmly as I can muster. Meanwhile, my heart is racing in my chest and I'm panicking a bit myself. But I can't let her see that, I must stay calm for her sake.

Right now, she actually needs me to be clear-headed and I'll do whatever it takes.

"Carter," she cries, "I don't think I can do this. It hurts too much. How did I let you talk me into this? This is your fault. How, how did I let you talk me into this? I don't know what I was thinking! I can't have these demons! They're tearing me up inside! What did you fucking do to me?"

Her words are cutting me up inside. She's been so happy these past months. Why, when she's in labor, is she back to thinking she should have never carried our children? I mean, the books, the experts and the doctors all warned that women can get a little exorcist-like when they are in labor, but this just cuts me deeply.

"Come on, Maggie," I coax, "you don't mean all that. It's just the pain talking. Let's get you up and dressed so we can get to the hospital. They'll be able to give you something for the pain and you'll be happy again." At this point, I don't know if I'm trying to convince her or me. Not that I matter, she's the one in pain and getting ready to give birth to our children.

"No," she tells me and rolls over. "I'm not having them. They can stay in there and die for all I care. I'm not going to the hospital to have these things, you can't make me."

She doesn't mean that, I know she doesn't. There's no way in hell she means what she's saying. She's just a little hysterical. That has to be it.

"Maggie, love," I soothe, "those babies are coming whether you want them to or not. You don't have a choice in the matter. Just the amount of pain you're in tells me we need to get to the hospital right away. How long have you been having contractions? Have you timed them to see how far apart they are?"

"I'm not having contractions, Carter!" she yells. I'm confused a bit, but she continues on, "It's not labor pains I'm having. This pain isn't from contractions. This pain is something else. I don't know what it is, but it's not contractions."

Now, I know I must get her to the hospital immediately. I grab my phone out of my pocket and dial nine-one-one. I don't think I can get her down the stairs and into the car without help, so I call for an ambulance to come and transport her there.

"Hello, nine-one-one please tell me your emergency," the operator answers.

"Hello, my wife is thirty-four pregnant with triplets and is experiencing a lot of abdominal pain. She says it's not contractions, but she is screaming in pain. I need an ambulance right away," I inform the operator as level-headed as possible. Inside, I'm not calm at all. If something is wrong with my babies, I'll die inside, I just know it.

"Okay, sir, it looks like you have nine-one-one tracking enabled your phone, so I've been able to track your location through your phone carrier and have an ambulance on route. Please stay on the line until they get there. Can you tell me where she is experiencing the pain? I will get your obstetrician on the line to assist us," she informs me. Wow, she is thorough, I'll give her that.

"Maggie," I say calmly, "I need you to tell me where the pain is, love. I have your doctor on the line and they are trying to help."

"It's all over," Maggie cries. Tears are streaming down her face and suddenly, she lets out a scream that I swear pierces not only mine but also the operator's ear drums.

"Oh my God!" she yells and then has a look of horror on her face. She whips off the blanket and I just about fall to the floor.

The bed is full of blood! My babies! What is happening?

"Blood!" I yell into the phone. "There's blood everywhere! Help! Help! Oh my God, please help us!" Forget staying calm, this is more than I imagined was happening. We can't lose our babies, not now, not after all we've been through to have them.

"Carter, this is Doctor Hall, I need you to calm down for a minute, can you do that?" I faintly hear come over the line. "Carter, I need you to check Maggie and see where the blood is coming from."

I look at Maggie and want to hurt something. She's in so much pain I didn't want this for her. No matter how much I wanted our babies, this isn't something I wanted for her.

"Maggie, love, I'm so sorry, so fucking sorry," I cry. "The doctor is on the line now, she asked me to check you to see where the blood is coming from. Can I touch you, please?"

She doesn't answer, she just nods her head.

I lift the blanket that remains on her and notice she's completely naked. I slowly look over her lower body and see that the blood is coming from her vagina. I inform the doctor of such and they say the ambulance is pulling into my driveway now and that she must get to the hospital immediately.

I rush to the closet and grab a clean sheet and throw it over Maggie. I can't let them see her this way, it'll devastate her.

I rush downstairs and throw the door open. The EMT's are already rushing to the door with a stretcher in tow.

"Hello, sir," one of the EMTs say. "Can you please take me to the location of the patient? We've been updated by the emergency operator on the patient's condition."

"Follow me," I tell them, and head back upstairs.

"We received updates from the emergency operator. We will check the patient and get her safely to the hospital as quickly as possible."

"Thank you," I answer. "Am I allowed to ride with her?" I ask as I open the door to the room to hear Maggie moaning in pain. Though, I don't think they heard me as they were solely concentrating on taking care of Maggie and assessing her pain.

"Ma'am," the EMT starts, "we are here to help you. Can you please tell us where it hurts and what happened?"

"It just hurts!" Maggie screams and begins crying heavily.

"Can I check you out?" the EMT asks. He's being cautious, treating Maggie with extreme care and his professionalism makes me happy.

"Yes," she moans. "Make it quick, I can't take this anymore."

The EMT examines Maggie and surmises that, yes, Maggie is in labor and needs to get to the hospital right away.

"Sir," the EMT turns to me, "I need to get her to the hospital, will you follow us, or will you ride along?"

"I'd like to ride along," I answer, then look at Maggie, "Is that okay?"

"I don't fucking care," she screams at me. "Just get these fucking demons out of me and stop fucking up my life!"

The EMT gives me a look of sympathy as he and his partner try as gently as possible to get Maggie on the stretcher. It's a bit of work getting her down the stairs, but they manage with the help of a few police officers who have also shown up.

As soon as we get to the hospital, Maggie is rushed straight into a labor and delivery room. As the doctor performs a quick examination of Maggie's cervix, she looks very concerned and informs us that they have to get the babies out of Maggie immediately or both Maggie and the babies could lose their lives.

I'm growing more uneasy by the second here. I'm praying Maggie and our babies will be okay and pull through this.

"Maggie, Carter, it looks like the placenta is covering the cervix," the doctor begins to tell us. "This can cause major complications. I'm going to need to perform a c-section, quickly, to get the babies out. We don't have much time. I will have the babies out in less than five minutes, but we need to get to the operating room now."

"Get them out!" Maggie yells. "I don't care what you have to do!"

"Mr. Montgomery," a nurse I didn't even realize was in the room with us says to me. "I need you to put these scrubs on and follow me. We'll let you in the room as soon as the doctor is ready to begin."

I put the medical gear they hand me as quickly as possible and rush to the operating room to be there for Maggie and our babies. I have to wait for a nurse to come out and get me but am losing patience. The nurse finally comes out and I see Maggie strapped to a table and a sheet hung halfway down her body, covering her lower half. I rush to her side and sit on the small seat next to her head. Maggie's eyes are closed, but there are tears coming down her face. I gently wipe one away. I don't talk, I understand her pain.

Within a minute of me arriving in the room, I hear the scream of the first of my children. Then not a minute later, I hear another. When I don't hear the third one, I immediately panic. I see them hand the last baby off to a medical team and they are working diligently on the baby. I still don't even know what gender my babies are, but I see them all being worked on by more doctors than I would ever imagine being in one room.

Finally, after about two minutes, I hear the last baby cry. I sag with relief and look over at Maggie who is pale as a ghost.

"Congrats Maggie and Carter," the doctor says. "You have three beautiful little girls. But, Carter, you're going to have to leave the room. Maggie, your uterus tore, and we need to repair it in order to stop the bleeding. We're going to put you under completely. Would you like to hold your girls for a moment before we do that?" the doctor asks.

Maggie shakes her head no and closes her eyes again. She must just be in too much pain, that's all I can think as to why she doesn't want to hold them.

"I'd like to hold them," I say to the doctor.

She looks at me then nods her head to the nurses holding the babies.

"Carter, you can hold them for a few seconds, then I need you to go with the nurses to the Neonatal Intensive Care Unit, so the babies can be fully assessed, and I can finish repairing Maggie's uterus. You will have to leave the room and Maggie will go under full sedation."

I nod my head and reach out for the babies. The nurses each hand me one and I look at all three of my beautiful girls and I am in awe. I don't ever want to give them up. They are gorgeous, just like their mother.

All too soon, the nurses take the babies from my arms and rush out of the room.

I stand up and kiss Maggie on the head. "Thank you," I whisper and then turn to catch up to the nurses and my newborns daughters.

IT'S BEEN a full day since the babies were born and Maggie still hasn't seen them. She's in a lot of pain since her surgery and hasn't been awake much. I know she needs sleep to heal, but I really wish I could bring the girls in to see their mother. We need to decide on names, and I don't want to do that without her seeing them to make sure each name fits. I have a few names in mind, but I don't want to make the decision without Maggie. It's just not fair to her after all she's endured.

Finally, Maggie wakes up and looks at me. She doesn't look happy at all to see me in her room.

"What are you doing here, Carter?" she asks, throwing me for a loop.

"Where else would I be, Maggie? I ask.

"With your precious babies," she spits out. "The ones you insisted on having, the ones that have ruined my body completely! Look at my stomach, Carter! They didn't just give me all these fucking stretch marks, they scarred me for life! Not even plastic surgery can fix the scars they've created! They had to cut me open. How will I ever get rid of those scars? This is all your fucking fault! Just get out and take those fucking demons with you!"

She doesn't mean what she's saying. She can't. But, hastily, I comply and leave her room. But I'm not leaving her room just to leave. I'm going to get the babies and bring them back to her. I'm sure once she sees the beauties we created and she nurtured for the last eight months, she'll change her mind.

I walk back in the room with a nurse following me. I have two babies in my arms and the nurse is wheeling the bassinet holding the third behind me. She puts the bassinet near Maggie's bed and quickly leaves the room.

"Maggie," I say, gently, "meet our daughters."

I lay the two girls on her chest then reach over to grab the third. She looks down at them and a tear escapes her eye.

"They are beautiful," she whispers, looking at the babies with awe. "Just what you wanted."

"We need to give them names," I tell her. I knew she'd change her mind as soon as she saw them. The look on her face is the one I had hoped to see during the last nine months. It's such a relief to see.

She looks at the first baby, then up to me. She smirks then states, "Felicia Haley."

"Okay," I say. "Felicia Haley. Okay, I can do that." Although it's taking everything in me not to say no way. Felicia and Haley are two of Maggie's old friends. They hate me. They always have, and she's told me many times the shit they say about me as she laughs about it. But, now is not the time to fight with her on this.

"How about the other two girls?" I ask. "What will we name them?"

She looks at them and then shrugs her shoulders. "I don't care what you name them, they're yours. But this one, her name will be the one I gave her, understood?"

I'm not going to argue. I look at all of my girls and decide.

I pick up the smallest of the three—she is a tiny little thing—not that they all aren't but she only weighed three pounds eight ounces when she came into this world yesterday. She's the one the doctors had to work on to get her to breathe. But once she did, she showed them she was going to have a voice and be a fighter.

"Sofia Marie," I declare looking into my beautiful daughter's eyes. "That's what your name will be my little sprite. And you," I continue as I pick up my other daughter in my other arm, "you will be called Isabella Lynn."

I look at Maggie and it appears she has fallen asleep again. She is holding Felicia to her chest and it makes me happy.

The nurse comes back in and tells me the girls will have to go back to the NICU now. They shouldn't really have left but she broke the rules, so Maggie could see them. Because of their small size, they will spend some time in the NICU until they gain some weight. Felicia and Isabella will be able to come home soon, but Sofia will probably spend about a month in the hospital. I don't want to have to separate them but there's nothing I can do.

Felicia Haley was born at four pounds ten ounces and Isabella Lynn was our chunky monkey out of the three weighing five pounds three ounces. I know that's really not big, but compared to how small Sofia is, she definitely looks the chunkiest.

CHAPTER FIVE
CARTER

UNDONE

4 MONTHS LATER

MAGGIE, Felicia and Isabella came home from the hospital a week after the girls were born. Maggie was assured by the doctor that if she chooses to have more children, that she would be able to, but if she wanted to have her tubes tied, like she had been insisting throughout her pregnancy, that she would have to wait until her body heals. Because of the complications of the girls' birth and the surgery she needed immediately following, they weren't able to perform the procedure as originally planned.

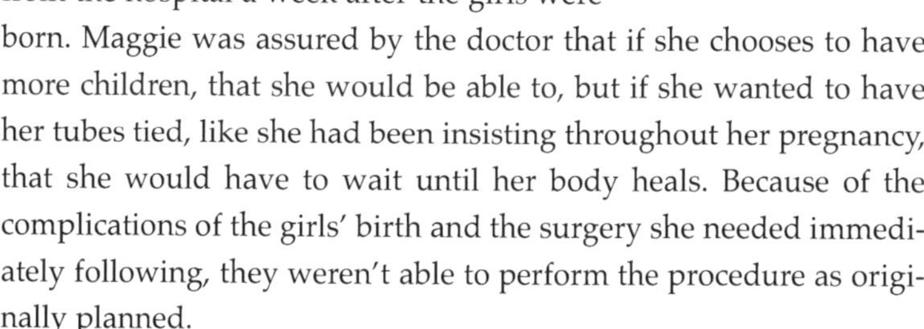

Maggie was a very attentive mother with Felicia but would barely bother with Isabella. She refused to breastfeed the babies because she didn't want them 'ruining her breasts like they did her stomach.'

I hired both a nurse and a nanny to take care of Maggie and the girls at home. Freyda, our new nanny, is an older woman, whose family lives far away. She's an amazing addition to our family and the kind of grandmother I'd always hoped my mother would have been. Maggie had a lot of healing to do and the girls would need a lot of care.

I spent every day at the hospital with Sofia. I couldn't stand the fact that one of my girls had to be left behind. I needed for her to know that her parents loved her and would never leave her alone.

It took a month, but Sofia was finally healthy enough to come home and be with her sisters again. The transition wasn't easy for her or her sisters. They all had to get used to being together again.

I kept a bassinet in my room and Maggie had the nursery for the girls when they were with her, though that wasn't very often.

Slowly, her relationship with Felicia began to dwindle and soon she would complain if any of the girls made a sound. I did my best, as did the nanny, to keep the girls happy, fed and clean. Maggie got tired of the nanny going in and out of her room to get to the nursery to care for the girls and made me switch rooms with her. She moved all of her stuff down to the guest room and I moved back into the master suite. It was a good move for me, because now that the girls were growing fast, they no longer fit in the bassinet I had purchased for my room. I would have needed to buy another crib for my room had she not made that choice.

When it came time for me to go back to work at the office, I often took the girls with me. Maggie would not only not pay attention to the girls, but she would also give the nanny a hard time when Freyda would try to take care of them. The best thing for all of us, was me taking the girls and their nanny with me to the daycare I had installed at the office.

Everyone at work loved my girls. They were hardly ever in the daycare because my employees would go in and steal them to spend some time with them. I didn't complain, I loved that everyone loved my girls.

Mikael came to the office often to spend some time with the girls. He, like me, had become enamored with his nieces. He only came to see them at the office because he refused to be anywhere near Maggie. His relationship with Maggie had completely died in the months after the non-wedding. He did try, I give him that much credit, to tolerate her remaining in my life, but she made it so he would never forgive her each time he came by. My best friend hasn't stepped foot in my house in months.

Maggie went back to her workouts as soon as the doctor gave her permission to do so. She spends most of her days in the home gym and sometimes some nights. She was so happy the day Marco came back to train her, I was a little jealous. She literally ran and jumped into his arms when he walked in the door. I thought I'd surprise her by bringing him back to train her, but I didn't expect her to act that way toward him. I was a bit shocked, to say the least.

Any time I call her to discuss something at home or with the girls, she's in the middle of a workout or getting a massage and refuses to stop and talk to me. It's a bit worrisome, but I'm afraid it's exactly what I asked for when I begged her not to terminate her pregnancy and to give our children a chance at life.

She's seen three plastic surgeons so far to correct both her stretch marks, which are vast and to try and lessen the scar she has from the C-section.

She never lets me forget how much of her body she sacrificed to have our girls, so I made sure to keep my promise and let her do what she needs to feel happy again. I don't know if she'll ever be truly happy with me again, but Lord knows I'm trying with everything I have to make that happen.

This morning, when I was getting the girls ready to go to work with me, Felicia seemed a little off. I've checked on her a few times in the daycare and the nanny has assured me that she's okay.

As I get ready for a meeting, Freyda walks in with Felicia in her arms. "Felicia has started to run a fever," she informs me.

"Freyda, when did this start?" I ask.

"About an hour ago," she answers as she hands me my beautiful girl.

"Hey Licia, my beauty, Daddy's gonna take you home to Mommy, okay?" I tell my girl. Then I look back up at the nanny and tell her to get the other girls ready, so I can take them all home.

She leaves to do as I've asked, and I sit back down in my chair with Felicia in my arms. I pick up my phone to call my assistant.

"Hello, Mr. Montgomery," Catherine, my assistant, greets when she answers. "What can I help you with?"

"Catherine," I answer. "Felicia isn't feeling well, I'm going to be taking the girls home. Please reschedule any appointments I have and send anything that needs my attention to my email."

"Will do, Mr. Montgomery. I hope she feels better," she tells me and hangs up. She's a great assistant and doesn't need more direction to do what I've asked.

I grab my jacket and head to the nursery to pick up the other two girls and everything else we will need.

Freyda buckles Isabella into her car seat and I put the Felicia and Sofia in theirs. I tell her that she can go home for the day and I'll take care of the girls by myself. She nods and heads to her car. She knows not to argue when I want to take care of my girls on my own. She tells me it's important for them to spend quality time with such a loving parent. I just wish they had two loving parents.

When I get home, I hear noises coming from the exercise room. Marco must be here training Maggie again. They are always training it seems. She's also hired another trainer, Ivan. She told me that there were days that Marco wasn't available, so she needed to hire someone else to cover those days. If this was making her happy, there was no way I was going to argue. It's what I had agreed to, wasn't it?

The training is obviously working because Maggie looks to be in better shape now than she ever was before she became pregnant with our children.

I decide to head upstairs first and put the girls in the nursery before I bother Maggie and let her know that Felicia is sick. Since Felicia is the only one that she has paid any attention to since they were born, although she's backed away from her, I'm sure she's going to want to know that she's sick.

I click the video app on my phone for the baby monitor I installed in the nursery and turn the sound up so that I can hear the girls if they wake up before I come back. They fell asleep in the car on the way home, so I'll let them sleep in their car seats until they wake up.

I head downstairs and head straight for the workout room. Maggie's moans are a bit louder now and they don't sound like moans you'd hear from someone who is working out or getting a massage.

What the fuck is going on in there?

I try to open the door but find it to be locked. *Why the fuck would this door be locked while Maggie is in there with her trainer?* I don't understand what is going on right now, though the picture is starting to come to me. Maybe it's denial, but there's no way, that what my imagination is putting together, could be the reason that those noises are coming from behind this locked door.

I grab the keys from my pocket and quickly find the one to this door. I finally get the door open and stop dead in my tracks. My eyes show me that what I imagined, is actually worse than I thought, but even still, my brain isn't processing what's happening right before my eyes. Have I been blind this whole fucking time?

Maggie isn't working out, and she sure as fuck isn't getting a massage, nope, nothing of the sort.

Maggie is splayed across the weight bench with both Marco and Ivan drilling into her. This is the same woman who told me that due to her postpartum, she couldn't find herself ever being sexually active with me or anyone else again.

Yet, here she is, stark naked getting drilled by not one, but two men at the same time.

Both men are steadily pumping in and out of her. One fucking her cunt and the other fucking her ass, a place she never once let me go. And they are rocking into her so hard, it's like they are trying to break her.

And Maggie, she looks like she's in a state of fucking euphoria. I've never seen her look that way when I was making love to her or even when we went beyond that and I was fucking her. She looks like she's lost in a state of bliss that she doesn't want to come back from. She's looking straight into the mirror but I'm sure she's not seeing what's in the reflection. If she did, she'd see me standing here with my hands fisted and my heart shattering.

"What the fuck?" I suddenly hear myself screaming.

They don't seem to hear me, at least not at first.

I scream again, "What the fuck are you doing?"

All three startle, and finally acknowledging my presence.

Marco and Ivan both look up with horror in their eyes and quickly pull their dicks out of Maggie. They scramble to pull their clothes back on and rush right by me and out of the room. They say nothing in their haste and soon after, I hear the front door slamming behind them as they make their quick exit.

I look over to Maggie and watch as she slowly gets dressed. She doesn't even seem phased that I just caught her fucking both of her trainers in our house. She actually has a look that expresses that me being here is an inconvenience to her.

"What are you doing home?" she snidely asks as she finishes getting dressed.

"Excuse me?" I ask. That's the first thing she has to say after I just caught her fucking the help?

CHAPTER SIX
CARTER

MY WORLD IS FALLING APART

AFTER MAGGIE FINISHES DRESSING, she walks past me and out of the workout room.

I go to grab her wrist but quickly snatch my hand back. I don't want to touch her after what I just witnessed.

"Maggie," I manage to call to her retreating form. My heart is shattered, I'm not sure what I want to say to her.

"What, Carter?" she replies as she whips around to face me. She puts her hands on her hips and continues, "Why are you even here? Why are you disrupting my day and disturbing my workout? What's so important that you had to break into my space and ruin my daily routine? Why do you even have a key to that door? I thought you built that room for me, so if it were mine, why would you need a key to it?"

Is this woman for real? She's pissed at me? That's what she calls a workout? And she's questioning why I would have a key to a door in my own fucking house?

"Workout? How is you being fucked by two men, that I fucking employ need I add, a workout, Maggie?" I yell. I can't believe the gall of this woman. Calling what she was participating in a fucking workout!

"Oh, Carter, please," she starts. "That, what you just saw in there, was nothing. That was a light workout compared to most days," she chuckles as she shakes her head in disbelief.

"This isn't a fucking joke, Maggie!" I'm yelling louder now. I can't believe what is coming out of her mouth.

"How did you think I was getting back into shape, Carter?" she asks with humor lacing her voice. "Marco has been fucking me into shape for years, way before you and I even met. Didn't you see what a god-like figure that man has? Just damn. I knew the moment I saw him, I needed him to fuck me. And I wasn't wrong. He knew just how to work my body. He's been working me out like this for years. Unfortunately, it was starting to feel a little too routine for me and I needed something different, plus, I didn't feel like it was working as well anymore. So, I first suggested to Marco that we part ways and I find a new coach. He wasn't happy about my decision so I decided I had to give him a little bit of a chance after how long we've been together and he came up with the perfect solution. He had a friend he was fucking, well, not just fucking, he also liked to share women with him. So, he had me meet his friend Ivan. Ivan was a god himself with all those muscles and that amazing physique, so I let Ivan fuck me to see if he was what I needed to get this to work. I wasn't completely satisfied, although Ivan definitely knew what he was doing, so Marco suggested I try to fuck them both at the same time. Not being one to just say no, I decided if they were up to it, I'd try fucking both of them right then and there, and see if it worked better for me. And Oh. My. Lord, I never felt that good in all my life. So, instead of finding a new workout buddy and firing Marco like I originally intended, we decided to add Ivan to the mix. I never realized how much I would love being fucked for hours by two extremely hot men. The workouts we've had, have been amazing. Look at this body. All I need now is that plastic surgery you promised me, so I can get rid of this fucking scar and extra skin your devil spawn caused me."

I realize, then and there, she's fucking serious. She's been fucking these men right here in my house, the place I thought we were making our forever home. And I've been the fucking fool paying them to do so. She's denied me for over a year, and here I was thinking she too was suffering from the lack of sex she's denied me. Man, I was a fucking fool.

"How could you do this to me, Maggie, do this to us, our family?" I gasp as a tear escapes and falls down my face. I don't want to cry. I'm angry and I'm hurt but I don't want to give her the satisfaction of seeing me cry.

"Oh, please. Do you not remember how sexual I am, Carter?" she asks. "Actually, you probably don't really know, now that I think about it. You see, I've been fucking multiple men for years. I've never been satisfied having just one man to do my bidding. You were one of many, Carter. You were never the only man I was with. As a matter of fact, Carter, *love,* I was in the middle of fucking Marco in that bed you are sleeping in when our babies almost died. Do you remember that day, Carter? Do you know why I never let you in my room? Why you were never allowed to even see the nursery? It was because Marco was living in there. He never left. He stayed on as my plaything all along. You were paying him to stay away, but I would never let that happen. I needed to be fucked. All. The. Time. All times of the day. Do you know how much my fucking sex drive picked up from being pregnant? I was always so fucking horny, no matter how many times I fucked someone in a day. Some days, I'd have two or three of my friends come over to satisfy me, I was that horny.

"Sometimes I'd grab one of the construction guys you had building the nursery and the home gym if I couldn't get in touch with one of my regulars. Eventually, though, it got to be too much and started to hurt because of how big I was getting, so I stopped fucking some of the other guys. I never stopped fucking Marco, even after the doctor told me it was too dangerous to have sex. Those spawn of yours tried ruining my sex life, Carter, but I refused to let them. First, it was a bit painful and difficult, but then Marco and I figured out how to make it work. So, he would take me from behind. Oh my, when I learned the pleasures of him fucking me in the ass, oh my God, Carter. No wonder you always wanted to try it. As a matter of fact, you should try it sometime. It was quite the euphoria. The day we tried to have regular sex again was the day you broke into my room and found me in pain, naked on the bed. Didn't you ever wonder why I was completely naked? Well, I guess not since I hadn't let you touch me or be near me in so long. Obviously we were a little careless and caused a problem. I just wanted to try to remember what it was like for Marco to fuck my pussy instead of my ass. If it weren't for the fact that I was in so much pain, I would have let him continue. I never cared for those things you made me carry. If I had lost them, oh well, I needed to have that orgasm, that's what was most important to me," she finishes with a shrug.

As if she couldn't make things worse than they already were, she continues on, completely obliterating any love I thought I'd ever felt for her. Destroying everything I thought we ever could have had.

"You know, the day I found out I was pregnant, I didn't know what to do. I sat there trying to figure out who the asshole was that did this to me. There were so many to choose from. Some of them, I didn't even remember their names. There were times I went out with Haley and Felicia and we shared multiple men that we brought home from the bar. Do you know that's why they hated you so much? Because I was never willing to share you with them. I didn't want them to have access to you and your bank account on the off chance that maybe you'd like one of them better and stop spending your money on me. Not that they wouldn't share with me like I always have with them.

"Anyway, I sat at my dining room table with Haley and Felicia and we tried to figure out what to do. Then, like a light bulb turning on, I figured it all out. See, you always wanted your family, Carter. You would constantly drone on about how you always wanted kids. And I knew right then and there, you were the only one that had the wallet to make me happy. I knew that all I had to do was play poor little me and you'd fully support any decision I made. Then I decided that if I had this baby, I'd make you pay me for it. But things weren't working out the way I wanted them to. When that high-priced doctor you paid for did those tests and we found out there was more than one baby, I knew there was no way I was going to have them. After the appointment, I went home to Haley and Felicia, and we three talked it out. We decided that while they stayed home in our apartment you bought us, oh, yeah, they live there too, if you haven't figured that out yet. They love spending your money as much as I do. Anyway, we figured out that I could move in here and you could buy all the things we wanted. You could continue to support me and pay for everything. The plan was to walk out of the wedding and have an abortion. But when you threw more money at me, on top of those amazing credit cards you gave us, well, I couldn't turn that down, now could I? So, I continued having my fun while the three of us, well, four, because Marco was there too. We laughed at how far and how much you'd let me walk all over you just for three fucking brats that would do nothing but cry and shit all day."

I'm no longer standing at this point. Halfway through her diatribe, I fell to my knees on the floor, not believing that this woman, or any woman, could be this evil. I don't know that I want her to continue, but at the same time, I feel I need to hear the rest of what she has to say.

"Wait," I somehow manage to choke out, just realizing something she said in her spew, "what do you mean you weren't sure who the father was? Are you trying to tell me those beautiful girls up there might not be mine?"

No, no, no. This can't be happening. She can't tell me that those aren't my babies up there. No, they're mine, I just know they are.

She has to be lying. She's just trying to hurt me more. Well, she can stop now because I don't know how much more I can take of this. Obviously, she doesn't care about the pain she's causing me and continues, yet again.

"No, Carter, I have no doubt those girls are *not* yours. I'm sure they belong to someone else. You just don't have triplets when there's no family history, or medical intervention at play in order to get pregnant. How dumb are you?" She begins to laugh like a fucking hyena.

This may be funny to her, but this really is no laughing matter. I thought my heart was breaking before, but now, *now,* I know that was nothing compared to the feelings I am experiencing. I grab at my chest thinking I'm having a heart attack, my heart hurts so much. I don't think I've ever experienced this much pain in my entire life.

She can't take my girls away from me. They are mine, she's wrong. I did read up on triplets when we found out. There's a very slight chance it could happen to a family who has no history of multiples and even though it is very slight, I believe that because of my desire to have a large family, that it actually happened for us. I got my three girls because God knew that I deserved them.

"Get out," I tell her in a low voice. I'm sure if I don't keep my voice steady, I'll yell and say things that I'm not ready to say to her right now. I no longer care about her affairs. She can fuck whoever she wants.

"Oh, no, Carter, I'm not going anywhere," she answers with a chuckle. "You see, you promised me things if I had those three demons, and you *are* going to pay up. I won't allow you to back out of it. If you even consider it, I will walk out the fucking door with those three girls and you'll never see them again. I will take them where you'll never find them, put them up for adoption, and make sure you never get to see them again. I don't want them, but I'm sure someone other than you, does. I'll be damned if you're going to have them after everything you've put me through and if you don't come through with what you promised me."

Oh, fuck no. What I put her through? Is she fucking delusional right now?

"Like hell you'll walk out of this house with my children, you vile fucking slut!" I scream so loud, I'm afraid I many have woken the babies.

I can no longer control my temper. I manage to get back to my feet and get directly in her face. She's pulled the last string inside me, I can't hold back any longer.

"You will never take my children away from me you fucking pathetic creature! How dare you talk to me this way! I've given you fucking everything and for what? You have no fucking feelings! You are a waste of a woman! All this beauty you try so hard to maintain is a fucking waste! You're the ugliest thing to walk this fucking planet! Your insides are so rotten, I doubt you even have a fucking heart! How I even fucking thought I loved you is beyond me! You want your surgery, go fucking have it. Good fucking riddance, it won't change how disgusting you are on the inside! I'll deposit money into your bank account right fucking now and you'll walk out of *my* house and never fucking return! You'll sign away all rights to my daughters and you'll never fucking see them again! You'll pack your shit and get the… Fuck. Out. Of. My. House!"

My temper is flaring to a point that I don't even recognize myself. If I don't move away from her, I'm afraid I'm going to strangle her. As I back away, she looks at me and chuckles.

"That wasn't so hard. Humph. Haley and Felicia bet me you'd fight a bit more about this. Guess they were wrong. Fine, I'll move out as soon as I get my money and you'll get to keep those bastards. I hope they never get sick and you need to find their real father, though. I couldn't even begin to tell you where to look should they need any desperate medical care."

With that, she turns and walks into the guest room. She looks back at me and waves and then slams the door.

I run straight up the stairs and stare into the crib at my beautiful sleeping girls. I keep them in the same crib for now, as was recommended by their pediatrician. It's supposed to be better for them to be together, reminding them of the closeness of being in the womb.

There's no way they're not mine. I don't care what she says. They are mine and no one will ever hurt them again.

I know Felicia is sick and I should just leave her be, but I can't stay here. I pack them up nice and warm and call Mikael. I have to get out of here. The only place I know the girls will be safe is at Mikael's house. His place is like a fucking fortress and he'd know if anyone was near his property faster than they could get to the front door.

As I walk out the door, I turn around to take a look at the place. No, I won't return here, even after that vile creature is gone. She's ruined too many things in this house. It's no longer my forever home. I can't have her tainting my memories or my girls' future. The house will go on the market first thing tomorrow morning.

CHAPTER SEVEN
CARTER

GOOD RIDDANCE

MIKAEL IS SITTING OUTSIDE on his steps when I pull up to his house. He either saw me on the security feed or he has been waiting for me on the front steps since my call to him. My bet would be that he's been there since we hung up.

He walks over to the car, goes to the back door and takes two of the girls out of their car seats. He doesn't ask any questions, he just grabs them and walks into the house.

I get out of the car and reach in the back seat for Sofia. She coos at me as I take her out of her seat and my heart melts just a little. This girl has me so wrapped around her finger, it isn't even funny. That month she had to stay in the hospital longer than her sisters made our bond a little stronger than the bond I have with Felicia and Isabella.

Don't get me wrong, I love all my girls the same, but Sofia and I had spent more time together alone than I've been able to spend with each of the other two.

After I grab the bag filled with stuff for the girls, I lock my car and head into the house.

Mikael has set up a playpen in the living room. My best friend knows me so well that he knew we were going to need a place to sleep, temporarily at least.

I called him as I left the house and told him I needed to come over. He didn't ask any questions, he just said he'd get everything ready for when I got there. I guess he realized this day was coming sooner than I did and prepared for it.

I wish I had been more prepared. Maybe then I wouldn't feel like my heart had just been run over by a Mack truck over and over again.

I gently lay Sofia in the pen with Isabella and Felicia and they immediately start talking to each other in that baby babble they use. They seem to understand each other well and continue their conversation, leaving me in the dust.

I walk over to the kitchen table, where Mikael is seated in front of a laptop. He's steadily tapping away on it, lost in whatever he's doing.

"Hey, man," I say, "thanks for letting me and the girls come over and crash. I may need to stay a little while, I hope that's okay."

Mikael looks up at me then flips his laptop around for me to see.

"I already knew," he says. "Take a look."

I look down at the computer and see my house on the screen. When did he put cameras up? I had never noticed them.

"When Maggie was pregnant with the girls, I came over to see you one day," he begins. "I didn't realize you had run to the office. When I came in, Maggie was sitting on the couch conspicuously close to that trainer of hers. Her friend, Haley, suddenly came out of the back room, half naked and hadn't realized I was there. She licked her lips and looked at Maggie and told her it was her turn. I didn't know what they were talking about and they didn't know I was there. When I looked back to the direction Haley was coming from, I saw Felicia in the doorway making out with some dude. I was confused as to why Haley was telling Maggie it was her turn. She was with you, having your babies, and living in your home, after all.

"When Maggie turned around and saw me standing there, she got up off the couch and sauntered over to me. I don't know what she was thinking, but she strode over to me and immediately grabbed my crotch. She asked me if I wanted to play with her and her friends. That there were only two men and I was the perfect third."

Mikael continues to look me in the eye as he's telling me this. *Why hadn't he told me before? He's my best friend, my brother, why wouldn't he have told me?* Instead of interrupting him, I let him continue.

"I pulled her hand off my dick and asked her what the fuck she was doing. She said she was horny and needed to get laid and that I was the perfect candidate. I thought she was fucking joking but she was deadly serious. I told her that she better get those people out of your house and that she needed to get her shit together and get out. I told her I was going to call you and tell you what she was doing and that you were going to throw her ass to the curb just as fast as you moved her in."

He starts shaking his head, as though to clear it of something. When he looks back at me, I see he has tears in his eyes.

"She told me… she told me that if I wanted to keep my best friend happy, that I'd never tell you. She told me that the babies weren't yours and that if I told you what she had done, that she would just leave and disappear with the children. I knew how much you already loved those babies and I would never do anything to hurt you."

I know he means what he says, he would never lie to me and I see how much this is hurting him. How much it must've been killing him living with this secret all this time. Just to protect me.

That cunt made my best friend lie to me for months and I had no idea. He was trying to protect me, but in the end, I still got hurt.

"Mikael, it's not your fault," I tell him. I mean it. I could be mad at him for not telling me, but I can't honestly say if I was in that situation that I wouldn't have done the same.

"After that day, I couldn't go back to your house and face her again. I started gathering evidence I would need to help you if you ever found out, and for you to be able to stay here with the kids if you needed to."

That's why he has all this baby stuff. I look around and see box after box of baby items that I didn't even notice when I walked through the door.

"I went there one day when you two went for one of your appointments. I placed some hidden cameras around the property, so I could gather any evidence you needed when the time came." He points to the laptop in front of me.

"You have everything you need, right there in living color to help you win those girls if she even tries to fight you. You have every indiscretion she's had since that day all on video. There was a video camera in the workout room as well, since I thought it odd that she suddenly needed more than one trainer. Be careful though. If you do decide to watch those, you're not going to like what you see. There's some sick shit in there.

"I know you and I have had some sexual exploits and fantasies, but the things that woman has done even turns my stomach."

Wow, and the hits just keep on coming.

"I've also contacted a lawyer for you and paid him a retainer for when the time came. Here's his number," he says as he hands me a business card.

"I don't know what to say, man," I reply, honestly.

Because I truly don't know what to say. All these months, he's had to live with knowing that she was cheating, that she would try to take my babies if he told me. That she even lied about the babies being mine. I can't imagine how much it hurt him to have to keep this from me all this time. It would kill me inside and I likely would have snapped and told him everything a long time ago had the shoe been on the other foot.

"Don't thank me, dude," he says solemnly. "I should've told you sooner, I'm as much to blame as she is, for hiding it from you for so long.

No fucking way am I letting him take the blame for any of this.

"No, Mikael," I tell him. "None of this is your fault. You were trying to protect me. I get it man, I truly do. And I thank you. I don't know what I'd do without you."

And I mean every word I say. This man has been my rock through everything I've had to deal with in my life.

He gets up and goes to the refrigerator. He pulls out two beers, hands me one and walks out of the room.

I know what he's doing. He's trying to give me time to figure shit out. I look at the computer screen and notice the time stamp at the bottom. This is actually live feed of my house right now.

There's a moving truck in front of it. What the fuck is that about?

Suddenly, I see three guys coming out of the house carrying my sofa. Why are they touching my shit? Then, I see her. She's standing there all sweet, dressed in practically nothing. She's pointing inside the house at something or someone. Then, that fuck Marco walks out, grabs her ass and kisses her. She pushes him away and laughs. I move the screen and see the workout room. There are people in there taking all the equipment apart. What the fuck is this woman doing?

You know what, I don't care. She can take every-fucking-thing. I was going to get rid of it all anyway. Payback is a motherfucker and that mother fucker's name is Carter Montgomery. She'll regret the day she fucked with me and my family, that's a promise I vow to keep.

I close the laptop and look at the card in my hand. I flip it over a few times then decide it's time to make this phone call.

Two hours later, I walk into the living room to see my best friend lying on the floor with the girls. He has them giggling away and my heart feels better than it has all day. Hearing the girls laugh makes so much of the bad go away.

"How'd it go?" Mikael asks without even looking at me. He has Sofia on top of his chest while he's lying there. She doesn't look like she's wanting to move any time soon.

"She robbed me blind as soon as I left," I answer. Not sure which subject he's asking me about.

"Fuck her," he says. "I'm talking about Robert. How'd the call go?"

Ah, he wants to know about the lawyer. He's not going to be happy with me when I tell him what I decided but I know he'll stand by my side as he always has.

"Well, he's going to draw up an agreement for me."

"An agreement? What the fuck are you talking about?" he asks as removes Sofia from his chest and puts her down next to her sisters.

"I'm giving her a million, making her sign away her rights and selling the house," I tell him. I wait for his reaction.

He stands and points to the kitchen then walks away. I follow him. I know he's trying to protect the girls from hearing what he has to say but it's not like they would understand or remember anyway.

I walk into the kitchen and Mikael is standing in front of the stove looking like he's ready to break something.

"What the fuck do you mean you're giving her a million?" he asks in a deadly low voice. Yeah, he's mad. He's pissed actually. I get it, but this is what I have to do to ensure I keep my girls. I'll do anything not to lose them.

"I'm not losing my girls, Mikael," I start to explain. "I'm going to give her whatever she wants to make her go away. I don't want her to do anything to try and take my girls away from me. I don't care what she told you. Those are my babies and I will not lose them."

He shakes his head, likely trying to keep calm and not blow up. He knows what my girls mean to me. He knows I'd do anything to protect them.

"You know you have to take the test, right Carter?" he asks, as gently as he can muster.

"I know," I say, resigned to the fact that I need to know if my girls really belong to me or not. They'll always be my girls and I'll always be their dad, but the need to know if my blood is the blood that actually flows through their veins is heightening. I know I'll regret it if I don't know the truth, and I don't want to regret anything when it comes to my babies.

CHAPTER EIGHT
CARTER

CONTRACTS AND DNA TESTS

TODAY, I'm on my way to see Robert Pinto, the lawyer that Mikael found for my case. He is supposedly one of the best family lawyers in the state. I could've fished around for other lawyers but believe that my best friend found the one that he knew would suit my needs. He did all the legwork, even before the shit hit the proverbial fan.

Mikael stayed home with the nanny and the girls. Mikael not only had a playpen for the girls, he had his own nursery for them with a spare bed inside for me. Freyda has been a blessing, even more now than she was when I first brought her on. She clearly loves my girls, the way a mother, or grandmother is supposed to.

I sure wish my mom was still with us. I know she would have spoiled my girls to no end. She probably would've moved in with me just to take care of them. That's what kind of woman she was. I'm sure if I have Freyda the option, she'd do the same.

From the time I was twelve years old, my mom raised me on her own. My father died of a sudden heart attack from a drug overdose.

Neither my mother nor I even knew he was using drugs; he kept that well hidden from us. Apparently, he never wanted us to see his pain and hid behind drugs to get him through. I don't blame him, nor do I understand his choices, unfortunately, I'll never get the chance to find out what hurt him so much he made the choice to turn to drugs.

My mother was an amazing woman. She took such great care of me and never let me want for anything. Her parents had invested a small fortune for her when she was young and her parents gifted it to her when my father passed.

She was never a big spender. Sure, she had the means, but we lived a pretty frugal life. She always told me that money can't buy happiness. I wish someone would have taught Maggie that.

When she passed away from cancer two years ago, I found out exactly how much money my mother had. Let me tell you, with the money she reinvested, my daughters' daughters will never have to work. Though I plan on following my mother's footsteps and teaching my daughters that hard work pays off.

I choose to live my life a little like my mother, but a lot less like her at the same time. I don't spend unnecessarily, yet I don't want for anything either. If I see something I want, I usually get it.

I forgot about that lifestyle when I was trying to convince Maggie to stay with me. It was like I was desperate to start a family instead of being patient and waiting for the right woman to come along. To say Maggie had me pussy whipped is an understatement. That woman had me wrapped around her finger the moment she let me put my cock in her pussy.

There's a lot I look back on, now that I've had a moment to think, that shows all the signs I never noticed. The excuses, the times I called her, and she was out of breath. The so-called bruises she had from working out. Now, I know they were fucking hickeys. Her workouts were just fuck sessions, not real workouts.

Pulling into the driveway of the address Robert gave me when we spoke on the phone, I note that it's a private residence instead of a normal business office. I understand the lure of working at home, so it doesn't make me concerned.

I knock on the door and a man I'm assuming is Robert opens it up.

"Hello, Carter, I'm Robert," he says making my presumption correct. "Glad you found your way here without issue. Let's get started."

"Hi," I reply and follow him into the house.

We walk past a living room and down a hall. He opens the door in front of him and I see it's his office. He walks in and sits in a chair behind his desk. There's nothing on his desk but a stack of papers. There's no computer or anything to be seen. I note immediately the man is a neat freak, which means that everything he's done for me, will be written to perfection.

"Take a seat," he states as he waves to the chair I'm standing in front of. "I've taken the liberty of writing up all the contracts. Take a look at everything. I've also contacted Miss Lucia and asked her to meet us here in an hour. She will be required to provide her DNA as well as sign all of these documents. This page here terminates her rights as a mother to the children in question and gives you the right to have a DNA test performed to discover the children's paternity. This contract here states that you will pay Miss Lucia the total sum of one million dollars, paid to her in installments, to cover the previously discussed plastic surgery, and the balance to be used however she sees fit. She will have no contact with you or the children. If she does contact you, she will forfeit her right to the money and have to return everything she's received."

I look up at the man astounded, he's very thorough, that's for sure.

"Thank you," I say. "I didn't realize that we'd do everything this quickly."

"Why waste time?" He shrugs.

"You're right." I hand him the first cashier's check that I had made out for Maggie in the amount of five hundred thousand. I decided to give her half up front and the rest of the money in installments, just to be a dick. I know she won't fight me. She's getting everything she's ever wanted.

Robert hands me the stack of papers and tells me to read through them. That if I want anything changed to let him know right way. He walks out of his office and closes the door behind him.

I look down at the papers in my hands and can't believe this is really happening. I'm numb right now and can't believe this is my life.

I read through each page slowly and carefully. Any mistake in these papers could cause me to lose my children and I'm not taking any chances. I'm sure Robert was thorough but it's not his children's lives at stake, it's mine. So, I have to make sure all the i's are dotted, and all the t's are crossed. Satisfied with all I've read, I put the papers down on the desk in front of me. I look at the time and see I have less than five minutes before that bitch arrives.

I stand up and stretch a little, trying to prepare myself for having to sit next to her while she sign these papers. I'll do what I have to do to get this woman out of our lives for good.

I startle at a knock on the door. Robert opens the door, sees that I'm no longer reading, and leads Maggie into the room.

Maggie looks at me and smiles.

I just glare at her and turn toward my attorney.

"Have a seat Miss Lucia," Robert instructs her.

She struts over to the chair next to me and sits down.

"Hi, Carter, how are my girls?" she asks. I know she's trying to get a rise out of me, but I won't let her. I just ignore her and wait for my attorney to speak again.

"Miss Lucia, here is a copy of the contract I drew up." He hands her the copy I just read through. "This was reviewed thoroughly by my client and myself. As I told you when I spoke to you on the phone yesterday, Mr. Montgomery has set up a stipend for you as the two of you agreed upon. Mr. Montgomery has brought in a cashier's check in the amount of five hundred thousand dollars that is in my possession and I will give it to you as soon as all the papers are signed, and a sample of your DNA is taken. I have a nurse waiting just outside who will come in and take the sample as soon as you give your okay. You will receive the first check today, and every month for the next eight months, you will receive fifty thousand dollars. At the end of the eight months, you will receive a final payment of one hundred thousand dollars to complete the one million dollars Mr. Montgomery has promised you. Do you have any questions?"

"I didn't agree to payments, Carter, you know this, what are you trying to do here?" Maggie asks me. I don't look at her, I'm letting my attorney handle it all.

"Miss Lucia, I assure you, it is in your best interest to take the money as Mr. Montgomery and I have worked out. Mr. Montgomery needs time to have the DNA tests run and to move his family into a safer environment. You have no worries that you'll receive the money. It's already been set up to transfer immediately into your bank account and you can see on the last page, your bank has already confirmed those receipts."

Robert continues to explain the details of the contract and the money while I tune them out. I know what the papers say. I know this bitch is getting more than she deserves. But I don't care. I just want her to disappear.

Suddenly, I realize that a nurse is taking a blood sample from Maggie, so I guess she signed the contracts. Good, this is going to happen just as I planned.

"Miss Lucia, thank you for coming in. Here's your check, you can see yourself out. I have additional things I need to discuss with my client." Robert stands and hands Maggie the check.

She happily takes the check and traipses to the door. She opens the door and looks back. "Take care of my babies for me, won't ya, Carter? I'll just take care of this." She waves the check at me and leaves.

She just had to get the last word in, didn't she? Well, she thought she did, anyway.

I turn and look at Robert, who has a smile on his face.

"She didn't read anything, did she?" I ask, a smile starting to form.

"Nope, she trusted everything we told her," he states then chuckles.

"So, in nine months, when her apartment goes on the market, she won't see it coming, will she?" I laugh. We stipulated in the contract that the money she was receiving was payment for buying the apartment back from her. She was so sure she was getting away with everything, but really, I'm going to get my money back, one way or another.

"Thank you so much, Robert," I say as I stand and shake his hand. "I've got to go get my girls. We have another appointment today that I'm not looking forward to. I don't want to see my girls cry when they take their blood for this DNA test. They can do anything they want to me, but I don't want them hurting my girls."

"Oh, that," Robert chuckles. "They don't have to take their blood. I just decided to do it this way with her because I wanted her to experience a little discomfort. That nurse, she was just a student. You turned your head, so you didn't see how many times she pricked Miss Lucia before she was able to find a vein and get her blood. It was quite comical, if I do say so myself. Your girls will just have the insides of their cheeks swabbed, as will you."

I have to give it to Robert, that was quite genius on his part. Maybe I shouldn't have dazed out and paid more attention. I would have loved to see Maggie in pain.

I thank Robert again and head home to get my girls.

Picking up the girls from Mikael's house, I head over to the clinic. I want to get this test over and done with so that I can enjoy my babies. I no longer have to worry about ever sharing them with anyone else.

The nurse at the clinic quickly does the tests and we're on our way.

I'm taking the girls with me out to the property I want to build our new home on. I decided not to buy another home but to build one to my specifications. This one *will* be our forever home and I want it to be perfect. The land I chose is twenty miles away from the place we used to call home. I tried to get as far away from that place as possible but not too far from my office. I really am going to need to get back to work soon, and I don't want to be far from the girls. They won't be coming with me as often because Freyda won't have to worry about Maggie complaining anymore.

The land is perfect. I go to the trunk and take out the stroller. Then, I carefully unlatch their car seats from the bases, and attach them to the stroller, knowing that I wouldn't be able to carry all three at one time, and walk to the center of the plot where I plan to build the house. I, then, remove each of them, one by one and lay them on a blanket I laid out for the four of us. They sit there looking at me with the cutest grins on their faces. It's like they know and they approve. Yeah, it may not be how I planned my life to be with my children, but I know this will be perfect.

PART TWO

CHAPTER NINE
CARTER

PERFECT CHAOS

3 YEARS LATER

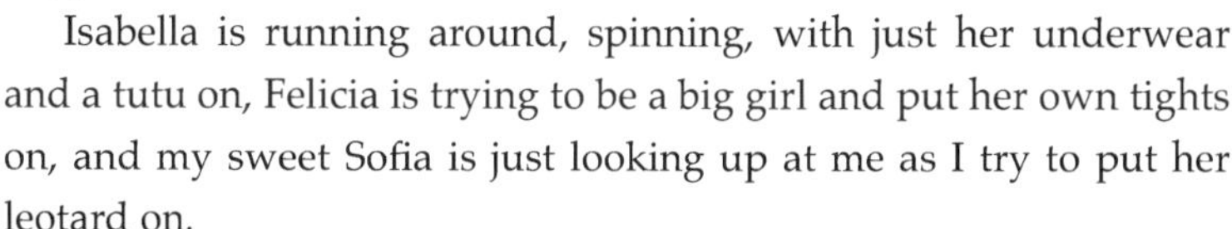

CHAOS, utter chaos. And I couldn't be happier.

Isabella is running around, spinning, with just her underwear and a tutu on, Felicia is trying to be a big girl and put her own tights on, and my sweet Sofia is just looking up at me as I try to put her leotard on.

My girls, they've made my life both chaotic and amazing these past three years. They are my little angels and I don't know what I'd do without them.

I know I made the right decision all those years ago when I decided to not look at the results of the paternity test we'd taken.

The day that envelope came in the mail, Freyda looked at my face and scooped the girls up and took them outside. She didn't ask any questions, she just knew I needed that time alone to process what I was holding in my hands.

I swear, it seemed like hours that I just sat there staring at that envelope. I know I should have opened it. But, these are my girls. I didn't care what that piece of paper said. There was no way that these precious gifts weren't mine. I made the decision right there and then that unless it was a life or death emergency, I'd never open that envelope.

I walked into my office and opened my safe. There were only important documents in this safe. Freyda and Mikael knew the combination to get in, but no one bothered touching anything, there was no need. The girls' birth certificates, my legal custody papers, my will giving Mikael custody of the girls should anything happen to me, the papers for the trust funds set up for my girls, and other things of that nature lived in this metal box. And now, this paper will reside there. I put the envelope way in the bottom of the safe, under everything else, so if someone needed to access the safe, they wouldn't accidentally stumble upon it.

I closed the safe and locked it. I decided to pretend that envelope didn't even exist. I looked back at the safe in the wall before I left the room and wondered if maybe I should have just taken it out and burned it. It's not like it's going to tell me who shares their blood if it's not mine. Maggie made sure everyone knew that she had no idea who could possibly be the person who impregnated her. If I had known what kind of woman she was back then, I would've never got involved with her. But then again, I wouldn't have those three precious little girls who fill my life with so much love.

Mikael thought I was crazy buying such a large plot of land so far away, but I knew my girls would need a lot of space to run and play.

I looked outside and saw Freyda pushing the girls on the swing set I had installed. It's a beautiful fall day and my girls love being outside as much as possible. They are barely ever inside if it's nice out. I think I'm raising three nature lovers, and that's fine with me. Again, those are my girls, and no one can ever change that, not in my mind and not in my heart.

Freyda saw me in the window and looked at me questioningly, I just shrugged my shoulders. She chuckled and went back to playing with my babies. Those girls have her wrapped around their fingers as much as the rest of us. She loves them like they were her own grandchildren. She had mentioned to me many times how much she wished she'd have had grand-children of her own to spoil. If it weren't for her insisting on living in her own place, she wouldn't let me pay her to take care of the girls. That's how much she loves them.

God, I miss Freyda. She was such a blessing to me and the girls. When she decided to stop working because she thought she was getting sick, I made sure she'd have everything she'd ever need. I paid for all the doctors I sent her to, so we could get her healed and back to her girls. Then, when she passed on so suddenly, I paid for her entire funeral. It broke my heart. She had the best service and the nicest casket I could find. I placed her within my family vault, because to me, she was my family.

Just thinking about her now, breaks my heart all over again. She was more than a nanny. She was our cook; she helped clean, and she was the girls' only grandparent. She was my sounding board. She was there for the girls' appointments and helped me design their room.

She was my voice of reason when I thought giving the girls each their own room was necessary. She told me I could build them each a separate room, but she was putting her foot down and I was not to separate them until they wanted to be separated. She thought it was important they remain as one as long as possible. So, even though my new home has a bedroom for each of my girls, they don't use them. They all sleep together in one room and have never even asked for their own. Most mornings when I go in to wake them, I find all three sleeping together in one bed. I know the time will come, and now, I dread the day they want to be apart.

For quite some time, my girls missed their nanny. They were only a little over a year old when she passed away and they couldn't understand why she didn't come back. Eventually, they stopped asking for her, realizing it was just going to be us four from there on.

I never hired another nanny for them. I didn't have the heart to replace someone who meant so much to us. It wasn't fair to either Freyda or my girls. I knew that I needed to do this all on my own. It's what I wanted after all.

Not only did I not replace their nanny, I decided that I'd never replace their mother. They didn't need women walking in and out of their lives. I was better off being alone with my girls for the rest of my life.

Mikael tried to convince me to go out and get laid a few times, but I never felt I needed to. Who needed another mistake like Maggie? Taking another chance with my heart wasn't in the cards for me. I was resigned to being alone for the rest of my life. I didn't need the heartache another woman could bring to my already shattered heart.

Sofia giggles and it pulls me out of my memories.

"What's so funny Sofie, girl?" I ask my baby girl.

"You're doing it wrong, Daddy," she replies. The angelic lack of an audible 'r' in her admonishment, making me grin.

I look at the leotard in my hand, and yup, I was trying to put it on backwards.

"I thought it was opposite day, silly me," I tell her and start to tickle her.

The other two girls stop what they're doing and start laughing hysterically at my mistake. They always seem to think I'm the funniest person in the world. And I'll let them continue thinking that until they realize I'm just really corny.

I finish getting the girls dressed and head out to the car.

They love their dance school. It keeps them social since they don't have another place to interact with other children.

When Freyda passed away, I decided to move my office into my house. The company can basically run itself, but I like to keep a handle on it. I basically took my role as a single father and made it my full-time job.

I buckle each girl into their seat and slide behind the wheel to get on our way. We can't be late for their first recital, that would break their hearts.

Driving down the road, the girls are steadily chatting away with each other. They get a bit loud at times, trying to talk over one another, but I don't quiet them. These are the best days of my life, and I'm going to enjoy every moment with my girls.

In two weeks, the girls will be turning four. Oh, how the time has flown by. They don't know it yet, but they will also be starting school in two weeks. I put them into a Pre-K class for four-year-olds so they can start their schooling early. Not that they haven't been schooled at home by yours truly, but they need the social aspect of attending school.

I didn't go with private schooling, much to Mikael's dismay. He thought his girls needed a private school and only the best. But I believe that the public school system has as much to offer them and they won't be limited in their interactions.

My mom made me live a humble life, and I will do the same for the girls. I had to go to public schools, I had to get scholarships for college and pay my own way. Hell, I even had to live in a rundown apartment when I first started out, until I earned my way to buy my first house. My mom wouldn't budge on that. She told me in order to appreciate what I had; I had to earn it first.

It was a lesson in life I'll surely pass down to my daughters. Although, I will probably give them a bit more than I started with. And I'm quite sure Uncle Mikael will give them whatever they ask him for. They have him wrapped very tightly around their chubby little fingers.

I'm ripped out of my reverie by a strange sound coming from the front of my Audi. I just had the car serviced last week, so I don't know what it could be. Suddenly, before I even get a chance to pull off to the side of the road, the car just stops. I try over and over to get the engine to turn over, but nothing is happening.

"Why you stops, Daddy?" asks Isabella from the back seat.

"Yeah, Daddy, why stop?" comes from Felicia.

"Something is wrong with the car, girls," I tell them. "Give Daddy a minute and we'll be back on our way."

I get out of the car and walk to the front. I pop the latch on the hood and lift it up. I don't see anything broken and there's no smoke or fluids coming out of the engine. I teeter around a bit more but can't find anything. I mean, I'm not a mechanic so it's not like I know exactly what I'm looking for, but I'm not an idiot either so I can make do most of the time.

Since I can't figure out what's wrong with the car, I go to the back and take out the safety cones I store in case of emergencies, such as this one. I take the cones and surround the SUV with them. I don't need anyone coming down the road and accidentally hitting us because they don't realize I'm broken down. I have to think of my girls' safety and this will hopefully ensure we'll be safe while we wait.

I get back in the car and call roadside assistance. This is gonna suck, my girls can't be late for their recital, it'll gut them. They were so excited to show me everything they have learned.

I'm happy I built in extra time to get to the recital hall this afternoon. We left a lot earlier than we needed to because I was going to surprise the girls and take them for lunch and ice cream before the recital. We don't eat out much but today is a special occasion, so I wanted to surprise them. Roadside assistance tells me they should have someone out here in about thirty minutes, so maybe we can still make it for ice cream at least before the show.

I look into the back and Isabella and Felicia are steadily babbling away to each other. Meanwhile, Sofia has a little book in her hands and an inquisitive expression on her face as she tries to decipher the words. She's so smart, that little one. She can already read and has been trying to do math as well. The other two girls, although they can manage a few things when trying to read don't really care much for it. They'd rather be pretty and do fun things while Sofia is always wanting to learn.

Isabella and Felicia remind me so much of their mother sometimes it hurts. She's had no influence at all on how they've been raised so far but they do have a lot of her traits. I try my hardest to sway them, but it never lasts long.

Yes, I want my girls to be who they are going to be, but they need to always know that being pretty on the outside doesn't mean you're pretty on the inside. I try my hardest to make sure all of my girls use proper manners. They are very respectful and I'm glad that Isabella and Felicia at least have that going for them.

"What are you reading, Sofie girl?" I ask my youngest.

"The *Cat in the Hat*," she says as she shows me the front of her book. "Why would a fox be in a box? That's kind of silly."

"Yes, Sofie girl, it is silly," I reply. "But Dr. Seuss is always silly, just like you, my silly girl." I reach back and tickle her stomach as I say this.

"Me, Daddy," laughs Isabella, wanting in on the tickle fest. I happily oblige.

All three click the seatbelt on their booster seats and get out to join me up front, where I start tickling them. They're laughing so much and it warms my heart.

I try to keep their mind off the time because I don't want them to panic about being late. We're having so much fun; it's hard to believe we're stuck in the middle of the road with somewhere to be.

CHAPTER TEN
ELIZABETH

CHANGING PLANS

I'M EXCITED TODAY. It's my first day off in I can't even remember when. I don't need the full day, but thought I'd spoil myself for once anyway.

Today, my godson, Alfonso, will be singing in his first solo performance. He may only be ten years old, but I swear that boy has the voice of an angel. He's been singing ever since he was a baby. He always sang his words when he first started talking instead of speaking them. It was the cutest thing ever. This was probably the result of his mother always having music on. No matter what was going on, Angela always had music playing. His voice has always been precious, but he sure as hell didn't get it from his mother, my best friend.

Angela couldn't hold a tune if her life depended on it. As a matter of fact, I'm pretty sure the last time she even tried to sing, even with my fingers stuck in my ears, I heard all the dogs in a ten-mile radius howling along with her. Okay, I might be exaggerating a little, maybe it wasn't that bad. It was probably more like a five-mile radius. Yes, her voice is *that* bad.

I'm sitting here at my kitchen table sipping on my cup of coffee, debating upon what time I should arrive at the concert hall. I want to get there nice and early. I want to be front and center, so Alfie can see me cheering him on. I know if I don't get there early, I'll never find a good seat. Knowing his mother, they will get to the hall with less than seconds to spare and she won't be able to find a seat. Maybe, if I'm feeling generous, I'll save her a seat right next to me. Maybe. Who am I kidding? We both know I will.

Angie has been my best friend forever. I don't remember a time when she wasn't in my life. She's been there by my side through it all, from losing my parents, to losing what I believed to be the love of my life. She was there when I made the decision to open my own garage and helped me buy my first tow truck.

My dad, God I miss him, taught me many things in life. I was his only child and he was a mechanic himself. I was always there, right beside him whenever he worked on his cars, whether it be cars at the shop or our own at home. He taught me everything he knew. He always told me that unless I knew how to fix my own car, I didn't have any business driving one. I took that to heart.

He passed away when I was sixteen. I was home with my mother cooking when we got the phone call. My father was under a car, fixing the brake lines when the lift in the garage broke. The hydraulics stopped working and the lift fell, crushing and killing him on impact. That was one of the hardest days of my life. We were later told that his friend, George, who had been working with him that day, tried to get him out, but it was too late.

My mother, she mentally checked out that day. Her mental state was always in question – she was bipolar and well medicated – but the day she lost the love of her life, it was all over. Shortly after my father's funeral, my mother checked herself into St. Mary's Mental Institution. She knew she needed help and finally wanted to make sure she could manage her illness long term.

Well, here it is twelve years later and she's still there. What she thought was going to turn out for the best, actually made her worse. She's barely recognizable these days. She doesn't know who I am most times and is always asking for my father. I still see her weekly, though my heart breaks every time.

I love my mother. She was a great mom before her mental break. She may have had mental health issues, but she never let them get in the way of taking care of me. She made sure to take her medication daily, so she'd never suffered a mental breakdown that I ever remember. And I do remember a lot from my childhood.

I remember the days of sitting on the counter and making chocolate chip cookies together. We would both be wearing more flour than went into the cookies. My father would come home from work and find us in the kitchen having flour fights. He'd laugh and join in sometimes. Other times, he'd break us up, send us to clean ourselves up while he cleaned the mess we had made himself. I really did have amazing parents.

Angie was there, right by my side through it all. Her family took me in immediately following my mother's breakdown. They never asked me for anything in return. They took care of me like I was their own child. They even offered to pay for my wedding when I married the man I believed I would be with forever.

When my marriage fell apart, Angie was there. It didn't matter that she had a four-year-old to deal with at the time. Her parents took her son, Alfonso, and sent her straight to me. They loved their grandson and their daughter so much. They always told me they loved me as if I were their own and wanted to make sure my sister was always there for me when I needed her.

Alfonso, my Alfie, is the greatest child you'd ever know. He may not have been planned and may be the outcome of something horrific that happened to Angie when we were just seventeen, but she's never made him feel it or acted like he was anything but perfect. She's loved her little boy from the moment she found out she was pregnant with him.

Alfie, thank goodness, will never know his father. That bastard raped my best friend at a party one night and then wrecked his car, killing a family. At first, he tried to blame everything on Angie, but she was the one who was hurt. He even tried to convince her to drop the rape charges, saying he was drunk and didn't know what he had done. That he got into his car after he realized what he did to her and that's why he got into the accident that killed that family, while drinking and driving.

He was held without bail for a while before he went through two separate trials. We made sure to be there for both. He was convicted of four counts of vehicular homicide in his first trial, one count for each of the family members he killed. Then he was convicted of rape in the second for what he did to my best friend. All together he will face more than fifty years in jail, without the chance for parole. He'll never get the chance to know his son, and Alfie's so much better off for it.

When Angie found out she was pregnant, unlike most people who have been raped, she believed that the child she was carrying was the light that came out of all the dark that happened that fateful night. When she gave birth, at just eighteen, she named her son after the family her rapist had killed to honor them and to give their name the life that bastard took away from them. She's one of the most honorable women I'll ever meet. She's been the best mom you can imagine, and her parents supported her decision wholeheartedly.

I love my best friend. I don't think there is anyone as strong as she is. I'm in complete awe of her heart, her soul and her perseverance.

I'm staring at the photo of my best friend and her son that I have saved on my phone, when it suddenly rings in my hand. I don't recognize the number so at first, I'm hesitant to answer it.

I'm used to calls from strange numbers all hours of the day and night. It's what happens when you run your own tow service, but I took the day off. The workers at my garage know this is a rarity, so they wouldn't let anyone bother me.

Reluctantly, I answer the phone. It was in my nature to work and even though I promised myself I wouldn't today, I have to, because my employees must've thought it important if they passed the call through to my phone. Otherwise, they would've taken care of it all themselves and not taken the chance of pissing me off by bothering me. Not that I get pissed off, either, that's another rarity. I'm always the calm one. I've learned to take one day at a time and live in the moment.

"Hello, Grace Family Auto Service, how can I help you?" I answer right before I know it would go to voicemail. That's the name I use for my garage. I know technically I don't have a 'family', but I still use my family name. I use it to honor my father and everything he taught me. If it weren't for him, I wouldn't be able to do what I do today.

When I turned eighteen, a lawyer came to see me. Apparently, my father was still taking care of me after his death. He had purchased the shop where he had worked, and no one knew. He set up a fund and the shop paid for itself until I turned eighteen. At that point, the shop and everything that went with it became mine. There wasn't much money left at that point, but it was enough that I could make some changes. Angie's family helped me out with the rest of what I needed. I've run a lucrative business ever since.

"Hey, Elizabeth, this is Tony down at the Audi dealership. I'm sorry to bother you today. Your workers said you were unreachable, but I have a vehicle broke down in the middle of the road down on Sumpter and really need a flatbed to tow it. You're the only one I know with a flatbed in the area, so I didn't have much of a choice. I really don't want to inconvenience you."

It's not out of the norm for me to get calls from the dealerships around town. You'd think that with how many vehicles they have to tow and how often they need it, they'd get their own tow trucks. I won't be the one to complain that they don't have the equipment they need, however, because they pay me well when I tow vehicles for them.

I know, without a doubt, that I'll take this tow job. Money is money, and I'm always in need of extra funds. Plus, he said the vehicle in question is in the middle of the road. I can't in good conscience leave a vehicle stuck in the middle of the damn road. Thankfully, it's on my way to the concert hall, so I guess I'm going to be trading in my Miata for the flatbed and will need extra parking at the concert hall. This will take up the extra time I thought I had to get to the venue.

"It's fine, Tony," I reply. "I'm on my way. Give me the details of the vehicle and the issue. I'll get out there and get them on their way," I say and wait for his reply before I hang up.

Ugh. I want to bang my head against the table. Rich assholes and their expensive vehicles. They buy a car they don't know how to fix and that irks me so much. I just wish people would learn about their cars before they get in them. It only takes a few minutes to look over everything before you get in it and drive away. If people would be more cognizant of their vehicle's needs, there would be a hell of a lot fewer breakdowns, which would result in a hell of a lot less traffic delays.

Thank goodness Sumpter is basically an abandoned road because I couldn't imagine the amount of backed-up traffic that would cause on a Saturday afternoon. The road would be blocked for miles and that would take so much more time for me to be able to get to them.

I grab the keys off the hook by the door, hop up into Old Mack, and get on my way.

CHAPTER ELEVEN
ELIZABETH

HOW CAN I SAY NO?

I CAN'T BELIEVE I have to work on the day I promised myself I wouldn't. Fucking pricks with their expensive cars. I bet the guy thought the car would just run and fix itself and never bothered to take it in for maintenance.

I don't take time off and the one and only day I wanted to dedicate solely to my nephew, I don't have much of a choice but to go out there and rescue someone who probably shouldn't even be driving the car they are. Pretentious dicks.

I take a left onto Sumpter and don't see anything right away. Of course, they would likely be all the way down at the end of the road. This will take even more time away from my day. This road seems to go on forever. There aren't many homes on this road, it leads to a dead end and marks the edge of town.

All the anger and frustration I was feeling quickly leaves me as I start to laugh at the site in front of me. Someone went way overboard with safety cones, I see. There has to be at least a dozen cones surrounding the white Audi SUV that's broken down in the middle of the road. It's not like the dude had anything to worry about it, he's probably the only person to be this far down the road since there's no one else that lives anywhere close.

I snap a picture and send it to Angie before I get out of the truck. This will make us laugh for days to come.

I look around the vehicle and over in the grass on the side but don't see anyone. It would've made more sense for whoever is in that car to stay over on the grass instead of staying in their car. When I walk up to the car, I see a man in the driver's seat and some children in the front playing with him.

Well, ain't that quite the sight? It's not a normal one anyway. It's pretty entertaining watching these little girls jumping all over him, and the smile on his face tells me he is truly enjoying himself.

Hesitantly, because disturbing the scene in front of me should be a sin, I knock on the window. I feel bad interrupting their playtime, but I have somewhere to be and just need to get this over and done with.

The girls jump and dive into the backseat as the man slowly opens his window. He's quite the looker, wow. His eyes are a piercing green which complements his dark brown hair that is short but styled just right. His jaw seems a little crooked, but the five o'clock shadow he's sporting tells me he doesn't care. He has a look that makes him seem off-limits but immediately my libido kicks into high gear.

"Hi," he says, and that voice just melts right through me. I forget for a moment why I'm here.

"Is that's your truck?" says one of the sweet angels from the back seat. My smile grows even larger when I hear her toddler-speak.

"Sofia, give Daddy a minute, sweetheart," the man replies. He looks at the girl with so much love in his eyes, I'm a little jealous. Huh, where in the hell did that come from?

"Hello," I finally manage to say. "I heard you were broken down and need assistance. Can you tell me what happened? Maybe I can fix you up real quick and get you on your way." I look into the back once again and notice that the three little girls in the back are practically identical. They have to be the most adorable twins and little sister I've ever seen. Their mom must be an exquisite beauty because these girls take my breath away.

"I don't know what's wrong with the car," the gentleman says. "I just had her serviced the other day and I was told everything looked good. We were on our way to the girls' first recital and the car just stopped. I looked under the hood and didn't see anything out of the norm, so I don't understand what happened."

"Okay, can you please pop the hood for me?" I ask. I look back at the girls again and smile. The two that look identical won't look at me but the little one is all smiles. She may just be the prettiest thing I've ever seen.

"Yeah," he answers. "Girls, you stay here and behave. Daddy is going to check out the car with this young lady, is that okay?"

"Yes, Daddy," all three reply at the same time.

Oh, how cute!

"Hi, I'm Elizabeth," I introduce myself once he steps out of the car. I have to look up at him as he's got to be almost six feet tall. He's not too tall, but when you're only five foot two, everyone is tall.

"I'm Carter," he replies as he takes my proffered hand. "I'm sorry to bother you, it looks like you were in the middle of something." He points to my outfit.

Shit, in my haste to get things rolling, I completely forgot that I was in a skirt and heels. Oh well, I'm not going to run back home to change now.

"Yes, my nephew has a concert today," I answer. Why am I explaining myself to him? I have no idea, but I prattle on. "I was on my way there when I got the call to come and rescue you. We have to make this quick or I'm going to be late. Plus," I add, "it looks like you have somewhere to be as well."

I noticed that his girls were in leotards and tutus. They must be heading to some kind of dance class.

"Yeah, I have to hurry too," he starts to explain. "Today is the girls' first dance recital and they've been so excited. I can't let them down. They've been looking forward to this for so long and I don't like my girls to be disappointed."

His love for his girls is so evident on his face and in his voice. You don't find many dedicated fathers out there like this one.

"Is your wife on her way?" I ask. "I can just tow the car and she can pick you up, so you won't have to go with the car. I don't want to keep you from what you have to do."

"No wife," he answers abruptly. "It's only me and my girls."

I don't normally allow people to just leave their cars with me. Usually, they have to come with me or follow me to ensure the car gets to where it needs to go. For some strange reason, I want to make an exception here. I don't want those precious babies to miss their dance recital.

It takes me a moment, but I just realized he said there's no wife. I wonder if maybe he just has the girls for his weekly visit, but something about the way he looks at those girls and the way they look at him tells me being a part-time dad isn't something he's doing. Maybe the wife passed away or something.

I haven't let a man get under my skin in so long but this man, or his daughters' really, have me doing things I would never do.

"How old are they?" I hear myself ask. "They're twins, correct?" I ask as I point to the two bigger girls.

"No," he answers. At my perplexed look, he continues, "They're triplets. Sofia was much smaller when she was born and has always been smaller than Isabella and Felicia. She's also much smarter than her sisters, but they are triplets."

Wow. I would've never guessed triplets, but looking at them again, I do see it. He must really have his hands full with the three girls. I'm going to ease his stress today. I'm sure any little thing helps him these days.

"Okay, it's against policy," I begin, "but, please take the girls and put them in the cab of my truck. I'm going to put your car on the flatbed and then drop you off where you need to go. I shouldn't have them in the truck, but since I own it, I'll make an exception. I mean, who is going to yell at me? I have somewhere to be myself, so after my nephew's concert, I'll drop your car off at the dealership. Is that okay?"

"You'd really do that?" he asks with a bit of wonder in his voice. "Thank you."

He walks back to his truck and opens the back door. All three girls jump out of the car and now I really see how much they look alike. The smallest of the three looks up at me and waves. I can't help but wave back and break out into a smile.

I hook up his SUV and lock it into place on the flatbed while he puts the girls' booster seats in the extended cab of the truck. He's such an attentive dad and I get lost for a minute just watching how he makes sure all three are nice and secure in the seats.

The drive to the dance hall is full of chatter. The little one, who told me her name was Sofia Marie, asks so many questions. She's a very inquisitive little girl and now I see why Carter said she was so smart. The other two girls talk about their clothes and their hair. They are just as precious as their sister but not as friendly. I'm sure once they know someone they are more like little Sofia, but they just met me, so I understand their hesitance.

When I get to the dance hall, I hand Carter my card and tell him that the Audi dealership will contact him once his car is ready. He asks me how much he owes me, but I tell him that I'm paid by the dealership and he has nothing to worry about. I let him know I'll put the girls' seats back in his car so he won't have to carry them around.

He gets the girls out of their seats, and to my surprise, Sofia jumps into my arms and hugs me. She thanks me for saving them and then goes back to her dad who gently lowers her to the sidewalk.

I think I just fell in love with that little girl. Too bad this will probably be the only time I ever see her. My heart hurts at that thought.

"Thank you again," Carter says and reaches his hand out to shake mine. He looks down while my hand is in his and smiles. "She's never like that. She's the shyest one of my girls, but obviously she sees something in you that the other two don't. Thank you for being so patient and answering all of her questions."

I'm choked up now. That little girl is the shy one? I never, in a million years, would have guessed that.

"Have a great day," I reply. There's nothing else that I can get out. My heart is in my throat and I don't think I could talk without crying.

CHAPTER TWELVE
CARTER

I CAN'T FEEL

I STAND HERE on the curb staring at the tow truck pulling away with my SUV on the bed. I'll convince myself that it's my car I'm watching but in reality, it's the woman behind the wheel that has my interest. I haven't felt something for another woman in so long and my body is definitely reacting to the tow truck driver.

"Daddy, come on." Isabella pulls on my pant leg and pulls me out of my thoughts. "Miss Jenny is gonna be mads because we're late."

The girls aren't late, we're still a little early but I guess their young minds think because we broke down that we'd be late today.

"We're not late, Isabella," I gently tell her. "Daddy was going to surprise you girls and that's why we left the house so early. We still have a little time, so what do you think if we go grab some ice cream from the shop across the street before we come back for the recital?"

All three girls start jumping up and down. They sure do love their ice cream.

"Yes, Daddy, come on!" all three yell, excitedly.

I lift Sofia into my arms first, since she's so tiny compared to the other two. She wraps her arms around my neck and holds on tight, like we've done in the past and I reach both hands down to grab Felicia and Isabella's hands. Being a single parent of triplets, I had to learn how to make things work when I needed to hold on to all three at one time. It was easier when they were babies, but now that they are older, we've learned to maneuver ourselves to make it work. They know they must always hold my hand when we are out. Especially if we are going to cross the street. I'm lucky in the fact that none of them have ever tried to pull away from me. They know they don't have many rules, but the simple ones I have they must follow.

We walk across the street and I find an open booth in the ice cream shop. I settle all three of them into their seats and let them know I'll be watching them while I get their ice cream. My girls are well behaved enough that I know I can trust them not to move from the table while I get their ice cream.

I walk up to the counter and order my girls their favorites. This is one thing they completely differ on. Each girl has their own favorite ice cream, so I always have to order them their own cones instead of just one for them to share. I decide that this time, I'll just order three small bowls because I don't want to take a chance of them getting ice cream all over themselves if I order cones. Maybe I should've thought twice about putting them in their costumes before I left the house knowing we were getting ice cream first. I know if any of them get even a little bit on themselves, it's going to be a disaster. They will all have major meltdowns and with the way this day has turned out so far, I don't think I can handle a tantrum from any of them, let alone all three.

I order Isabella strawberry ice cream with rainbow sprinkles. Sofia gets vanilla ice cream with chocolate sprinkles, and Felicia gets, my personal favorite, chocolate chip mint ice cream with whip cream. Felicia is a girl after my own belly. She eats many of the things I eat, whereas I have to fight most days with Isabella and Sofia about what they eat. I swear those two kill me sometimes. I always have to cook two different meals for dinner because Isabella and Sofia rarely eat anything that Felicia and I like to eat. If those two had a choice, we'd all live on grilled chicken and mashed potatoes every day. I like something different every night, and so does Felicia.

When I get back to the table, Sofia is talking animatedly to Isabella and Felicia about the tow truck driver. I don't think she heard Elizabeth introduce herself, so Sofia just keeps referring to her as the lady driver. She's so cute about it. I've never seen Sofia act this way towards another woman. Usually she's so standoffish and refuses to give anyone a chance.

When I first signed the girls up for dance, Isabella and Felicia jumped right in. My beautiful Isabella is a natural. She truly feels the music and moves with such grace already. Felicia and Sofia are quite a bit behind Isabella but they're always happy to go and learn.

I honestly believe each girl's paths are already set out for them. Isabella will be my prima ballerina, while Felicia will be my personal chef, and Sofia will be the scholar.

Felicia loves to help her daddy cook. She's always front and center when I'm making their meals. She doesn't care if she was playing or watching a movie, as soon as she sees me head to the kitchen to make some food, she drops everything so she can be right there with me.

Miss Jenny, the girls dance teacher, has asked me many times if she can move Isabella up to the more advanced class. I haven't let her yet because I don't want Felicia and Sofia to feel like they're not as important as their sister. Although, I don't know if this is hurting Isabella in her training. Miss Jenny always tells me that Isabella is such a natural and she picks up immediately on anything the girls are taught.

I prefer that my girls stay together as long as possible. I know this might not be a good thing, but I feel the longer they stay together the closer they will be and hopefully they won't resent one another for anything as they grow up.

I grew up an only child. Mikael is the closest thing to a brother that I have. I don't know how I would have survived the last three years without him and I can't imagine how much better life would have been growing up if he were my real sibling.

Speaking of Mikael, here he comes. Strutting in the door like he doesn't have a care in the world. I knew he would be here today; he's never missed anything when it comes to the girls. He loves his role as the doting uncle and I believe with my whole heart that he loves my girls as if they were his own.

"Uncle Mik," all three girls squeal at once. He leans over the table and gives each girl a hug and a kiss on the head.

"How are my favorite girls?" he asks as he takes a seat. "Are you ready to dance for your favorite uncle?"

"Yes!" they all exclaim in unison, again. They truly do love their uncle, especially since he's so involved in their lives. There's never been anything he hasn't been present for.

"Hey, bro," he says to me and holds out his fist. "I grabbed the girls' booster seats on my way here. Sorry about your car, I'll give you guys a ride home when the recital is over."

I called Mikael while the girls and I were waiting for the tow truck. I knew I'd need a ride after the recital. I knew without a doubt Mikael would give me a ride, so I had to call and give him a heads up so he could grab the spare seats he keeps for them.

Mikael starts talking to the girls and although I normally make myself part of the conversation, I tune them all out.

That woman. Where did she come from? And why is Sofia so enamored by her? I have no idea.

I swore when all that shit went down with Maggie, I'd never let a woman near me or the girls again. But something about that sprite just got to me. She made my girls feel comfortable. She looked at them with a look only a mother could have. Well, any mother but their own of course.

Oh, that bitch. I was so happy when she just disappeared without a fight. It was the best day of my life when she signed those papers. I expected to hear from her when nine months after she signed the papers, we changed the locks and put her apartment up for sale. I was waiting for the fight that was sure to happen. I was prepared for it. Unfortunately, she let me down once again. I was so disappointed, but hey, by then I should've been used to her not doing what I expected.

My dick begins to deflate just thinking of that bitch. It's yelling at me to get back to that no more than five-foot-tall woman that came to our rescue today. Usually, someone like her would have never turned me on. The cute little pixie cut that framed her square face. Those deep brown eyes with the slight slant tells me she's either got some Native American or Asian in her ancestry. Her cute ass, which I couldn't help but look at while she was bent overlooking at my engine. I just wanted to lift the bottom of that skirt she was wearing to find out if she wore a thong or was going commando underneath. If I were a betting man, I'd go with commando. There was not one line that would've told me she was wearing anything under that skirt. Trust me; I examined it very well with my eyes.

Oh, these thoughts are going to get me in trouble. I can't get a hard-on while sitting here with my three babies waiting to go to their recital. I shift, uncomfortably to try to calm my wayward dick down. Mikael shoots his eyes to mine quickly then turns his attention back to the girls. I'm sure he'll have questions later since he can't say anything in front of the children. I have to get this woman out of my mind before I drive myself crazy and do something I swore I'd never do again.

CHAPTER THIRTEEN
ELIZABETH

CONCERT AND BABIES

WHEN CARTER GOT out of the truck and closed the door behind him, I had to pull away as fast as I could. If I didn't, I may have said or done something I'd likely regret. Like snatch up all three of those babies and take them home with me. Give them the mommy that Carter implied they didn't have.

Those were three of the most precious little girls I've ever had the pleasure of meeting. Not only were they beautiful, but they were kind, respectful and very well mannered.

And that little one, be still my beating heart. She may be the most precious one of the whole bunch. She's tiny and reminds me so much of myself.

All three are very well spoken for their age. If Carter didn't tell me they were triplets, I would've put the bigger two at about four and the little one at three at the most. But, my guess is they are all closer to four.

Then, when he said it was just him and his girls, and implied he was doing this on his own, it was everything I could not to let my jaw drop to the floor. That's something you hardly ever see. A single father who has custody of his kids and doing it all on his own.

That does a little something to my insides. It awakens something inside of me that I thought had died long ago.

I know I should go straight to the concert hall, but I have to pull over to the side of the road for a few minutes to get my heart and emotions under control.

It's both a blessing and a shame that I'll probably never see the four of them again. I don't know if it would be possible to not throw myself shamefully at that man. Even if I did, just to be able to be a part of his children's lives. Not that he wouldn't be a bad prize himself, but really, it's all about those babies for me. I always wanted to be a mother, but those dreams were squashed. Just a few minutes with those three girls brought the longing right back to me.

I can't imagine ever growing up without my mom. Like, how does he teach them things a little lady should know? Who bakes cookies with them and has flour fights with them like my mom and I always had? My heart breaks a bit for the girls and I wish like anything they had a mother in their lives.

Not that they look like they're missing out. I can't help but wonder what happened to her. Did she pass away? Something tragic? I can't imagine she would have just abandoned those precious gifts. No woman I've ever known would ever leave their babies behind. Angie is a shining example of that. Her baby was created through a disgusting act, but the mom instinct in her kicked in and she's raised that precious boy with all the love she has.

Obviously there has to be someone who helps them. Little girls need someone to help them learn fashion, to brush and maintain their hair, to teach them about boys and the heartbreak they can cause. They did appear to be well taken care of, from their hair to their clothes to the way they act. Maybe they have a nanny or something. That would make sense. The rich usually do have nannies for their kids. Andrew would tell me all the time about all the nannies he had growing up.

I have to get my shit together. I need to get to the concert hall and I can't do that if I don't let this go. I made a promise to Alfonso and I refuse to break it. I'd never do anything to make him feel like he isn't number one in my book. I would never want him to feel let down.

I quickly wonder again if Carter feels the same way about his girls.

I put the truck back in gear and head down to the hall. When I get there, I see that the lot is filling up quickly. Shit. My rig is going to take up a lot more room than my car would have so I'm going to have to park it way in the back.

When I finally make it inside, the front of the auditorium is already full. It takes me a while, but eventually I find a decent seat. Not the seats I wanted, but at least Alfie will still be able to see me. And even if he can't, I'm sure he'll hear me cheering him on.

I look around as the auditorium continues to fill up, searching for Angie. I know she's got to be here by now as the concert is ready to begin but don't see her anywhere. I would get up to look for her, but I'm not losing these seats. No sooner than I have that last thought, I feel a body slump down in the seat next to me. I look over and Angie's appearance is all frazzled.

"Thanks for the seat," she drones.

"What made you think that seat was for you?" I laugh as I sit back down.

"Who else would you save it for?" she asks, brow raised like she's daring me to answer. "It's not like you've got any other friends but me, so obviously it's mine."

She's not wrong, so I'll let it go. Normally I'd banter with her back and forth, but my mind is lost on other things right now.

"Why are you late?" I ask her. Not that I don't know. Angie will be late for her own damn funeral.

"I'm here on time. I don't know what you're talking about," she answers. "You obviously were late being as we're not in the front row like we normally are. You're always here so early, it guarantees us seats up front. Do you know how long it took me to find you back here because I was looking all through the front rows for you?"

Of course, she would catch on to that. Before I have a chance to answer, the lights go down and the Master of Ceremonies steps on the stage.

MY BOY WAS AMAZING! He's always amazing but tonight, tonight was really his night to shine!

"Auntie Elizabeth," he yells, excitedly. "Did you see me? Did you see everyone stand up when I was done? Oh my God, Auntie Elizabeth, that was amazing."

He's very excited and rightfully so.

"I saw you, Alfie!" I reply. "You were the most amazing singer tonight. No one else was even half as good as you were. You're gonna do big things kid!" I take my hand and I ruffle his hair with my last statement.

I mean what I say. He is going to go somewhere with that voice of his. His dream one day is to go to Julliard in New York. I can definitely see that happening sooner rather than later. I've set up a college fund for him, so he won't ever have to worry about having the means to do so.

This boy is going to blow up the billboards one day and, come hell or high water, I'm going to be there to help make it happen.

"Hey, Mom," he looks back to his mother, "Mr. Donaldson wants to talk to you about a project he wants me to work on with him. He has a few students that he wants to take with him to the White House to sing for the President and I'm one of them. Can I, Mom, can I? Please, I promise I'll do all my chores and I'll get good grades. Please, Mom, it'll mean everything to me."

"Stop, Alfonso," Angie says as she puts her hand up, the smile adorning her face showing the pride she has in her son. "Of course, I'll let you go. You don't have to drone on and on and make all of these promises. I'd never keep you from something this important. Stay here with Aunt Elizabeth and I'll go talk to your vocal coach."

"Thanks, Mom, you're the best!" Alfie exclaims as he throws his arms around her in a big hug.

I'm in awe of Angie's relationship with her son. It could have turned out so much different with the circumstances surrounding Alfie's conception but Angie has never let any pain from that show. I'm so proud of my best friend. I don't think I would have been able to make the decision she did had I been in her shoes.

"Come on," I say to Alfie as I grab his hand. "Let's get away from all of these people and wait for your mom over by the snack station."

Alfie loves his snacks. That he gets from me. I'm the bad influence when it comes to food. I love my chocolate and my sugar. If Angie wasn't so strict when I'm not around, I'm sure Alfie would be as big as a house. If it weren't for two hours' worth of gym time a day for me, I sure as fuck would be.

We head over to the snack table and each grab a plate full of goodies. Alfie tells me all about this upcoming trip to the White House and how his coach asked him to do a solo. He's so excited and I'm just as excited for him. This is a once in a lifetime chance he'll have and no doubt he'll blow the entire cabinet away.

CHAPTER FOURTEEN
CARTER

RECITAL

MY BABIES, they are truly amazing. They were absolutely perfect. I may be a little biased, but hey, I had three girls up on that stage that looked absolutely incredible.

Isabella, though. After what I witnessed tonight, I realize that I may be dishonoring her talent by holding her back to stay with her sisters. She truly is a shining light on that stage and should be moved up. I will speak with Miss Jenny and let her know she was right. I hope this doesn't affect the other two, but I can no longer deny that Isabella is a natural and should be training more than the other two.

"Man, you've got your work cut out for you with that one," Mikael states from behind me. "She's going to be phenomenal. You're likely going to have to pay a small fortune in training alone for her. But don't worry, if you refuse, I'll be happy to become her favorite person and do it for her."

Like hell, he'll become my girls' favorite person. They'll all always be Daddy's girls if I have anything to say about it.

"Not happening, dude. You'll never be the light their daddy is. However, if you insist on paying for her training, you're more than welcome." I know he'd really do it if I let him.

Mikael gives me a look and then just shrugs his shoulders.

I'd never make him pay for anything for my girls and he knows it. But I had to agree just to see if he'd take the bait.

I head off to the backstage area so I can speak to their instructor and so I can retrieve my girls.

"Miss Jenny," I say as I lightly touch her arm to get her attention.

"Oh, Mr. Montgomery, did you see how beautiful your girls were tonight. Did you see Isabella lead everyone into perfection? That girl, I'm telling you Mr. Montgomery, she has it. She really has it."

"I know," I reply. "That's what I wanted to talk to you about. I think you are right, and I am holding Isabella back. I'd like for you to go ahead and advance her. I'll explain it to all the girls later, but please, plan on Isabella being in the advanced class from here on out."

"Thank you, Mr. Montgomery. I'm excited to get to work with her more. She's gonna be a damn fine ballerina one day, take my word for it."

"Thank you. Now, let me go find the girls."

I walk away, looking at all the adorable little faces just chattering on and on. These little girls love what they do, and they look so cute doing it. I turn my head and spot my girls. They are talking to each other and laughing. My girls are always laughing about something.

"What's so funny?" I ask from behind them, startling them.

"Daddy," all three yell and jump up to get in my arms.

Good thing they are still little, and I can still carry all three at one time. I pick them all up and give each girl a nuzzle.

"You girls were beautiful out there tonight," I tell them excitedly.

"Especially Isabella!" Sofia exclaims.

"Yes, Isabella was the star!" shouts Felicia.

Wow, even my girls recognize how good their sister is. They are very excited for her. And here I thought they'd be upset they're not at her level.

I put all three of them down and look into their adorable faces.

"Isabella," I start, "what do you think about starting advanced classes? Miss Jenny thinks you should be doing more and after what Daddy saw tonight, I have to agree. So, would you be you okay not dancing with your sisters anymore?"

Isabella looks very thoughtful as she processes what I'm saying to her. Instead of answering me, she looks to her sisters. Her thoughtfulness is astounding. She's studying their faces for disappointment, but that's not what she gets. Both Felicia and Sofia are nodding their heads at her excitedly.

"Do it," they both yell to encourage her.

"Okay, Daddy," she finally answers. "I'll do it."

All three of the girls start jumping up and down in each other's arms. I love their support of one another.

"I don't wanna dance anymore." I suddenly hear one of my girls say softly. It's Sofia, and this is a big surprise to me. I thought she loved it.

I bend down again and grab my baby.

"What's wrong baby girl? Are you upset Isabella isn't going to dance with you anymore? Why don't you want to dance anymore? I thought you loved dancing."

"No, Daddy, I still want to learn. I like to dance but I don't want to do it all the time. Can't I just dance when I want to?" Sofia, my little adult at the age of three.

"Of course you can, baby girl," I reply and then turn to Felicia. "What about you, princess, do you still want to dance?"

"Yes, Daddy. But I don't want to be a ballerina like Isabella. I want to dance like thems." She points to the hip hop girls in the corner. It doesn't surprise me. She's always changing the music at home to something more upbeat.

"You can do whatever you want," I reply to not only Felicia, but to all three of them.

"Let's get out of here; I hear Uncle Mik wants to buy us dinner."

"Yay!" all three yell and run off in Mikael's direction.

On my way out, I see Miss Jenny and decide to let her know what's going on. I explain that Isabella has agreed to move up. I also inform her that Felicia wants to change classes and Sofia won't be dancing anymore.

I can't believe my girls are already separating themselves from each other. They probably don't even realize this will cause them to spend less time together. If they change their minds and all want to be together again, I'll do everything I can to make it happen.

By the time we make it home, the girls are beyond tired. I quickly give them a bath and put them to bed. The great thing about them being triplets is I can just throw the three of them in the tub at once. People may think it's hard getting three girls bathed and to bed, but it's a pretty easy task for me.

Once I tuck the girls in for the night, I head back downstairs to the kitchen. After the day we've all had, I need a drink. I don't imbibe too much. I have my children who only have me to depend on, but some nights I need a little bourbon to relax me.

I take the bottle down from the cabinet above the fridge and pour myself three fingers. I look at the bottle, longingly, as I wish I could just drink until I stop thinking.

I can't get that woman out of my damn mind. The image of her smiling has been playing on repeat in my head. When she bent over the front of my SUV, and when she hugged and kissed my girls goodbye like she's known them all their lives.

I bet that woman is going to be a great mom. The kind of mom I wish my girls had sometimes. I wonder if she's single. I didn't notice a ring on her finger, trust me, I looked. Although some men don't care if there's a ring, I'm not one of them. I won't be the cause of someone else's heartache.

It took a long time for me to stop hurting after learning the truth about Maggie. I don't think my heart will ever fully heal and I don't think I'll ever be able to trust another woman, either.

It's been almost five years since I've been with a woman. I plain old gave up even trying. Sure, I probably could've gone out there and had a one-night stand or a dozen, but I never felt the need after being hurt so deeply.

I think Elizabeth could be a game changer. I can see myself making love to her for hours. The problem is I'm sure one time wouldn't be enough with a woman like her. I'd be hooked the first time and want to go back for seconds, thirds, hundreds. Too bad, I'm not willing to open myself up to something like that again. I have my girls to think about and there's no way in hell I'll bring another woman around them.

I look down at the card in my hand. I hadn't even realized I pulled it out of my pocket and wonder what Elizabeth is doing now. Is she thinking of me like I'm thinking of her? Was she able to walk away and not look back?

I go to take a sip of my drink and look at the glass in bewilderment. I didn't even taste the first sip, never mind realize that I drank the whole thing. Reluctantly, I put the glass in the sink and decide to head to bed. Tomorrow is another day and I have to find out what's going on with my car.

I guess I'm going into the office to work tomorrow. The girls will enjoy that. They haven't been there in quite a while, since I moved my office to the house. But they do love going there and playing in the daycare whenever I don't have a choice but to be there. It'll be easier working in the city, since I have access to the daycare, so I'll be able to either get my car or a rental, rather than have to go back and forth, between there and home and not have to drag the girls all around with me.

I grab my phone and put an order in with the car service to pick me and the girls up in the morning. They'll have car seats available for the girls since theirs are in the SUV and I didn't think to ask Mikael to borrow his. It'll be safer than calling a cab.

With everything taken care of for tomorrow, I put my phone on my charger and head to my bedroom. I guess I'll get to bed, tomorrow is already looking like it's going to be another long day.

CHAPTER FIFTEEN
CARTER

RESTLESS NIGHTS AND NIGHTMARES COME TO LIFE

SLEEP DIDN'T COME easy last night. I spent most of the night tossing and turning, trying to get the images my mind was conjuring up of Elizabeth out of my head.

My imagination was sure getting the best of me and I had to keep forcing myself awake to get rid of those thoughts. It's been ages since I've been intimate with a woman, but the things that were happening in my dreams last night make me believe that I'd never been out of practice. Who knows? Maybe when they say it's like riding a bike, they're right. I know one thing for sure, if I ever get my hands on that woman… I won't last long. At least not the first time. Being celibate for so long will cause my stamina to be nil.

Deciding I can't let these thoughts linger, I get out of bed and head for the shower. I have to work out this fucking hard on I just gave myself again. I swear my hand and cock have become very well acquainted these last twenty-four hours.

Shower done and a tiny bit satisfied, I head downstairs to get some coffee and to start breakfast for my girls.

Freyda taught me early in the girls lives that breakfast was the most important meal of the day. I missed making them breakfast one day and boy were those three cranky for the rest of the day. Freyda also convinced me that making my girls a homemade breakfast was also very important. It keeps routine for them and keeps them healthy. The one day I forgot breakfast, I gave them cereal instead. Again, it was not a good day, to say the least.

Looking through the pantry, I decide waffles and breakfast sausage will be a good start today. I grab all the ingredients I need from the pantry, the sausage from the freezer and get to work.

No sooner do I grab the last waffle out of the waffle iron, then I hear the girls chuckling upstairs. Taking the steps, two at a time, I head straight to their room. The girls are sitting on the floor together playing with their dolls. They are so incredibly adorable right now.

I'm so blessed with these three; I don't know what I'd do without them in my life. They hardly ever give me a hard time, well, except when I forget to feed them a wholesome, homemade breakfast. That won't ever happen again.

Felicia notices me standing by the door first and jumps up and runs straight for me. I lean down and snatch her up in my arms and begin tickling and kissing her all over. She laughs and laughs. Soon, the other two are trying to tackle me to the floor to save their sister. I oblige, of course, and pretend to fall to the floor where all three try to tickle me. I smother them all with kisses and hugs and tickles. This, right here, is what life is all about. It's the happiness on my girls' faces; it's the love they give to me and each other so freely.

Knowing that I can't be too long, I scoop all three up in my arms and head down to the kitchen to feed them. When the girls see that I made them waffles, they get so excited I feel like I'm going to drop them. I gently put each of them in their seats at the table and serve them up their food. While they eat, I cut up some fresh fruit for them since I know I have to give them a little healthy snack on top of the meal I made them.

After breakfast, I call the Audi dealership to find out about my car. I'm very confused when they say they never received it. Elizabeth told me she was bringing it there right after she was done with what she needed to do for the day. I'm going to have to search for that card she gave me yesterday and find out where my car is.

With that thought, I get the girls ready and head into the office.

I GET to the office with the girls and they are so excited to be able to go to the daycare and play. The workers I've hired love when the girls come to see them. Everyone here loves my girls.

I head towards my office but stop to see Mikael first. I need to talk to him and let him know we'll be here for the day.

"Hey, bro," I say as I open his door. He's on the phone but as soon as he sees me, he tells whomever he's talking to that he'll call them back.

"Why didn't you tell me you were coming to the office?" he asks as he's putting the phone back on the cradle.

"I called the car service because of the girls," I begin. "I forgot to ask you to leave me their seats, so I had to call the service to come get us. I didn't want to bother you again today after all you did for us yesterday."

"Bullshit." He's not happy and it shows. "You know those are my girls as much as they are yours. Don't fill me with that crap."

"I have too much to do today and have to get my car back. I just didn't want to be a bother to anyone," I respond, honestly.

He seems to believe me this time and sits back in his chair.

"Listen," I say, "I need to find out where my car is. I may need to leave here for a little while. You know I hate to leave my girls at any time but I don't think I should drag them around with me today.

Would you mind keeping your eye on them until I get everything figured out?"

Mikael really is the only person besides myself I'd ever trust with my girls. I may have the daycare center here but I've always been onsite. If there was ever an emergency, I would never leave unless I knew Mikael was in the building. His security firm is run out of my building and neither he nor I would ever think of moving it anywhere else.

"You don't even have to ask," he answers. And I know he means that. They really are his girls too.

I head to my office, so I can call Elizabeth to find out what happened with my car.

I work for a little while, so I can get my head together before I decide to head to the address Elizabeth gave me to pick up my car.

Apparently, she decided it was best to fix my car herself, instead of me paying the dealership to fix an issue I should've never had in the first place.

There was a recall the dealership should have caught the last time they had my car. It was a faulty part which caused it to stop running. She told me that with my last maintenance check, they had that information on hand and should have taken action to correct the issue. She was quite upset it wasn't done and decided to take on the task herself. Free of cost, she said. So she thinks. There's no way I won't pay her for going above and beyond.

Her claims that it was for my girls and that she didn't want to have to see me in that situation again made my heart a little softer where she was concerned. The more I try to get her out of my head, the harder she becomes embedded in it. I can't take chances on someone coming into my life. I have to quickly get my car so I can get her out of my life as abruptly as she appeared.

Instead of heading right over, I decide to use my ensuite bathroom to take care of a pressing matter that was affecting the front of my trousers. I haven't had to jack off this much since Maggie was pregnant with the girls. My dick hasn't been satisfied with just my hand ever since Elizabeth showed up to help me and the girls. He'll have to deal with it, however, because I don't plan on ever letting a woman in my life or bed again.

Before I take leave, I stop in the daycare to see the girls. They are always my first priority and I want to make sure they are not driving the daycare personnel crazy. The three of them can be a handful if you're not prepared. I've already called for a car and I'm sure they are waiting outside, but I pay them enough, they can wait for me. If they want to complain or leave, then that will be the last time I use this service. The girls look like they are having a blast, so instead of interrupting them, I just observe them for a moment and head out.

As suspected, there's a car idling at the curb. As soon as the driver sees me come out of the building, he rushes to the back and opens my door. He doesn't ask any questions as I've already given his company all the information they need to get me where I'm going. I sit in the back seat, contemplating things I shouldn't be.

I wonder what it would be like to have a woman like Elizabeth in my life. I could see so much potential in her. She's already shown more care for the girls in the five minutes she's known them than their mother ever did. No doubt in my mind she would make an amazing mother. I briefly wonder if she'd be open to becoming the girls' mother, then chide myself for letting my thoughts head in that direction.

I don't realize how much time has passed, but next thing I know, we're pulling up to a garage. I see my SUV inside one of the bays and wonder if I came here too early. Although Elizabeth told me on the phone the car was done already, I wonder if she thought I was coming later and had to scramble to complete the job.

Entering the front of the bay, I don't see anyone around. I hear some laughter coming from somewhere in the back and head that way. I know normally you shouldn't enter a garage because of liability issues, but I ignore that thought.

The laughter gets louder as I approach what looks to be an office. One of the voices I'm sure is hers, but I don't know the other.

Peeking into the office, I see Elizabeth behind the desk and another female standing behind her looking at a computer. She takes my breath away the moment my eyes land on her. That smudge of grease on her face makes her more attractive to me than when she was all dressed up the other day. I've never found women like her attractive before, but right now, my dick is telling me he needs more action.

Ignoring him, as I have been, I lightly knock on the door. Both women jump when they hear me, and it looks like Elizabeth is scrambling to turn off her monitor. Hmm…I'm curious now to know what they were looking at.

"Hello, Elizabeth," I say with a smile.

"Hello, Carter," she replies. "I wasn't expecting you until later, I'm sorry. Angie, this is the gentleman I was telling you about who has those three precious girls. Carter, this is my best friend Angela. She's the mom of my amazing nephew who blew the roof of the concert hall I was heading to yesterday, before I got the call to tow you."

She's cute and rambling a little. I can see the nervousness in her eyes and I wonder if she can see that she has the same effect on me.

"Nice to meet you." I reach out my hand to shake Angela's. She's almost as beautiful as Elizabeth and I wonder what Mikael would think if he ever met her. Maybe I should set them up.

I stop myself, yet again. I can't go there. Mikael and Angela hitting it off would mean me seeing more of Elizabeth and my dick would never forgive me for that unless he was getting to bury himself inside her.

Fuck, there he goes again.

"Do you need more time with my car?" I ask as I point out to the bay.

"Oh, no," Elizabeth replies. "She's all done. I can't believe those assholes didn't catch the recall and put you and your girls at risk like that."

"Oh, I thought maybe because it was still in the air, that it wasn't done." I tell her honestly.

"No, not at all. I just didn't want it parked on the street, so I just left it in the bay. Let me grab your keys."

I turn around to leave and notice that Angela is no longer anywhere in sight. That's weird. It's like she just disappeared. I didn't even hear her walk away.

Elizabeth meets me back out by the car and hands me my keys.

"I hope I didn't chase your friend away," I tell her. "I didn't want to interrupt, but the girls are in daycare and I have to get back to the office."

Now I'm the one rambling.

"I could've brought the car to you," she shyly tells me. "You didn't have to come here. I would've loved to see your girls one last time."

If I didn't have an iron gate around my heart, I swear this woman may have just wormed her way into it.

"I didn't want you to go out of your way," I tell her. "You've done so much for us already; I don't think I could ever thank you enough. Here, take this." I hand her an envelope with what I figure to be a little more than a fair rate for the work she's done. I may have given more than a little, but in reality, I don't think it will be enough.

"No," she tries to refuse the envelope, "I can't accept that."

"Okay," I say making her believe that she'll get away with it.

I get in my car to leave and slowly back out. As I'm leaving, I call out for her. When she approaches my window, I toss the money out and she catches it. I pull away without speaking. She can't refuse it if I'm not there.

When I get back to the office, I head straight for the daycare. I'm going to grab my girls and head home. They'll be happy to be back home again, and truth be told, sharing them for as long as I did today is taking a toll on me.

When I get to the daycare, I notice the girls sitting on the floor talking to someone. This woman is not someone I hired to be here, so I head over immediately to find out who she is. As I get closer to the girls, the hairs on my arms stand, my hackles are raised. I realize, not soon enough, that the woman sitting with *my* children is Maggie. How fucking dare she?

I look around and notice Natalie sitting at her desk. I wave her over, and she jumps up immediately.

"Who the fuck let her in here?" I question, very angrily.

"Um, she said she was the girls' mother, I didn't think that was an issue," she replies, and I just about blow a fuse.

Everyone who was hired here was carefully vetted either by me or Mikael. Everyone should know that no one, and I mean no one, is allowed near the girls that doesn't work here.

"No, that's not okay, Natalie," I answer, my anger building. "You need to get the girls, right now, and bring them to Mikael's office. Afterwards, I would appreciate you gathering your things because you will no longer be employed here. The rules have always been the same. Unless you work here, you are not allowed access to my children. I don't care who they say they are. You should've called me or Mikael if there was a question, and this is something you definitely should've questioned. You've put my girls at risk, and that is immediate grounds for termination. Do you understand?"

"Yes," she answers. I see tears form in her eyes, but don't have it in me at the moment to sympathize with her.

She walks up to the girls and instructs them to go with her. When they look up at her, they seem confused. She tells them again they need to go and reluctantly, they get up. Each of my girls hugs Maggie. I'm beyond angry now. Someone will pay for this! As soon as the girls leave, I point to the office behind Maggie and she follows me in.

"What the fuck are you doing here?" I bellow. Yeah, I couldn't ask calmly, there's no calm anywhere in me right now.

"Oh relax, Carter," Maggie answers with a coolness that has my blood boiling even more. "I came to see my children. I need them to get to know me. You know, it's time for me to have my children back."

"Over my dead body," I reply. "What fucking makes you think you have any rights to my children? You signed away your rights to them years ago. You have no right to even be here."

"Well, I may have signed some papers, but you know it was against my will."

"What the fuck are you talking about, against your will?"

"Oh, you remember, you forced me to sign those papers."

Is she fucking serious? I made her sign those papers? I think not. She didn't want our children, she said so many times.

"I don't think so, Maggie." She's fucking even crazier now than she was back then. "You wanted money, that's all you wanted. I had to fucking beg you to even have my children. You are fucking delusional if you think I made you do anything."

"Well, take this as your warning, Carter," she starts. "I'm asking the court for custody of my children. I will prove to them how much you abused us then and continue to abuse them now. I will have my girls and you are the one who will never see them again."

"Get out," I answer with all the strength I can muster. "Get out and never come near me or my girls again."

I don't know where she got the gall to accuse me of such things, but I know if she doesn't leave right now, I may do something that I'll not only regret but that will cost me my girls.

Right at the perfect time, Mikael walks into the daycare with three of his security officers in tow.

"Maggie," Mikael says, "you need to leave. If you don't leave right now, my officers will happily escort you from the premises."

"Fine," she mutters. "But this isn't over. Not by a long shot. You'll pay, Carter. That I promise you."

With that final statement, she picks her purse up off the floor and leaves the daycare. Mikael waves to his officers and they follow her to ensure she leaves the building.

"What the fuck was that?" Mikael asks.

"Not now," I reply. "Where are the girls? I have to get them home."

I don't have time to explain to Mikael what happened, but I'm sure once he secures the building he'll be at my house. He knows not to fuck around when it comes to the girls. He gets on his radio and not two minutes later my girls come running into the room and straight into my arms.

"She said she was our mommy," Isabella says and starts crying.

"Don't cry baby," I gently croon. "Daddy will make sure that lady doesn't come near you again."

With that last statement, I grab all three girls and head home.

CHAPTER SIXTEEN
CARTER

I'LL DO ANYTHING TO KEEP MY GIRLS SAFE

ONCE I GET HOME with the girls, I head straight to their playroom. I need time with them after that monster was near them. They need my reassurance that everything is going to be okay, or maybe it was me that needed the reassurance.

I sit right in the middle of the floor and the girls join me. This is our special place and where we spent our special time. Plus, this is where I've taught the girls they can share anything that is on their minds and they would never get in trouble. I aimed to give them a special spot, so they knew they could always speak their minds. It's my hope that as they get older and more mature, that they will carry this forward in life and always know they can come to me without judgement.

"Hey girls," I start. Even though we've been together for the last hour, I have always started our time in this spot like this.

"Hi, Daddy," all three reply at once. They were always so in sync whenever they'd answer me. It was like it was rehearsed. Well, I guess it kind of was since we did this weekly.

"So," I continue, "I know you have questions about that lady you saw today, and since this is our safe place, you can tell me anything. If you feel something, I can help you. Who wants to go first?" I try to remain as calm as possible, though there is a strong battle raging within me.

"Is she really our mom?" This comes from Isabella. She doesn't look me in the eye like she normally does, though. She's looking at the floor.

"She is the woman who gave birth to you, yes," I answer honestly.

"Is she going to take us away from you, Daddy?" This is Felicia and she nearly breaks my heart when she asks that. I want to reach for her, but know it isn't the time yet. We aren't done with honest time and I have to wait until everyone gets their feelings out of the way.

"No, Daddy will never let her take you away from me." It was an honest answer for sure. There's no way I'd ever let her near my girls, again.

"Will she come live with us and be our mommy again?" Sofia's turn to ask a question makes me angrier than I thought I'd be.

"No, pretty girl, she will not."

"Why not? Doesn't she loves us like other mommies love their children?"

"Daddy loves you more than anything. I can't answer for that woman, or how she feels, but aren't you happy here with just Daddy?" My girls have no idea how much this is gutting me. I thought I had my heart broken before, when Maggie spewed her evil, but this was a hundred times worse.

"But," Sofia cries, "why can't we have a mommy like the other kids?" She's starting to shake she's crying so hard. It takes everything in me to not snatch her up. Even Isabella and Felicia are starting to cry now.

Fuck it, I grab all three and hold them close to me, thank goodness I have long arms that I can wrap them all up at once. This is breaking their hearts. Something I never wanted for them. My girls are so sensitive and so smart beyond their years. I can't handle this.

All four of us just sit here and cry. Well, the girls cry. I'll cry later when they aren't around. My girls can't see how much them hurting is breaking my heart too.

"Knock, knock," comes from the door. It's Mikael.

I knew he'd follow us here as soon as he secured the building. I'm sure his security team received some harsh scrutiny from him. He was just as hard as I was when it came to these girls.

"Can Uncle Mik get a hug from my girls?" he asks. Looking at all three of them crying in my arms, I'm sure his heart is breaking as much as mine.

"Okay," Sofia tells him as she slowly wedges herself out of my arms.

Isabella and Felicia just hold onto me tighter. They aren't ready to let go. That is fine with me. If I had my way, I'd hold all of them in my arms and shield them from pain forever.

"Come on to Uncle Mik," Mikael says as he reaches down and picks Sofia up into his arms.

With her in his arms, he walks over to where we are sitting and sits down beside us.

"Did I miss honest time?" he asks looking at the two holding tightly to me with their faces buried in each side of my neck.

"No," I hear Isabella mumble. Seems she is coming out of her sobbing fit now. Sniffling and wiping her nose on her sleeve. I guess raising them as I had been doing wasn't teaching them to be ladies, after all.

"No?" Mikael asks. "Okay, so here's my honest then. Uncle Mik will never let anyone hurt you again. I'm going to make sure you won't get scared again by any strange ladies."

"She was our mom," Felicia states as she climbs out of my arms and sits back down next to me.

"No," I reply, "she's not your mom."

"But, Daddy, you said she was?" Sofia asks.

"No, sweetheart," I reply and motion for Sofia to sit on the floor. If we were going back into honest time, she needs to be seated on the floor and not in her uncle's lap. She looks at Mikael like he is going to contradict me then reluctantly sit back down on the floor.

"She did give birth to you, yes," I continue, "but your mom she is not. She gave up that right when you guys were babies. She wasn't ready to be a mother and decided to allow me to raise you on my own. You can't call a woman like that Mom."

"But, why didn't she want to be with us?" Isabella asks.

"That's not an answer I can give you right now. Right now you're way too young to understand. My hope was that you wouldn't ever have to deal with what happened when you three were just wee babies. When you are older, you are more than welcome to ask again. But for now, know that Daddy isn't going to tell you everything."

Mikael looks at me, sorrow in his eyes.

"Know that your daddy has done everything to make sure you girls are always safe and happy," Mikael tells them. "As have I. I failed you today and that wasn't okay. You guys trust Uncle Mik, right?"

All three nod at his question.

"Then trust me and your daddy when we tell you what happened isn't something you ever want to know. Trust that we would only do what's best for you. Know that we don't *ever* want to see you cry or hurt."

With that, all three girls look around at us, then each other and nod their heads.

"Can we play now?" Sofia asks.

"Yes," I answer. "Do you want Uncle Mik and me to play with you too?"

"We can play dollies," Isabella yells excitedly.

Felicia gets up off the floor and runs to the doll bin. She grabs the bin and wobbles back over to us. Once she gets to where everyone is sitting, she dumps the entire bin on the floor. I hold back a chuckle, wink at Mikael and both of us grab a doll and begin to play with the girls.

MIKAEL and I played with the girls for a few hours before they started to get tired. I ordered a couple of pizzas and we sat on the playroom floor to eat. While the girls were eating, I noticed their eyes getting droopy. I picked up Isabella and Sofia to wash them up and get them ready for bed. Mikael grabbed Felicia and followed along, getting her ready too. The girls went out quickly as the day was more emotional than they'd ever had, and they tired faster than they would normally have.

Mikael follows me as I walk into the kitchen. I reach on top of the sink and reach for the good stuff. I know I can't drink like I want to because of the girls, so I at least need top shelf to enjoy.

I pour Mikael and myself each three fingers of the bourbon and sit down at the island. Mikael doesn't say anything. He just sits down at the opposite side and takes a sip of his whiskey. He, too, needs to gather his thoughts, so we both sit in silence.

"I don't know what to do," I start. "She can't take my girls. Robert made sure the contract was ironclad. What does she have up her sleeve that she's come around after all this time?"

"I already got my tech looking into where she's been all these years," Mikael answers. I knew he'd be on this before I even asked.

"She's up to something," I say to Mikael, looking him straight in the eye. "She wouldn't just come around out of nowhere. Not unless she needs money and is up to something."

"I know," he answers. "But why now? I thought she'd come around after you locked her out of that apartment, but she didn't. I don't know anything, I'm sorry. I failed you, Carter. My job is to keep you and those girls safe and I failed you, again."

"No, you didn't. Stop that shit, man. This isn't on you. It was never your fault. Not even close. I don't blame you at all."

"But I blame myself!" he yells and stands up. "I watched her for over a year after she left. I know you don't know that, but I didn't want her coming back fucking up your head again. When I was sure she was done playing games with you, I stopped! But, she wasn't fucking done, now was she?"

Mikael can't blame himself for this shitshow. This is all on me for getting involved with that woman in the first place. I know I should be upset he never told me he was following her, but I'm not. I'm actually a bit relieved that he thought to protect us when I didn't.

"Not on you, man," I tell him. "Not on you at all. I never imagined she would come back here, ever. What we need to do now is figure out how to stop her, again."

"I wish I had the answers," he says and looks at his phone. He must've put it on silent because I didn't hear it ring.

"Yeah," he says as he answers. "No, fuck, yeah, thanks. Follow them. No, don't let them out of your fucking sight, do you hear me? If you lose them, you'll lose your fucking job, hear me? Yeah, okay. Keep me updated. No, wake me from my fucking sleep if something happens. No, I said fucking wake me. I don't care what time it is. Yeah, okay. Gotta go."

I couldn't hear the other side of that conversation, but it doesn't sound like it was a good one. Fuck, I don't want to hear what he has to say. Instead of talking to me when he hangs up the phone, he walks out of the kitchen. Grabbing the bourbon and our glasses, I follow. He is sitting on the couch when I find him, running his hands through his hair. He clearly walked away to take a minute to himself.

I put his glass down in front of him and top it off. I'd have more, but I can't take the chance and am just going to finish what was in my glass.

"She's married, man," he says then takes a gulp from his glass. "She's fucking married. I think that's why suddenly she thinks she has a right to the girls. I know she signed those papers, but if she's saying you forced her, the courts will want to investigate the circumstances. We didn't keep anything she did after she was gone for a few years. I didn't think it was necessary anymore. We thought we were free and clear of her. Her being married will show the courts she has some stability. She can use that to her advantage. The courts will probably side with you because of her giving up her parental rights, but she's got to have something else up her sleeve if she came after you. I don't know what it is yet, but the boys are looking into it. The courts may order temporary visitation until they make a final decision."

"Fuck!" I bellow. "This can't be fucking happening! She can't have my babies. There's no way." I cringe a little, realizing how loud I am. I can't wake the girls after the day they've had.

I look at the bottle on the table. I really want more. Mikael must hear my silent plea and pours more into my glass.

"I can't," I start.

"I'm here. There are four men outside," he states. "They know no one can come near. I don't plan on drinking much more because I need to get updates from my men. Just imbibe, man. This one time. You deserve it. I'm here. Drink."

I started the glass he poured before he even finished talking. He knew what I needed, and I knew that if I did drink too much, he would take care of the girls.

Mikael and I sit with our glasses in our hand, staring out into nowhere. We both, I'm sure, are thinking of ways to stop Maggie. This took us all by surprise and I don't know what I could do to thwart her attempts.

Finally, a wayward thought comes to my head.

"I need a wife," I blurt out. Mikael's head shoots up and looks at me with confusion.

"What the fuck?" he asks.

"I need a wife. Someone who could be the mom the girls need. At least for now, until this shit gets straightened out."

I know exactly who would fit the bill. It's going to take all the strength I could muster not to give in to her, but I have the perfect candidate in mind.

"Elizabeth," I state.

"Who?" Mikael asks, genuinely confused now. I hadn't told him yet about the sexy as fuck mechanic who has captured my eye and makes me sport a semi every damn time I think about her.

"My mechanic," I answer. She really isn't my mechanic, but I am definitely going to claim her now.

"No, man," Mikael pleads. "You don't need a wife. Stop this thought. Let's not make any hasty decisions. Let my team find out what the fuck that bitch is up to first."

"If I'm married, like she is, there is no way the courts can judge us differently," I tell him. I believe this, with all my heart. If I have a wife, the courts would see a whole family, the same as Maggie was going to try to portray. "I need to do this, to ensure my girls stay with me. After we get things settled in court, we'll get a divorce. I can do this. I need to do this – for my girls. I saw the way Elizabeth was with my girls, just that one day, for a quick moment in time. I'm sure she would look really good to the courts."

"No, man," Mikael states once again. "We'll figure this out without you going to that extreme. Just give me some time. If I can't get the answers you need, then you can consider doing something else. But, just give me and my team a chance."

"No, I'm doing this."

And with that thought, I walk out of the room and head to grab my phone. I need to make a call and I'm sure it wouldn't be an easy one.

CHAPTER SEVENTEEN
CARTER

CONVINCING ELIZABETH

WALKING OUT ON MY DECK, I give myself a little mental prepping. This is a big deal for me, and I know I'm not prepared for something this extreme. But I'll never be prepared to lose my girls and that is what needs to be my priority.

I look at my phone, trying to will myself to dial the number I know I need to dial. I'm hoping that calling the number she gave me goes straight to her and not to her business. I know that although I've prepared myself to speak to her, I'm not prepared to speak to someone else just to try to get in touch with her.

The phone rings. And rings.

Finally, her soft voice comes over the line, "Hello, you've reached Grace Family Auto Service, this is Elizabeth speaking, how can I help you?"

I don't answer. I get a bit tongue tied. Now that she's on the line, I don't know what to do.

"Hello," I hear once again. "Is anyone there?"

I try to answer but can't seem to find my voice.

"Hello, I can hear you breathing," she says angrily. "I don't appreciate crank calls. Please, don't call me again."

"Elizabeth," I answer before she has the chance to hang up. "It's Carter. Carter Montgomery."

"Oh, um, hi Carter. Is something wrong?" she asks, sounding concerned.

"Yes. I mean no. I mean yes." I don't know how to answer. Last time we spoke, it was about car problems. I don't want her to think she didn't fix the problem with my car, but I don't want her to think I'm okay either. I'm just so confused about how to answer the question.

"Is it your SUV?" she asks, concern clearly lining her voice.

Exactly what I didn't want to happen. Just then, a thought comes to me. She'll come out here if I tell her it's my car. If I tell her it's personal, she may not be as willing to listen to me. With my car, I know her concern would be genuine and will come quickly if I ask. With that thought in my mind, I continue.

"Yes," I lie. "I don't know what it is, and I have to get somewhere. The girls—"

I don't get to finish my sentence, she cuts me off.

"Tell me where you are, Carter," she says. "I'll be there as fast as I can." I feel a bit like a dick but this is what I need. This conversation shouldn't happen over the phone. She needs to see how serious I am and how serious this situation is. I give her my address and tell her that I'll be waiting.

Shit, now I have to figure out how to get rid of Mikael. He could ruin this for me.

I head into the house and see Mikael sitting on the couch, studying his phone.

"Hey, um," I start. "So, Elizabeth is on her way here. She thinks I'm having car problems. Do you think you can, like, um…" I point to the front door.

I really need him to leave.

"No fucking way," Mikael answers. "I'm not leaving you here. I'm not letting you do this, bro. There are other ways."

"Mik, this is my choice. It's what I want. Please, I need you to understand. You need to let me do this. Think of those babies you love so much," I say as I point upstairs.

He looks at me, resigned to my fate. "I'm not leaving. You can use me as an excuse if you have to. How you got from point A to point B, but I'm not leaving. I don't know this hooch, so I'm not letting you do this without at least vetting her."

I get what he's trying to say but I don't know that I want him to meet Elizabeth, yet. This could go the wrong way.

Five minutes later, the doorbell rings. Holy fuck that was quick.

I look at Mikael, and he just shrugs.

Guess I set myself up for this, might as well get it over with.

When I get to the door, I look back to where Mikael was sitting. He's no longer there though; he's literally standing right behind me.

"Do you mind?" I grind out.

"Not at all," he answers. "Answer the fucking door before you look like an asshole," he says and points to where Elizabeth is standing. Maybe getting a glass door wasn't the brightest idea. I put it on my mental checklist to change that.

"Hey," I say as I open the door. "This is my best friend, Mikael. He came over when I needed him." It's not a lie. "He's gonna watch the girls while we go talk outside."

The look Mikael gives me when I state that is priceless. I don't give him the time or the chance to grill Elizabeth. I walk outside and shut the door behind us.

"What's wrong with your car?" Elizabeth asks.

She looks beautiful. She's wearing some sexy jeans and a tank top. On her feet are a pair of chucks that match her tank top. She looks like she'd been working. Parked in my drive is a cute little Miata. Huh, my girl likes a little sport on the side with her big bad wrecker.

My girl. Where did that thought come from?

I look at Elizabeth again and smile. Yeah, she looks like she'll fit perfectly into my little land of chaos. I really hope she'll help me. I'll make it worth her while. Maybe in more than one way, too.

"I need your help," I tell her.

"That's why I'm here," she answers, looking up at me.

"No, not the kind of help you're thinking," I begin. "It's a lot more than just my car. As a matter of fact, my car is fine. There's something else I need. I noticed you're not wearing a wedding or engagement ring. Please tell me I assumed correctly, and you aren't married. Or seriously involved with someone?"

"Um, no, I'm not," she answers quizzically.

She should be confused. I've only met her twice, but I know in my heart she's the answer I need.

"I need you to be my wife," I quickly blurt out.

"Sorry?" she asks, bewildered.

"I need a wife. And my girls, they're already smitten with you after meeting you just that one time. I know you can do it. Please tell me you'll be my wife."

"That's not the way things happen, Carter. We don't know each other. We've never been out or spent time together, and how would you even think asking me to marry you would be appropriate. Here I was thinking something happened and you and your girls were in trouble. How dare you lure me out of here under such false pretenses."

She's angry, her voice getting louder with each statement. I didn't expect this. Hell, I don't know what I expected, but it sure as fuck wasn't this.

"Hold on," I say in a calming tone. I need to soothe the wild animal she's looking to become. She's a spunky little sprite. I find it turns me on even more. "Let me explain, please. You're right. I did lure you out here with a lie. But it wasn't all a lie. I do need you. I'm desperate and it could be damaging to the girls if I didn't. Please, hear me out."

I grab her arm before she walks away as I tell her this. She continues to glare at me, but I know I now have her attention.

"Can we walk over there?" I ask as I point to the playhouse. I don't want to take a chance of the girls waking up and hearing or seeing anything.

"Fine," she huffs and snatches her arm out of my grip and walks over to the playhouse.

"Elizabeth, I promise, you won't regret listening."

About a half hour later, I finish our story. Tears are running down Elizabeth's cheeks and I want to wipe them away. But she hasn't given me permission to touch her, so I won't.

"Are you serious? How… Just how can a mother do and say those things?" she finally asks. "I would've given anything to be a mother and have such beautiful girls. I can't believe a woman could be that evil."

She's right. I never, in a million years, would believe a story like my own had I not lived it. It's a horrendous one no one should ever endure. A woman that evil should only exist in horror movies. However, it is my reality and one that I need to keep my girls shielded from.

"It's true," I answer. "Not something I share often, but you needed to hear all of it to understand. She suddenly showed up today, at my office. She's insisting that she's going to get custody of my girls after all this time, even after signing away her rights. My best friend, he owns a security company. He has people who work for him that found out she's married. I know courts look at married couples more seriously than those who aren't married. Never mind the fact she's their mother. You know courts will more than likely side with a mother than they will a father. So, that brings me to why I called you. I saw how you were with my girls. I saw again tonight that one mention of me and the girls being in trouble, you ran over here quicker than I could blink. I know I'm making the right choice, but I need you to accept that also and help me. It's a huge responsibility, but I see an amazing mother in you and I can't lose my girls."

I know I'm babbling but I need her to understand the severity of the entire situation. I know I'm stating this as something temporary, but what I see in Elizabeth, I know I want so much more. I can see a lifetime with her. I know I just met her, but something inside me tells me she's it for me and my girls.

"I get it, Carter, I do." She looks up and then around. She walks away from me and starts roaming the property. I hope she's trying to see herself here. She can have anything she wants if she agrees.

"I'll pay you," I blurt out.

Those words sting more than I realize. I recall saying them years ago when Maggie was threatening to kill my girls, before they were even born. That thought, in and of itself, is what makes me sick to my stomach. I start to heave. I can't lose, I can't lose my babies.

I fold over, into myself. Oh, my God. What if she doesn't agree? What if she says no? Will I lose my girls?

I'm having a panic attack, I can feel it and don't know how to get myself out of it. I hear voices but can't clear my head.

My girls, they mean everything to me. I can't do this. I will leave this fucking country and disappear. I can't lose my girls.

"Breathe, brother." I faintly hear.

I realize then that Mikael is now outside with me. It's no longer Elizabeth. This makes my heartbeat pick up even more.

"No, she can't leave, don't let her leave," I beg my best friend. I realize then I'm on my knees and he's right beside me, trying to get me to stand. "Stop her, Mik, please."

"She's just inside, brother," Mikael tries to tell me calmly. "She ran inside to get me. You were screaming, and she couldn't get through to you so she came to get me."

I start to calm and realize that I must look like a pussy, but I don't care. These are my children we are talking about, my entire world.

"You woke the girls, bro," Mikael looks at me with sympathy in his eyes. "There's only one time I've ever seen you break like this. What happened?"

"I can't lose my girls," I choke out. The mantra is stuck in my head. I don't know how else to convey what I'm feeling.

He nods his head in understanding. "Come on, man, let's get you inside and cleaned up."

At that statement, I look down. I notice there's dirt and grass on my hands and my clothing. I really must've lost it… bad. I don't ever remember having such a break down. This is unacceptable. I need to be strong for my children. If anyone but Mikael, and hopefully, Elizabeth, had witnessed this, they could probably use this against me in court.

I mentally slap myself and stand. Time to put my fucking jock strap on and knock these fuckers down.

"Okay, I'm okay," I tell Mikael. "I need to get inside and see the girls."

Walking into the house, I get myself ready for a barrage of questions. My girls may be little, but they are very smart.

Instead, I hear laughing and giggling.

I look to Mikael and he just shrugs his shoulders and continues inside.

When I get to the playroom, my heart just about explodes, for a different reason than what just happened outside. Elizabeth is on the floor rolling around with the girls.

All three of them are on top of her trying to tickle her, it seems. She's playing with them the same way I do. It's like she knew what they liked. Like she already knows them.

"More," yells Sofia and I see Isabella and Felicia trying to hold onto Elizabeth's arms. They are trying to hold her down while Sofia tickles her.

And Elizabeth, she's letting them. I can see her pretending she's struggling but they are pretending to hold her back. She's trying to look serious as she tells the girls, "I'm gonna get you, you pretties. You'll all be mine. You can't keep me down."

This has to be one of the most precious moments I've ever seen with my girls when it comes to interaction with another female.

This sets my resolve. Now, I know I'm doing the right thing more than ever when I asked Elizabeth to marry me and become my girls' mother.

"Okay, girls, time to go back to bed," I say as I interrupt their playtime. It's very late and although I love how much Elizabeth is already bonding with the girls, I have to keep them on a routine. I can't let them run amok.

"But, Daddy," Felicia whines. She actually whines. My girls aren't normally whiners. They usually just listen and don't give me a hard time.

"Come on," Elizabeth tells them. "If you're good and listen to your daddy, maybe he'll let me read you a story."

Elizabeth gives me a look that dares me to disagree with her. She knows I'd do anything for my girls, so there's no way I'd be the bad guy and say no to her reading to them.

"Yay," all three squeal. Another noise I'm not used to hearing from them.

"Come on, let's go to our room," says Isabella as she grabs Elizabeth's hand and starts to drag her away.

"One story," I say. Not that they care what I have to say right now, and oddly, I'm okay with that.

Elizabeth turns to look at me as she walks out the door with my girls. They all look so happy. She gives me a wink and keeps walking.

I turn to Mikael, who has a shit eating grin on his face. "What the fuck just happened?" I ask. I'm truly confused by this turn of events.

"I think you just got your wish, buddy," Mikael answers. He turns and heads to the front door. After he opens it, he looks back at me. "Let me know how it all turns out."

CHAPTER EIGHTEEN
ELIZABETH

IS THIS A DREAM?

AFTER PUTTING the sweetest girls in the world to bed, I hurry to leave Carter's house. I don't want to face him right now. I need time to think.

Those girls, they were just the sweetest things ever. I ran into the house in a panic because I didn't know what was happening outside with Carter and I couldn't seem to get through to him.

When I entered the house, I saw a scene before me that just about broke my heart but soothed it at the same time.

Carter's friend had all three little girls on his lap, trying to soothe them. They must've heard their daddy outside and were crying for him. His friend, Mikael, was obviously close to the girls and thought he could handle them.

"Hi," I gently whispered. I didn't want to startle the children but was trying to make my presence known.

I didn't know what to do and needed someone's help.

"Is he okay?" he asked as he tilted his head toward the outside.

"Not really, he needs someone; can I help with the girls, so you can go out there?"

"Hi," the little one said as she raised her head and saw me standing there.

"Hi, pretty girl," I answered. "Do you mind if I play with you, so Mikael can help your daddy with something?"

"Okay," she answered softly. Slowly and easily, she climbed off Mikael's lap. "Can I show you our playroom? There's so much in there and you're a girl, we'll have so much fun."

Her mood seemed to be changing quickly and it eased me a little.

"How about you two?" I asked the other two girls.

"Okay," they both answered and climbed down off Mikael's lap to join their sister.

"This way," the biggest of the three said.

"Um…" I started, embarrassed. "Although I remember you girls, I seem to have forgotten who is who. You all look so much alike and silly me can't tell you apart."

I remembered the little one's name was Sofia, but the other two really do look alike and I can't tell them apart. I'm sure with time, it'll be easier for me to remember, but right now, I needed them to tell me.

"This is quite embarrassing," I quickly added on and did a little squirm which made the girls giggle.

"I'm Isabella," the one with her hair in a ponytail answered. "And that's Felicia, though Daddy calls her Licia."

"Okay," I replied. "I got it now. I promise I won't forget anymore." And I really hope I didn't. These girls are precious and if I consider doing what Carter has asked of me, I can't screw up their names. "So, where is this playroom? I'm ready to play already!"

"Come on," Isabella said and grabbed my hand.

Suddenly, all three girls were dragging me through the house. I took a quick peek back at Mikael and he mouthed a 'thank you' back to me before walking out the door.

I played with the girls for about thirty minutes before Mikael and

Carter came back and, I tell you, spending this little time with them was the highlight of my life. I've never been happier.

Even though these girls aren't mine, I love them already.

I recall everything Carter told me while we were outside, and suddenly, I completely understand his panic attack. I don't know what I would do if those girls were mine and someone was trying to take them away from me.

I call Angie and tell her I need her to meet me. I need a drink. And my best friend.

Someone needs to stop me before I make a mistake that could cost me the love of three little girls who've already captured my heart.

I get to the bar before Angie, so I order us each a drink and find us a table. I don't care how many drinks I have before she gets here, I am planning on getting drunk. And from the sound of her voice, it seems she may need to as well.

Angie's parents are likely watching Alfie for the night. I'm sure she even has them on standby as our DD's as well, knowing we are both having a bad day. It is a good thing her parents know how bad we could get and would come to get us once we are too hammered to get ourselves where we need to go.

I observe the people milling about and think about what their lives are like. Do they have practical strangers asking them to marry them and raise their kids? Do they know what they wanted in life? Are they happily married? Or are they out here planning on cheating on someone who thinks their life is perfect?

So many scenarios are running through my mind, I don't even notice Angie sit down at the table. I don't know how long she's been here, but she has already finished half of her drink. Apparently, she is waiting for me to get out of my own head and come back to reality.

"Bad day, huh," she asks while finishing off her martini. My girl is a vodka martini drinker. She doesn't like whiskey unlike me. She can't understand how I can drink the 'hard stuff' as she calls it.

Yeah, my best friend is obviously observant.

"You, too?" I ask in return.

It wasn't like Angie to need to come out and vent, but since she is apparently having as bad a day as I am and since she never complains, I know I have to listen to what is happening with her first.

"The asshole tried to contact me from jail," she begins. Immediately, my defenses rise.

"He's not allowed to do that!" I exclaim.

There is a restraining order on him, although he is in jail and has an order from the judge that he is never to try to contact Angie nor her child once he was born. That's what happens to rapists. They don't get to enjoy the child they created through a crime; they get to spend their lives miserable and in jail.

"I know," she answers meekly. "I just don't know what to do. Alfie has started asking questions and I don't know if I want to answer them myself. I think I want that asshole to tell his son what he did to me but then again, my boy is too young for this shit. I was going to reach out to the prosecutor who was on the case, but he's retired. My dad is looking into who we need to contact. I just don't know what to do. I don't want Alfie to hate me for him not having a father, but I don't want him to know his father is a rapist either, at least not until he's old enough to understand. I'm stuck, and I feel horrible that I'm going to disappoint my son."

Angie is babbling on. I don't know how to answer her. Although, it seems she knows what the answer should be, it isn't my place to tell her what to do. If it had been me, I don't think I could have ever gone through with having the child of the man who took my innocence and then blamed me for what transpired afterward.

"You don't have to do anything, Ang," I try to calmly explain. I know she knows this, but sometimes her parents and I have to reiterate it to her. "He has no rights. He's not allowed to contact you. This will give him more time in prison now that he's tried. He will never be allowed near you or Alfie and your parents and I will make sure he can't get near you. At this point, he likely will never see freedom, so you won't have to worry about Alfie ever having contact with him. You are an amazing mom and will find a way to explain things to your son without destroying him. I don't think he ever has to know how he was conceived, but that's on you. I don't think you should say anything. Personally, I wouldn't ever tell him if I were you. I'd let him find it all out on his own."

"I know you're right," Angie replies. This is what she needed. She needed a reminder that she is doing the right thing. I can't even imagine how hard all of this has to be on her. Yes, she has a strong support system, but I know that she needs reassurances once in a while.

"You are an amazing person, Ang. And an amazing mom. Stop overthinking shit. Don't let that fuckernut fuck with your head again. He's doing this shit on purpose because he knows it gets to you." I'm not sure I was right on this one. No one had any contact with that douchenut, but I need to sound as confident as I don't feel.

"I know, I know," she laments. "I just… I wish Alfie had a real father sometimes. I mean, my dad is amazing with him, but I just wish he had someone to look up to besides him."

I knew what she meant. I had an amazing father and it was a shame that if I ever did have the chance to have kids, they would never know him. I wished the triplets could've known him. That thought alone tells me my resolve is breaking and I ultimately know in my heart what I'm going to do, however, I'm still going to pretend I don't know what it is. Knowing my dad, the way he was, he would've loved them as if they were his own. I miss my dad, something terrible. I truly wish he were still here. There's so much left he could've taught me. So much more that we needed to resolve. So many more questions I wanted to ask. So much he could teach his grandchildren. Losing my dad had to be one of the hardest things I've ever been through. One of them. We don't bring ever up the other.

"One day, Ang, you will find someone who will love both you

and Alfie; he will become Alfie's dad and the most amazing man to him. He won't ever question who his biological father is again," I say, hoping it happens for her. It should happen. She deserves it more than anyone I know.

"Okay," she says and gives me a pointed look, "talk. You don't do this unless you really need to talk, so go. Enough about me and my problems."

I know I'm the one who called Angie to talk, but now I don't know that my issues are significant enough compared to hers. I want to just bottle up Carter's proposal and leave it be. Maybe if I act like it never happened, we can all forget it? Yeah, that's what I'm gonna do.

"I just wanted to spend time with you," I lie. To my own ears, I sound convincing. I hope Angie believes me.

"Nu-uh," she says.

Obviously, she doesn't. Crap. What am I gonna do now? Change tactics.

"When is Alfie's next concert? He really did an amazing job and I know he's gonna do great things," I tell her. Hopefully talking about her son is enough to thwart the conversation I don't really want to have right now. Though I know I need to. But, avoidance, that's my new tactic.

"Nope," she says, wagging her finger in my face. "Not happening. Don't you fucking dare change the subject. I know you called me for a reason, and it wasn't to discuss my son's amazing voice. So spill it, bitch."

The girl knows me all too well. Fuck. Why did I think calling Angie to talk about this while it's still so fresh was a good idea? I still need time to process it myself, never mind evaluating it with my best friend.

"I'm not ready," I answer, honestly.

"Nope. I'm not letting that happen either. Last time I let you dwell on something you just about wound up next to your mom in the institution. Now talk. I'm here for a reason. Don't make me insignificant. Please. Give me something else to focus on besides my own problems."

"Fine. Carter, that guy I had to tow last week, he's in a predicament and asked me to help him and I don't know what to do." I finally tell her what happened. I let it all spill out and watch her reactions.

"You know what you have to do, Elizabeth," she answers. This is what I was afraid of. Instead of telling me what I should do, she's gonna make me make come to my own conclusions. Shouldn't she know by now not to let me make decisions on my own? That only leads to bad mistakes and lots of heartache, take Andrew for instance. That will tell you all you need to know about what happens when I make choices on my own.

"I'm not sure, Ang," I tell her. "You know everything that happened with Andrew, I'm not sure I could handle that kind of heartache again. What happens if I get too attached and he wants me to leave?"

"Listen to yourself," Angie implores. "You're not even giving things a chance. What if this is exactly what you've been waiting for? What if this is what you've always been meant to do? Are you really going to let it slip away? All because of what that douchenut did? You never deserved any of that and he never deserved all you had to give."

"Will you cut it out with all the nuts, woman!" I laugh at Angie. She's always cussing someone using 'nut' as the ending. She's the one that's a damn nut.

All jokes aside, I know she's right, but it's so hard for me to trust anything, or any man. Andrew really caused damage to my heart and psyche. I don't know.

"I'll think on it," I answer. "I can't promise you more than that. Give me some time to weigh it all out."

"Not too much time. Don't get lost in your own head."

"I'll try not to."

We both know that is a near impossible task, but my best friend knows me and knows that me getting lost in my head will take damn near an act of God not to happen.

"Call me," Angie says. "I'm here for you anytime you need. You've been my rock for so long, now it's my turn to be there for you. I love you, Elizabeth." Angie pulls me into a big hug and continues, "You're the best person I know and if you were meant to become a wife to that man and a mother to his girls, you'll know it in your heart. Follow your heart; it won't lead you astray again."

We decided to end the night there and head home. I have a lot to think about and Angie has to find a way to get the man who fathered her child to leave them alone.

So much to do, but the safety and happiness of those little girls are at stake and we both knew what I really need to do.

CHAPTER NINETEEN
ELIZABETH

LIFE WITH ANDREW

GETTING drunk with Angela is never a good thing. I should know better, but I always make the same mistake and over indulge time and again.

Her parents came to pick us up, as I knew they would, and dropped me off at home.

Now, I'm sitting here in utter misery, trying for the life of me to decide what I should do next. I know what I want to do, but is it the right thing? Am I thinking with my libido, am I thinking with my heart or am I thinking clearly?

I don't know. And right now, I really don't want to know.

What I need to do is pass the fuck out and forget today ever happened. That is what would be for the best. To forget everything. To never have contact with Carter and those beautiful girls again.

But that's not what I do. Instead, I imagine what a life with them would be like. What it would be like to be a mom. How amazing it would be to have my own children love me and want to be with me.

Andrew stole all of that from me.

Or so I thought.

I have the chance of a lifetime to start all over and I am actually contemplating what I should do. What the fuck is wrong with me?

I walked in the door after a long day at the garage. I was both dreading and excited to find out if what I'd been wishing for, for so long, was true. I look around to see if Andrew was anywhere around but didn't see him. I wished he was here because I thought this was something we should be doing together.

Walking through the house, I pictured how much things will change if I'm correct and my dreams are coming true. I've always dreamed of being a mother and if my suspicions are correct, they will finally come to fruition. I was about two weeks late right now and the possibility of being pregnant was so exciting.

I looked at how much would change throughout the house and smiled. I couldn't wait to have to clean up after my little one when they made a mess. I couldn't wait for sleepless nights with a newborn baby. This has always been a dream of mine and I couldn't wait to celebrate with the news Andrew.

Thinking of him again, I knew he's going to be just as excited as I am. We have had long conversations about becoming parents. We've discussed many times how many children we would have together. I've always wanted at least three, but we'd compromised on two. Well, two only if we have a boy and a girl. If we have two children and they are both girls, we'll try one more time for a boy. Though, I'm convinced that our first child will be a boy.

As if conjuring him up, Andrew walked in the door whistling. It looked like someone else was in a good mood tonight, and I'm about to make his life even better… I hope.

"Hey," he said as he walked over to me and gave me a kiss on the head. He always did that, and it's the sweetest gesture. My heart melted every time.

"Hey," I said back and hugged him. I held him to me for a moment trying to get the courage to tell him our news.

"What's wrong?" he asked, suspicious of me holding onto him longer than I normally would have.

"Nothing," I answered honestly. Because if my suspicions were correct, nothing was wrong, and everything was perfect.

"So, what's up then?" he asked, changing his question, yet still inquiring about my motives for not letting go.

"I have something to tell you," I replied as I released him from my grasp. I grabbed his hand and led him to the couch. "I know we've talked about this a lot and I think we've finally got what we've always wanted." I smiled at him while I told him this, hoping that he would be as happy as I was right now.

"What's that?" he asked confusion clear on his face.

"I'm late," I told him.

"You made it home before me, so how do you figure?" he asked. Such a man thing to not understand what I was trying to convey.

"I'm two weeks late," I continued. "I'm never late. This is the first time in my life. I think we've finally created one of the lives we've always talked about having."

"Nope," he said, like it was a finality.

"What do you mean, nope?" I asked. Now I'm the one who was clearly confused.

"Can't be," he answered. What the fuck was he talking about?

"Andrew," I started, "I don't think you understand what I'm saying

here. I think I'm pregnant. I'm two weeks late. I bought a pregnancy test, so we can be together when I take it tonight. We've talked for a while about having children and I think our dreams are finally coming true."

I didn't understand his bewilderment or his certitude when he spoke. We've talked about this.

"Can't be. You're just late," he said. "There will never be any babies for us."

What the fuck was he talking about?

"Babe, I'm late for my period. I've never been late for my period in my entire life. We haven't used birth control in over a year. I'm sure I'm pregnant. What do you mean there will be no babies for us?" I stood up and started pacing the room. I was starting to get emotional here. I didn't understand his vehemence.

"There will never be kids for us, is what I'm saying," Andrew answered. "There's no way I would ever have children with a woman set on being a man. You're a fucking mechanic for Christ's sake. What kind of mother would you even be?"

I needed to sit down again. What the hell was Andrew saying? Who was this man? This wasn't the man who I planned to spend my life with.

"Andrew?" I questioned. I didn't even know what to ask. My life was shattering, and I couldn't fathom what this stranger in front of me was saying.

"Seriously." He started laughing. "What in the fucking world would make you think I'd ever trust you to mother of any child of mine? I have no intentions of ever having children with you. I can't even imagine a woman with your background being a good mother. I'd never want to put children through that. A mother needs to be soft and nurturing and all you ever do is work on fucking cars. You're more a man sometimes than even I am. If I were gay, you'd be the perfect father figure. I had a vasectomy six months ago to ensure that we'd never be able to have children. I thought you'd get over this macho bullshit and hoped we could plan a family one day. But then you went ahead and expanded that fucking place your father died in. When I finally realized you wouldn't ever give this shit up, I decided there was no way I'd ever take a chance of getting you pregnant."

My heart was shattering, and Andrew was acting like this wasn't even happening. Who was this man I married? He had always told me he supported my career and that he was proud of who I was.

"Don't act like that, Lizzie," Andrew continued. "I'm the man in this relationship, but you've been trying to emasculate me for years. If we ever had kids, I swear, they'd think you were their father and I was their mother. I couldn't in my right mind ever think that it was okay to have children with you. I'm a man. I need to be a man. One day, maybe, if you decided to ever be a real woman, we could discuss this again and I could have the procedure reversed. But right now, hell no. There's no way we're having any children. Besides, you love your job and your business. You'd never have time to be a mother, and I'd be damned if I would ever let someone else raise our children. A woman's place is at home, taking care of the kids, taking care of her husband. I never really liked that I was raised by nannies and wished my mother would have done her job as a mother. I expect the woman I have children with to be a full-time mother, something you obviously will never have the desire to be. I've accepted our fate, it's about time you do, too."

"What the fuck?" I finally found my voice. "If this was how you felt, why the fuck did you marry me in the first place, Drew? You knew my dream of having a family. You made me believe that you had the same dreams. How the fuck are you saying this now, when it's highly possible I could be pregnant? I haven't had a fucking period in six weeks, what the fuck else could it be? You don't want to have children with me, fine. Get the fuck out! If I am, indeed, pregnant, you can just fuck right the fuck off. I don't need you. I can raise this baby or any baby in my future alone."

I was fuming. Who the fuck did this man think he was? How did I not see his ways all of these years? Please, Lord, help me here.

"There's no fucking way you can be pregnant, Lizzie. I told you this. I had a vasectomy. I was guaranteed you couldn't get pregnant. So, unless you have something else to tell me, there's no way you could be having my child."

"Are you fucking serious? How else would I have gotten pregnant?"

"Maybe you fucked someone else," Andrew stated with a shrug of his shoulders, like it's the most likely answer possible.

"What?" I yelled. I swear I just heard myself shriek. "How the fuck dare you even suggest something like that?"

This man had lost his ever-fucking loving mind.

"I can't have kids, Lizzie," he stated. "How unclear is that? I had that possibility destroyed. If you are pregnant, there's no way in hell it's my child."

"You've got to be kidding me? Get the fuck out!" I yelled. I needed time to process all this new information. I also needed to figure out - if this man did have this procedure as he claimed - what the fuck was wrong with me. I'd had all the symptoms of pregnancy. I hadn't had a period in over a month, something had to be wrong with me.

"I'm not going anywhere," Andrew stated as if everything that had just happened, didn't.

"I told you to get the fuck out of my house," I stated, trying to stay as calm as possible. "This is my house; I own it free and clear of our marriage, so you need to leave. Please, Drew, just leave. I really don't need you to be here right now. I need to process."

I tried with everything in me to be as calm as I possibly could. This man that I married had just taken everything I believed we were and destroyed it. I had thought this was the rest of my life, but obviously, I had been mistaken. There's so much running through my mind that if I didn't have time alone, I didn't think I could be responsible for my actions. I didn't look good in orange after all.

"Fine," Andrew finally conceded. "Call me when you're feeling better and I can come home. I've had a long day and need to sleep. Once you calm down enough, we can go to bed."

I tried my damnedest not to reply. I seriously thought about changing my favorite color. If this man who I thought I was going to spend the rest of my life with, didn't walk out the door, I would have to go to jail, or on the run. Both were very strong possibilities.

After Andrew left, I decided to do some research. Andrew said he had a vasectomy so we couldn't have children, but I didn't want to think some-

thing else could have been wrong with me. I truly hadn't had a period in six weeks and was scared what all that could mean. If he couldn't have children, something had to be wrong with my body. My mind reeled with so many different scenarios, that I scared myself. This couldn't be happening to me. I had too much to live for. Too much of a life to live. Too many people who loved and needed me.

Okay, so I might not have that many people but I was sure Angie and Alfie would miss me and did need me around.

Hours go by and I was not a fan of WebMD. If my symptoms were correct, I was either really pregnant, dying of cancer, or my body was tricking me into a phantom pregnancy. I was betting on the latter because of how much I'd always wanted to be a mother. I decided then and there, that even if the tests were negative, I was going to make an appointment with my OB-Gyn. Hell, even if the tests were positive, I would still need to make an appointment to make sure everything was okay.

Going into the bathroom, I gathered my courage. No matter the results, I would be fine, I tried to convince myself. I did what I needed to do and set a timer on my phone. I couldn't stay in this bathroom and wait.

I went to the kitchen and went to pour myself a drink. I stopped myself before the first drop hit the glass. If a miracle occurred and I was actually pregnant, I couldn't drink alcohol and take any risks where my baby was concerned.

I stood at the counter and watched my phone. I swore this was like watching a pot trying to boil water. You know that saying 'a watched pot never boils'? Yeah, that's how I felt about time going by as I waited to read the results of the test.

When my phone alerted me that it was time to check the test, I grabbed my stomach and said a little prayer. I could do this alone if I got my miracle. I wouldn't let Andrew get me down. I'd be an amazing mother; I knew I would.

I walked into my bathroom with my eyes closed. I knew it was silly but I didn't want to see the results before I was ready.

I come out of my memory and wipe my eyes. The pain is still so real; I feel it like it just happened yesterday. I can't believe what I let that asshole put me through. What I allowed to happen. That I never saw his lies and betrayal. I was so happy when I believed he wanted the same things I did, but when I learned of his lies and deceit, it devastated me. The signs were there, I'm sure, but I was too blind to see them. That's what love does to you; it blinds you from the things that should be so clear.

And I did love him, that's one thing I'll never deny. He was a part of my heart. He may still be, but now he's the black hole part of it that'll never go away.

I conceded to the knowledge that I would never be able to have children of my own and hoped that one day, maybe, I'd adopt a few children who deserved a mother to care for them. There are so many babies in this world who are unwanted and have been given up. So many children grow up in the foster system, believing no one ever wants them.

I vowed to be someone who would show a child or two that they were more than they thought they were. That they meant something to someone. They were loved, and most of all worthy of love.

So many children grow up not knowing what real love is. I'd like to think I can make a difference, eventually, in one of their lives.

Now, I've been offered the chance of a lifetime. My dreams have a chance of coming to fruition. I have the chance to be the mother to three beautiful girls and I'm doubting my ability to do so. The dream I've held in my heart since before I can remember.

I mean, I don't really know them. I don't really know their father. I seriously doubt my ability to be able to be the person they need me to be. But that's what I was expecting to do anyway, wasn't it? Love children and earn their trust when they didn't know the first thing about me. To love a child who wasn't mine by blood but taken over by heart.

Then again, do I want to give up this dream and allow those girls to possibly be raised by that vile creature they have for their mother? Now that Carter told me all about her, I know I would never trust those girls to be raised by her.

Can I just give myself up to be a wife and a mother in the drop of a hat? Was I worthy enough to become the mother those three girls needed? Was I ready to leave my current life behind on a whim?

Those were the questions I really needed to ask myself. The questions, I already knew with every fiber of my being that I already knew the answers.

Now, it was just time I accepted my fate and did what I knew needed to be done.

CHAPTER TWENTY
CARTER

THE WEDDING

THREE WEEKS LATER

I KNOW they talk about pre-wedding jitters all the time, but I knew my anxiety had to be even worse than what they meant.

I was marrying a woman who was pretty much a stranger and bringing her into my girls' lives. I was committing myself to someone I didn't know anything about.

Sure, Elizabeth and I had spent some time together in these last few weeks, preparing for the changes our lives were going to take. We needed everything to look as real as possible to everyone around us. Only our closest friends knew what the real situation was, the whole two of them. It was a little crazy that the both of us were so guarded and each only had one person they were close to. I knew Mikael well enough that he would never do anything to hurt us, but I wasn't so sure about Elizabeth's friend Angela. She said she trusted her with everything and there were reasons, but she wasn't at liberty to tell me. It was Angela's story and if one day she wanted to share it with me, then I would be honored.

My girls are so excited to be Elizabeth's flower girls. They already love her. They ask for her every day.

Elizabeth and I decided that she would not move in until we were officially married. At first, we were planning a fake marriage, but Elizabeth had a clearer head than I. She thought it was too risky and would be too costly if we were caught.

So, now, here I am, standing in a little church in our town just a few weeks after my proposal. I was finally getting the church wedding I wanted. I just hoped that God didn't strike me down for making a mockery of his house.

Elizabeth has done everything to make this marriage look as real as possible. She wanted to make sure we had enough for the courts to make it all believable.

I stand here, waiting, sweat running down my back under my tux.

"Stop fidgeting," Mikael says behind me.

"I can't," I whisper back. "This isn't a mistake, right?"

Mikael doesn't answer. He knows I really don't want his answer. He's already told me how he feels about my marriage but is here with me and standing by my side in my decision. He, like me, only wants what is best for my family. It would destroy him as much as it would destroy me if I were ever to lose the girls to that incubator.

The music starts, and I look toward the closed doors. I know that at any moment, Elizabeth will head down the aisle with my three girls attached to her side. Elizabeth decided that all four of them would walk together instead of one at a time. She thought it would show how united she was with the girls. I happened to agree.

The doors open, and my breath gets caught in my chest. The sight before me is surreal.

Elizabeth's beauty is unbelievable.

I have definitely chosen wisely, but I have to remember to keep myself in line. This isn't a marriage out of love, but out of necessity.

Elizabeth has dressed my girls to look exactly like her. All four of them are in the same dress, but different sizes. Their hair is all the same and they are carrying the same bouquets. I don't think the photographer we hired will be able to do them any justice, to capture how beautiful this picture really is.

The girls start walking down the aisle and I see my girls counting as they take their steps. They have practiced walking down make-believe aisles ever since Elizabeth and I told them we were getting married. Good thing they are so young as they never found it strange I was marrying her after knowing her just a few weeks.

As the girls get closer to the altar, I chuckle. All four of them are in boots. Not shoes. And it's absolutely adorable.

Sofia, getting tired of waiting, breaks away from the others and comes running up to me. I lean down and snatch her up as soon as she reaches the front and smother her with kisses.

"Hi, Daddy," she yells excitedly.

"Hi Sofie Girl. You were supposed to wait and walk with Elizabeth, Felicia and Isabella," I mockingly scold her.

"I couldn't wait to get here," she fake whines. "It was taking just forever!"

I chuckle at that.

"Okay, Sofie Girl, you just stand here, next to Uncle Mik and let's wait for the others," I tell her as I put her down.

I look back down to where my bride is still walking with Felicia and Isabella. She's giggling herself, now holding their hands so that they also don't run up to the altar.

I'm still in awe of how she keeps my girls in place. She clearly has a love for them and they love her the same.

"Hi," she says when she finally reaches me.

"Hi," I return. I'm literally speechless at the moment.

"Hi, Daddy, we maked it!" Isabella yells, awe and excitement riddling her sweet voice.

I lean down and kiss her on her head and do the same with Felicia, who is looking unsure of herself.

I lower to one knee in front of her, "What's the matter Felicia?"

"Did I do it all right?" she whispers for only me to hear. "I didn't remember the routine like Isabella, and Sofia ranned away so I was scared."

"You did perfect, Licia," I reassure her and give her a hug.

When I stand, Elizabeth has a smile on her face.

"Are you ready?" she asks.

"Yes, let's do this," I answer.

ELIZABETH

I can't believe I'm marrying Carter. I can't believe I said yes to all of this. I've known this man for a month, max, and here I am, today, marrying him and becoming a mother figure to his children.

Sofia, Isabella and Felicia look so adorable in their dresses. I wanted all of us to match so no one would feel left out or different.

I know we are all individuals but when the girls saw that their dresses looked just like mine, they were excited that they were marrying their daddy just like me. I didn't have the heart to correct them. They were, in a sense, marrying me not their dad. I was the one being added to their family, not the other way around.

As we walk down the aisle, Sofia gets impatient and runs down to Carter. That makes me stumble in my step and stop. Just seeing how excited she is and how he makes sure to take care of her does something to my heart. After he puts her back down, I grab onto the other girls' hands and continue our walk.

When we get to the altar, Carter kneels down to say something to Felicia. He apparently sees something in her demeanor that I had missed. When she finally smiles at him and he stands back up, I know I can't turn back. We need to give these girls everything they didn't know they were missing.

I stare into Carter's eyes the entire time the minister speaks. I repeat all the words he tells me to speak. I watch in awe as Carter slips the ring he's purchased on my finger. I hadn't seen it before today as he wanted it to be a surprise, but apparently, he knew my style to perfection. It was all me.

Different, yet elegant and the stone, not a typical diamond like so many others. It was two rings that matched each other. The wedding band separate but the same as the other. The entire set is unique. A style I didn't know existed. It isn't even a gold or silver ring. It is black with blue stones. The whole thing has an elegance to it that I didn't realize existed. The rings are some kind of metal and woven in a way I didn't know was possible. It appears to be a lace weave and looks both gothic and vintage.

When I look at him in surprise, he simply states, "I never got you an engagement ring." It's just that simple to him. I don't have time to say anything else as the minister pronounces us husband and wife.

Wait, did I miss a part?

What happened to you may kiss your bride?

Doesn't he want to kiss me?

He just gave me these beautiful rings and we're skipping the kissing and solidifying our marriage part?

Carter clears his throat and looks between the minister and me. "Didn't you miss a step?" he inquires, a puzzled look appearing on his handsome face.

The minister looks a little perplexed by the question, but just as quickly turns a bright shade of red. "I'm sorry, it appears I have. Mr. Montgomery, you may now kiss your bride."

Carter doesn't wait for the minister to complete the sentence before he lands both hands on each side of my face and pulls me into a kiss that sweeps me off my feet. A kiss that I knew I'd want every day for the rest of my life. He clearly did want this kiss as much as I did.

We keep on kissing, not remembering that the kids and other guests are here. Suddenly, we hear the girls making gagging noises and giggling at the same time.

When we finally separate, I'm a bit flushed, and a little embarrassed by my behavior.

Our friends and family clap as we quickly grab all three girls' hands and walk out of the church.

We are having a small reception at Carter's house where everyone would meet us to cut down on the cost, even though Carter told me I could have anything I wanted. I'd thought a huge blowout was overindulging and unnecessary, especially having three young girls to take care of.

When we get back to the house, there aren't any people waiting for us. The catering vans are gone, and we are able to just relax for a moment. We have an hour before the guests arrive to give us some time to ourselves before the festivities begin.

I also have a surprise planned for Carter and the girls and need time before everyone arrives to pull it off.

I walk into the family room and have the girls follow me. They are all curious as to what is happening, but stop in their tracks when they walk in. I had the decorators put up some banners when we left for the wedding because I wanted the girls to be as much a part of this day as we were.

There, in the family room, a banner hung. On it, I'd had printed, "Felicia, Isabella, and Sofia, will you be my daughters?"

The girls look to the banner, then to their dad who is standing behind me with his mouth wide open, and finally, back to me. I knew they could read some, but now I was worried they didn't understand or that I went too far too fast. They just stand there as if they don't know what to do or say.

No one says anything, and I stand there feeling like a fool.

CHAPTER TWENTY-ONE
ELIZABETH

BECOMING MOMMY

IT FELT like a lifetime has passed when Carter puts his hands around my waist and his head on my shoulder. I try not to get caught up in the way that makes me feel, but I silently hope there would be more times like this.

"Thank you," he whispers in my ear for only me to hear. "This is incredible. You've literally made them speechless."

I don't quite feel like that is what they are feeling, but I let Carter think so.

But then, Sofia speaks, "I get to have a mommy?" she says softly and looks at me. There are tears in her eyes and I don't want to see that sweet baby cry. I immediately drop to my knees and pull her into my arms.

"I want to become your mommy one day, if that's okay with you," I explain to her. "I want us all to be a big, happy family, but I need to know that's what the three of you want as well," I continue.

"I always wanted a mommy," she whispers in her sweet little voice. It tears my heart apart that she's been missing this in her life.

"I'll be the mommy you want, if you let me," I say. Tears are now rolling down my face at her confession. "Is that what you all want?" I ask Felicia and Isabella who still haven't spoken.

"What about our other mommy?" Felicia asks a bit snidely. "She said she was our real mommy. What about her?" This breaks my heart.

"Honey," Carter says, "Maggie will always be the woman who gave you to me, but she wasn't able to be your mommy." He is trying to be careful about how he expresses her not being around. I understand it has to be very hard on him not to tell the girls the whole truth about that woman.

"I would like to have a mommy," Isabella finally says. "And if you want to be my mommy, too, I think I like that."

My heart is tearing apart. I feel like I have acceptance from only half of the girls. Sofia embraces me once again and I feel like my heart was being torn all over the place. Then, without warning, both Felicia and Isabella come over and hug me too.

Carter gathers us all in his arms and whispers, "Welcome to the family," for only me to hear.

IT'S BEEN three weeks since the wedding and I moved into Carter's house. We are trying to keep up pretenses, so we actually do share a bedroom. Too bad Carter doesn't seem to want to share the bed with me though. His room is big enough that we have a couch in there, and that's where he sleeps at night. I'm missing the excitement that comes along with being newlyweds.

I know I shouldn't be disappointed that we haven't consummated our marriage, but this is what I signed on for. He needed a wife and more importantly, the girls need a mother, so here I am.

As I make my way down to the kitchen, I hear the girls giggling.

Seems like Daddy Bear is up to his normal breakfast antics. He makes sure to get up nice and early with them every day now. He's gone back to work in the office to try and give me more private time with the girls. Though the girls seemed disappointed when he started that, they've now become adjusted.

"Again, Daddy, again!"

There goes Isabella. With her yelling like that, it tells me that Carter is again pretending he can be a ballerina. It's quite the scene when he dances around with Isabella as such.

Carter still takes Isabella to dance class every day. We wanted to maintain some of their normalcy, while making adjustments to having me around.

I walk into the kitchen and immediately start laughing. Carter is in there with a damn tutu on making believe he's dancing. Only, the thing he's doing makes me think he's trying to be a contortionist instead. There's no way that ballerinas move like that.

"What are you laughing at?" Carter asks as he attempts a plié.

"Carry on, I'll just be over here making breakfast," I say as I wave at him, continuing to laugh as I walk away.

"Are you working today?" Carter suddenly asks from right behind me.

As a wedding present, Carter surprised me with a new flatbed and invested some money into my shop. I was able to hire a few new employees and not have to go to work daily, which worked out with us trying to get the girls to bond with me. However, on the days I do go into the garage, Carter stays at home and works from his home office. After the incident with Maggie, which ultimately led to our marriage, he's been leery about taking them to the daycare he told me he has in his office building. I don't really blame him for that. I don't want the girls to go through that trauma again either.

"Yes, just for a few hours," I answer him. "I have to do payroll and pay the bills. Also, Tommy is sick, so I'm going to have to drive the new flatbed. No one else is qualified and I don't want to add another expense by hiring someone new."

"Okay, I'll call the office and tell them I'm staying home today," he says without question.

I'm not used to someone being so agreeable with me. Andrew would've had a fit if he had to change his plans for me. I smile at the man I've come to respect and care about.

"Mommy Elizabeth, will you make us breakfast today?" little Sofia asks. When she started calling me Mommy Elizabeth, my heart just about burst. I locked myself in the bathroom and sobbed like a baby. I love these little girls so much already, I can't imagine someone having them in their lives and not wanting them.

"Of course, Sofia," I reply. Trying to mask my voice so she doesn't see how much it affects me still when she says calls me mommy. And yes, it has an affect on me every time.

I go to the refrigerator and pull out some eggs and turkey bacon, then go to the pantry to pull out some flour and the rest of the ingredients I'll need to make some homemade pancakes. I used to use the boxed pancake mixes, but Carter taught me how to make them from scratch since he's tried very hard to make everything natural and healthy for his girls.

That's another trait of his that really has me wishing we could have a real marriage instead of an arrangement. My attraction to this man escalates daily. I just wish he felt the same.

There are times I lay in bed and watch him sleep. I have to talk myself out of going to him most nights and taking our relationship to another level. The only thing that holds me back is the embarrassment I'd feel if he turned me away. I bet being with Carter would be explosive. I imagine him holding me tight in his arms. I imagine the look in his eyes as he makes love to me, or hell, I'd even take him giving me a good, hard fuck. I can see the sinew of his muscles as he thrusts into me, the look on his face as he comes.

I see how loving he is with his children; I can't even imagine how loving he'd be with his wife. Damn it, I am his wife. I wish I knew how to make our relationship become one of a forever kind and not just an arrangement to help him with his girls... I wish I could figure out how to steer this arrangement towards a relationship that would last forever. Everything we do together already feels more like a real family, than the original agreement we made.

Waking up in his arms would be such a beautiful thing. I have a feeling, that making love would be slow and tortuous, but in a good way.

I shake myself out of these thoughts. Now is not the time for them, and the girls are waiting for their breakfast, so I won't have time for another cold shower.

When I get back to the counter, Felicia is there, ready and waiting. She's become quite the helper when it's time for me to cook. She's definitely going to be our little chef of the family. She's already retrieved the mixing bowls I'm going to need and is anxiously waiting to start.

"I'm ready, Elizabeth," she says, cheerfully. Although I'm happy that she's accepted me and this has become our thing, I'm sad that she's not as excited about me being her new mom as Sofia is. As a matter of fact, neither she nor Isabella has completely accepted my new role in their lives. I can only hope that one day I'll be everything they need and want as a mom.

Felicia and I quickly get breakfast ready while Carter carts Isabella and Sofia upstairs to get ready for the day. Even when the girls are home all day, the routine is to get ready early in the morning as if they were going to school, or us to work. Routine is key with such young ones and learning early in life will ensure they continue it when they are adults.

"We're ready, Elizabeth," Isabella states as she sits at the table. I look over to her and smile. She and Sofia tried so hard to set the table for breakfast and I want to laugh. Everything is haphazardly put together.

"Carter," I call. "Please come help the girls set the table properly."

"On it," he replies, laughter lighting his voice.

When he walks into the kitchen, he too chuckles at the job the girls did. Then he proceeds to 'help' them fix the table as it should be.

This family thing is everything. I don't ever want to lose it, though I know it's not really real. My heart can't distinguish the difference though and I know when this charade is over, my heart will truly be broken. I don't know that I'll ever heal after it comes time to let them all go. This will be worse than anything I've endured in the past.

I decide not to think about it all and just go with the flow. I don't want to be depressed in front of the girls and Carter. I'll leave that for later, when I'm in the shower and no one can hear me cry.

Felicia and I finish breakfast and bring everything carefully to the table. I made sure to make everyone's plates and Felicia decorated them like she sees on the TV show she loves to watch. I hope one day when I am able to have children of my own, that I'll be able to experience the same things with them.

MY WORKDAY WENT BY QUICKLY. I finished payroll before noon and then paid all outstanding bills for the shop. I even paid the bills that were due from my house. I haven't sold it yet, as I know I will need a place to live once this charade is all over.

Carter and I never really discussed what would happen once the arrangement was no longer necessary. I'm hoping he won't just boot me out on my ass. I've become so attached to him and the girls and it would kill me if I had to walk out of their lives. I have to believe he wouldn't have let me become so entwined with them only to rip them away. He has to see that he'd be doing not only me, but also them, an injustice if he did so.

He loves those girls with everything he has. I can't see him doing something so cruel. At least, I'm hoping he won't. If he does, he's not the man he's portrayed himself to be all this time.

There haven't been any calls for tows, so I decide to head home. Just in case, I drive the flatbed home. I know Carter doesn't like when I come home with the rig because if I happen to get a call in the middle of the night, the sound of the truck might wake up the girls, but this is my business and I can't screw it up. When he gets through this ordeal with his ex and he and I no longer need to play house, I will still have a business to run.

I walk into the house to complete silence. It's unusual for this time of day. Usually the girls are running rampant around the house and one of us is getting dinner ready. Don't get me wrong, the girls are very well behaved, but we do let them run around and blow off some steam. They are children after all.

I walk into the family room and what I see melts my heart.

Carter is asleep on the couch with all three girls sleeping in various positions on top of him. This is a picture-perfect moment, so I pull out my phone and snap one, or ten pictures, but who's counting? They really must've run him ragged today.

Instead of making any noise and waking them, I head into the kitchen to get a start on dinner. I might as well make myself useful since I'm sure it will now be a long night. When the girls nap this late in the day, getting them to bed at a decent hour is nearly impossible.

Carter walks into the kitchen about twenty minutes later. His hair is a mess and he has sleep lines all over his face. It's quite adorable.

"How long have you been home?" he asks, his voice a bit husky still from sleep.

"About a half hour," I respond. "I didn't want to wake you, you looked so peaceful with the girls. Are they still sleeping?"

"No, they went to the bathroom and to wash their faces," he answers. "Dinner smells good, what are you making?"

"I decided on something simple. Just grilled chicken, mac 'n' cheese and some broccoli."

"Sounds good. I'll set the table. I'm sorry we all fell asleep," he says sheepishly. "I know when you work, I'm supposed to cook dinner, but these girls had more energy today than they've had in a long time. I don't know what they were on, but make sure you don't give it to them tomorrow."

I chuckle at that statement. Those girls are getting older and becoming more and more active every day. He has no idea what we do during the day anymore. I have to force them to take naps around one o'clock every day just to make it through. But I'm not going to share my secret with him, he'll figure it out… or not.

The girls walk in the room, still looking sleepy. Joy, it's going to be a great night, said with no sarcasm whatsoever.

We all sit down and eat. As dinner goes on, the girls start to get their energy back and by the time they are done, they are literally bouncing in their seats. I excuse them from the table and they run straight to their playroom. At least that'll give me a few minutes to clean up and think of ways to get them into bed.

"I'll take cleanup since you cooked," Carter says from close behind me. I jump at his close proximity. The way he's leaning in behind me makes it seem like an intimate moment and I can't handle something like that with him. I'd want something permanent if we started anything. Hell, who am I fooling, I already do.

"Okay," I reply and walk away from him. When I turn back around, I notice a mix of confusion and hurt on his face. I don't want to hurt him, but I can't hurt me either.

"I noticed you brought home your rig, everything okay?" he asks as he starts to clear the table.

"Everything is fine. There weren't any calls all day, but we know how things can be at night. Tommy is sick, so he won't be able to answer if anything comes in. I want to make sure I'm prepared if I'm needed."

"You should really hire another driver. I love that you love what you do, but you shouldn't have to run out in the middle of the night. How about you just hire someone for the evenings? If money is an issue, I'll just help you out some more."

I know his question is innocent, but it just brings back memories of things Andrew used to say. I don't need anyone telling me what to do. I have to rein in my anger, though. That is not what he's trying to do. I do understand. So I just shrug and walk away. I need to breathe and know walking away is the best way to do it.

Suddenly, the doorbell rings. I'm not expecting anyone, so I look over to Carter who also looks bewildered.

We both walk to the door and Carter looks through the glass. His demeanor immediately changes, and he tells me to go be with the girls.

Not wanting to upset him but wanting to know what's going on, I step in front of him and look through the glass. I know this is his house, but I'm not going to be shooed away when someone comes to the door. I am legally his wife and have rights here.

What, or shall I say who, I see standing there knocks the wind right out of me.

CHAPTER TWENTY-TWO
ELIZABETH

AND THE BOMB DROPS

GETTING over my initial state of shock, I whip the door open. I don't think the person or persons on the other side expected to see me.

"What the fuck are you doing here?" I seethe.

"Excuse you, but my children are in there, what are you doing here?" the bitch in front of my ex answers.

"I'm not talking to you," I look her straight in the eye as I reply. "I'm talking to him." I continue as I point to the man standing behind her.

I can't believe Andrew is standing here with this bitch at the door to my home. How he even found out where I live is a concern.

"I'm not here for you Lizzie," he answers with a smug look on his face, "I'm here for my children."

"What the fuck are you talking about?" Carter asks.

"I am here for my children," Andrew states again.

Now, I'm more confused than ever. Andrew? Children? Those two things don't even go together, it's like an oxymoron.

"Yes," the bitch says. I totally forgot she was even there. "Andrew is the real father of my children and now we're here to take them home with us."

This cunt must've lost her damn mind. Andrew chose not to have children. He told me he had a vasectomy to prevent being able to have children. The whole scenario in front of me causes me to burst out with laughter.

"Are you laughing at me?" Twatface McCoward asks.

"No," I answer with as straight a face as I can. "This one is quite funny though. He can't have children. Now he's claiming he has fathered some. That's quite hysterical if you ask me."

"How do you even know my husband?" she asks.

"Husband?" I choke out. Oh my goodness. This can't be happening. This is some kind of joke right? It has to be. Not only is Andrew claiming to have children, but now he's married, too?

"Yes, Lizzie. Mags and I have been married for three years now. We had a somewhat casual relationship before and decided to make it permanent, but she never told me she had our girls until recently. Now, I'm ready to take them home and be the father they need. Mags made a mistake and now we're ready to raise our children together."

"This isn't fucking happening." I suddenly hear Carter growl from behind me. "You need to leave my property and never come back. You gave up your rights to my girls! You can't come back into their lives three years later and try to stake a claim to them. You have no rights. I have legal papers, you bitch!"

Holy hell, I've never seen Carter this mad. Yeah, we've only known each other a short while, but he's clearly losing his temper. The girls are in their room and don't need to hear him speak this way.

"Carter," I start as I turn around. "Calm down for a moment. The girls are in the playroom. You don't want them to witness this."

He looks at me for a moment then concedes.

"You two need to leave my house, right now, and not upset my wife or my children."

"Your wife?" Andrew questions then starts laughing. "This is fucking precious. Did you finally find someone willing to deal with your bullshit? Who likes being with someone who has a man's job? This is funny. I will *not* allow my children to be raised by two men!"

How dare he?

Carter speaks before I even have a chance.

"If you disrespect my wife, one more time, I swear to you, I just might forget that *my* children are inside and knock you the fuck out. You have exactly thirty seconds to get off my porch and get in your car. If you think you can take my children from me, just try it. I have everything I need to win this. Don't fuck with me, my children, or my wife!"

Trying to calm Carter down is senseless now. I'm seething mad myself, but I have those girls to think about. One of us has to maintain a clear head, and it's obviously not going to be Carter at the moment.

"Listen, everyone," I calmly start. "It's late and the girls need to be put to bed. Here and now is not the time for this. Let's all try to talk about this calmly, somewhere else. I'll call someone to come watch the girls, so we can all go and talk this through." I'm trying desperately to be the one with a clear head on my shoulders, though I know it won't take too much for me to snap. They've already tested my patience and I can't let them see how much they are really tearing me down already. *Fake it and don't let them break you* is on repeat in my head right now.

"Mikael is on his way," Carter whispers in my ear. A jolt burns through me at his proximity, but I have to ignore it. Now is definitely not the time for my body to acknowledge his,

When did he even call him I wonder?

"I'll tell you later," he says to me as if he heard the question that was in my head. He's developed this uncanny ability to read my thoughts lately and it's weird.

"Please, if you'll just go over to the pool house and wait for us there. As soon as Mikael gets here, we'll head over. Please, at least let's think of the girls' wellbeing before you start anything else." Carter is much calmer suddenly and he makes me very proud.

"Fine, whatever," Maggie says and turns on her heel. "Let's go Andy," she yells back.

Andrew gives me another look and then turns and follows her over to the pool house – like a dog following a bitch in heat. A laugh escapes me at the mental analogy.

"You've got to be fucking kidding me?" I exclaim as I turn around to face Carter again. "How the fuck is my ex married to your ex?"

"I don't know. Let's wait for Mik to get here and then we'll find out. His security immediately alerted him to Maggie showing up here. We have tons of cameras in place ever since she showed up at my company. They alert him to everything she does. As soon as he found out she was here, he sent a text and let me know he was on his way."

"That explains a lot. Though, I wish you would've told me about the cameras beforehand."

"I'm sorry. It just never came up, and I didn't think she'd ever be stupid enough to do something like this."

"I understand. Let's go check on the girls to make sure they didn't witness anything then wait for Mikael."

"Thank you," Carter says and hugs me. That's the first time he's touched me since we've been married, and my body alights at his touch. Now is not the time, but my body doesn't want to acknowledge that.

We go into the playroom and the girls are sound asleep on their little sofas. Huh, I guess bedtime was going to be easier than I'd originally thought. I'm relieved they are sleeping, not only because of their late naps but that means they didn't hear the commotion outside a few minutes ago. Relief obviously passes through Carter for the same reason.

He motions to the girls and picks up Sofia and Isabella. I walk over and pick up Felicia and we take them to their room. We quickly undress them and put them in their pajamas. Baths are going to have to wait for the morning and I'm okay with breaking their routine right now.

Once we finish with the girls, we go back to the front of the house. Mikael is walking in as soon as we hit the foyer. He never seems to knock, and I don't know how I feel about that. This is something that Carter and I will have to discuss at a different time.

"Go, get that bitch out of here," Mikael states. "You can explain everything afterwards."

"Thanks," both Carter and I reply at the same time. The three of us know there is no need for formalities right now. There's a much bigger fish to fry.

Mikael continues to walk by us and heads to the girls' room, I assume because he's out of sight quickly. Although, when I think about it, he could've gone to Carter's office in the house. That seems more likely since he'll probably want to get on a computer to watch the grounds until Carter and I get back.

"Are you ready for this?" Carter asks. "We knew there was a chance she would show up again but never once did I think she'd have the balls to show up with her husband demanding the girls. This is something I didn't see coming. I don't like to be blindsided and that's exactly what she's done to me, yet again."

"You and me both," I concede. "The sooner we get this over with, the better. I just don't understand how we have to deal with both these cuntsuckers at the same time."

Carter lets out a little snort and grabs my hand. "Let's go, my lovely bride."

When we get to the pool house, Andrew is pacing around like a mad man while Maggie is sitting on the couch checking her finger-nails as though she doesn't have a care in the world. If I were to make a wager, I would think this is something Andrew wants, and Maggie is just trying to make him happy. He's got an awfully fat wallet, and from what Carter has told me about her, this is probably her golden ticket to keep the lifestyle she loves so much.

"What the fuck are you doing with my children?" Andrew screams as soon as he sees me.

"I said watch how you fucking talk to my wife," Carter says in a low, angry voice.

"I told her she wasn't fit to raise kids, that's why I left her manly ass in the first place and now I find out she's playing mommy to three of my children anyway? This will not happen, I promise you that," Andrew continues.

"This woman here is the only mother *my* children have ever had and you don't get a say in that matter," Carter warns.

"Can we all please calm down and try to speak rationally?" I interject. Yelling, accusing, and demanding are not the way to get things accomplished. I just want these people out of my home and off my property. Wow, I realize, I'm finally starting to accept this place as my own. I'm not seeing it as just Carter's house anymore. It's my home too.

"Carter," Maggie sighs. "I told you they weren't yours years ago. You decided you wanted to keep them anyway, that's not my fault. But now, their real father wants them, and you can't stop him. You don't have an actual link to them and we can prove it. We want to be a family with our children. He never signed anything, so you can't use the papers I signed against him."

"He's not their father, I am!"

"No, you're not. You know this," Maggie laments.

Now I'm confused. He's not their father? How and when did this happen? And I'm still confused on how the fuck Andrew is claiming to have fathered these girls.

"You can't have kids," I state to Andrew.

"Ha, of course I can," he answers.

"How?"

"I lied to you. Obviously. I never wanted you to have my children so I told you something that wasn't true so you'd stop pushing me. I made sure to grind up birth control in your juice every morning to make sure you didn't get pregnant. I always wanted a family, just not one with you. I wanted my children to have a mother who knew how to be a woman, not one who thinks she's a man. My children need guidance not some butch bitch teaching them about cars and shit. They need someone prim and proper and who knows how to look good and be obedient to a man."

All this time, I thought what had happened was my fault. Now, I'm learning that this man not only lied to me, but he drugged me too? Is this why what happened after he left transpired? I thought I was finally over what he had done to me then he lands this blow on me? Who is this man? How did I ever think I truly loved him? I clearly knew nothing about him or what love was.

"Mags and I were together the whole time you and I were together. This sap right here didn't know either. We played it cool. Fucked when we could but didn't have anything committed. When she got pregnant, she thought I didn't want kids because I told her what had happened with you, so she decided to blame it on this one. She was afraid to tell me the truth when we got back together but finally fessed up. We've been working on fixing our relationship and now that we have, we want to raise our children together and there's not a damn thing you can do about it."

"Like hell, I can't," Carter yells. "These are my children. I was there when they were born. I have taken care of them all their lives. If you even dare try to take them away from me, I will fucking sink you, I promise you that. Now, you need to leave my fucking house and get off my fucking property or I will have you arrested for trespassing."

"I've filed for custody of my children," Andrew states, like he's already won. "Here's the paperwork with the court date. I will get my girls, and all you'll have is this piece of tra—"

Andrew doesn't get to finish his sentence before Carter's fist meets his face.

I gasp in surprise but chose not to interfere. Andrew deserves Carter's wrath, and so much more.

"You will pay for that," Andrew says as he grabs his jaw.

"No, you will pay for threatening me and disrespecting my wife. I gave you enough chances. Now, get the fuck off my property or I will personally drag you off." The energy coming off of Carter is getting scary and hot.

"Please leave our home," I try to be the calm once again. "We appreciate knowing about your claims and will be sure to be in court on the day we are summoned. There's no need to continue this conversation."

"Let's go, Andy," Maggie chimes in. "We'll have our girls soon enough, no need to be around this trash any longer."

She is looking me in the eye as she says that last part. But I decide to be the stronger person and not let things escalate any further. I walk over to the door and hold it open and wait for them to leave.

Once they are gone, I walk back over to my husband and hug him. He hugs me back and takes a deep breath. I know he is trying to calm down before we need to head back inside.

Mikael is there waiting for answers and we need to come up with a game plan. Now that Andrew is also involved in all this, I know I am going to try my hardest not to let them win. Over my dead body will they ever get their hands on our children.

CHAPTER TWENTY-THREE
CARTER

WITH SHAKING HANDS

HOLDING Elizabeth in my arms feels so right. I don't know why I waited so long just to hold her, but this is where she belongs, in my arms. I don't want to let go, but I know we need to head back to the house where Mikael is likely pacing my office waiting for answers.

"Let's head inside," I say as I reluctantly let her go.

We walk hand in hand back to the house and I'm hoping that this is a sign of what's to come for the two of us. That we'll finally be able to move on as a couple and no longer live as roommates.

I know this shouldn't be my top concern right now, but I don't believe that anything that Elizabeth and I do together will turn out badly. That includes fighting for our girls if it comes down to that.

There's a hard truth I'm going to have to face in the next few moments. Something I should have done years ago, but decided I never wanted to know.

Mikael is waiting for us as soon as we walk in the front door. I'm surprised he's right there and not waiting where I thought he would be.

"You know I have the pool house bugged, right," he asks.

Shit, this is worse than I thought it would be. I never told Mikael I didn't look at the DNA results. He always assumed I had, and we never discussed it.

"Why did you bug the pool house?" I ask, trying to divert the real reason he made that statement.

"You told me you wanted max security. The only place in this house that is not monitored is your bedroom and the bathrooms. Other than that, every place is under surveillance. Now, let's get back to the real reason I'm here and let's not get off subject. Why didn't you set that bitch straight with the DNA test you did on the girls?"

He stands in front of me with his arms crossed over his chest waiting on an answer. He's my best friend, my brother, he deserves the truth. I couldn't have done everything I've done for and with those girls had it not been for him.

"I never read the results. I didn't feel I needed to. Those girls are mine. She signed away her rights... They are mine. I didn't want to feel anything but them belonging exactly where they are. I felt that if for some odd reason the results weren't in my favor, I may not have given them my all," I try to explain.

"That's bullshit and you know it. You're a great father and you would've treated them exactly like you have all these years. They are your girls, I know it, you know it and that bitch knows it. I don't know what she's trying to pull, but we've gotta get this straightened out, as soon as possible." He's right. We do need to find out and then get this cleared up once and for all.

"Mik," I start, "I need to do this alone. I can't have you here when I look at those papers."

My best friend looks at me like I've just slapped him. I know he loves my girls as much as I love them, but this is something I can't do with him here. I can't watch his heart break when mine may be breaking at the same time. I wouldn't be able to handle both our worlds being torn apart.

Mikael looks at me again but doesn't say a word. I know he's hurt but I can't deal with his emotions right now too. I see his acceptance as his shoulders slump and he turns and walks out the door.

I'll fix this with him, I just need to do this by myself.

"You're not doing this alone," Elizabeth says as she wraps her arms around me.

I know she's my wife and will be there for me, but she can't understand why I need to do this alone.

"I need to do it alone," I tell her. "You don't understand. If I don't see what I want to see, I don't know how I'll handle it. I don't want anyone to see that from me. I need to know those girls are mine, and if there's something that can potentially rip them from the only home they've ever known… I just… I don't think I could handle it." I'm trying not to break down as I explain this to her, but I know she's not going to accept my answer.

"I'm doing this with you, you can't do it alone," she demands. "This is what I signed on for Carter, and you're not taking any part of it away from me. We'll deal with this together, like we've planned all along. I'm not letting you do it alone," she repeats.

I look at my wife and see that there's no way I'll be able to fight her on this. Mikael may have walked away, but I see Elizabeth's resolve and know there's no way I'll win.

Reluctantly, I turn and walk back to our bedroom. I know Elizabeth will follow me but I can't ask her to come.

When I get to our room, I head straight for my closet. In the back is the safe where I keep all my important documents. The dreaded DNA test is in there as well, hidden behind a bunch of papers that no one would have ever thought to look at. I take the sealed envelope out of the safe and walk back into the bedroom. Elizabeth is sitting on the bed waiting for me, so I take a seat next to her.

It feels like this envelope is burning a hole through my hands. My hands are shaking so badly. I really don't want to do this. Elizabeth grabs my hands to steady them. She grabs my face and turns it so I'm looking into her eyes instead of down at the dreaded document in my hands.

"No matter what, we're in this together. It's going to be okay," she tries to reassure me.

It's at this moment I realize that my feelings toward my wife are no longer of a marriage of convenience. I have real feelings for this woman by my side. I've somehow fallen for this woman who has only been in our lives for a short while but has shown us more love than the woman who actually mothered my children.

The envelope drops to the floor, momentarily forgotten, as I slowly raise my hands to Elizabeth's face. She looks over at me with reverence and I'm compelled to make this woman understand how I feel for her.

I lean in and slowly meet her lips with mine. The shock I feel when our lips touch reaches deep down to my soul. I feel Elizabeth react to my kiss and lick my tongue across her lips. Her taste is one I want to savor forever. She opens up to me and suddenly, I have a need to devour her.

Elizabeth's arms wrap around my shoulders. Right now, I need my wife. I need to be reassured that my entire life isn't about to fall apart. I know I have to slow this down. I don't want to rush through making love to feeling my wife for the first time. This needs to mean more, I need to show her she means everything.

I stand and lean over Elizabeth. The look on her face and the swell of her lips has me reaching for my shirt and unbuttoning it. When she sees my intentions, she stands in front of me and grabs my hands. She takes over unbuttoning my shirt and at that moment I realize it's not only me that needs her, but she needs me too.

I reach down to the hem of her top and lift it over her head as she tries to slide my shirt off my shoulders. After we lose our tops, I reach down and lift her into my arms. I walk over to the side of the bed and gently lay her on top of it. I want to take my time loving my wife and need to show her how much she's come to mean to me.

"Carter," she whispers.

"Elizabeth, my beautiful wife," I reply.

There are no more words to be said right now. I have a need to feel and taste her, so I slowly lay myself next to her body and kiss her again.

I make my way across her lips then begin to drag my tongue down her neck. She moans beneath me, feeling exactly hard I am for her. I slowly trail kisses down to her breasts which are encased in a soft pink bra. I see her hard nipples trying to poke through the soft lace and reach down and gently nip at one through her bra. She moans again and it's making it harder for me to take my time.

I reach behind her back and unclasp her bra. I watch as she sits up and removes it from her perfect breasts. My mouth waters at the thought of having those perfect pert nipples in my mouth and hands. I know she sees how I'm feeling for her at the moment and grabs my head and eases it down to her breasts.

I take one of her nipples into my mouth and gently suck. God, she tastes amazing. With my other hand, I start to knead and rub at her other breast. I can't leave one unattended while I feast at the other. She's moaning and writhing underneath me and suddenly I realize I can make her come just by sucking on her nipples alone. This makes my cock so hard, I know if I don't slow myself down, this won't last as long as I'd like it to.

Elizabeth reaches down between us and starts to rub me through my pants. I'm not going to be able to take much more so I grab her hands and hold them over her head. I make my way back up her beautiful body and latch myself on to her mouth.

Her kisses are hungry, and I know she doesn't want to wait much longer.

I stand from the bed and reach for the button of my pants. They are way too constricting and must go. She seems to have the same thought as she stands next to me and removes her pants at the same time.

Just seeing her there, completely naked realizing she wasn't wearing any panties underneath makes me wonder if that's how she is all the time. If not, I might request it of her, to give me easier access in the future.

She looks down as my pants fall to the floor. The look on her face is priceless as she realizes that I too, have gone commando.

Slowly, she climbs back on the bed and reaches for me. Who am I to deny her what she wants? I want it just as much as she does.

I climb onto the bed and hover over my beautiful wife. I can't believe how lucky I am that this woman wants me as much as I want her. As long as it's taken us to get to this point it seems like so much wasted time right now. This, I know, is where I was always meant to be.

"Elizabeth," I whisper as my cock hits the wet spot between her legs. He wants in just as much as I do. It's taking so much out of me to hold back and not just dive into the beautiful woman lying beneath me.

"Yes, Carter," she answers. She knows my question without me asking. She angles her hips upward, positioning my cock exactly where it wants to be.

I need to know that she is wanting and needing me as much as I do her. She knew just by me saying her name, I was asking permission to enter her.

Slowly, my cock finds entrance into her sweet heat and I groan in pleasure. I have to start out slow or this will be over much faster than I desire. I need to savor the feeling of this woman. The feel of her body wrapped around mine is something I want to treasure for the rest of my life. There's no need to rush our first time together. I've waited so long for this, I don't feel like it'll last long.

"This is it, us, forever," I say as I look into her eyes, sinking deeper inside her sweet body.

"Yes," she whispers back and starts to move with me.

We move slowly with each other. The way we move together feels as if we've done this all our lives. Our movements, our rhythm is in perfect sync with one another. I wrap my arm around her head and slowly kiss her. The rhythm of our mouths is in sync with our bodies. I feel so much right now that I never want it to end. We are both trying to hold back and savor this moment, together, but by looking into her eyes, I see she is as close as I am to letting go.

I feel Elizabeth reach down between us, and wrap her hand around the base of my cock. I know what she's doing. She's gently squeezing the base of my shaft to try and prevent me from coming too soon. This woman already knows my body and it's only our first time together.

Slowly, I pull out of her, needing more from this moment. I need to taste her; I need her essence on my lips. I need to savor her taste, to hold on to more.

She starts to protest, but when she feels me kissing down her body, she realizes my intentions. She writhes beneath me, her anticipation building. When I reach the apex of her thighs, her scent intoxicates me. Although I wanted to slow this down, I dive right in and shove my tongue in her pussy. I don't have the patience I thought I'd have with her. This first time, it's everything to me.

Her taste, it's like nothing I've ever tasted before. I begin to feast on her. I move my way up to her clit while taking two fingers and gently pumping into her. I can feel her climax building and know that I need to be inside of her the first time she comes. In the future, I'll make sure to make her come multiple times on my tongue before I do, but right now, this first time, it needs to be together while I'm buried balls deep inside of her.

She protests when I stop but emits a deep moan when I shove my cock back into her swollen pussy. I've never felt anything so amazing. I can't take this slowly anymore, the way her pussy is gripping me, I know I'm not going to last much longer. I begin to pound into her harder, deeper, chasing that climax we are both so desperate for.

As I pump in and out of her, she matches her rhythm with mine. She needs to get there as much as I do. I reach between us and pinch her clit between my fingers while I drive into her. She's almost there, I can feel her grip and know I'm going to go over the edge with her.

"Carter," she yells as she comes all over my dick. The feel of her coming makes me unload inside of her. I knew I wasn't going to last long and the feel of her pussy squeezing and milking my dick is like heaven on earth.

"Elizabeth," I groan as my cock just keeps exploding over and over. I don't remember coming so hard or so quickly, ever before in my life.

The aftershocks of our orgasms begin to steady, and I lie there on top of my wife not wanting to move. My cock hasn't gotten the message yet that he's spent, and wants more, but I know I don't have it in me at the moment. I need to get up and clean myself and her up, so we can get back to what we came into this bedroom for.

"Carter," she starts, "you're crushing me." She's giggling as she says this, and my cock wants more attention from her body when she begins to shake while she laughs.

Slowly, I pull out of her and look down into her loving eyes. I see something there I've never seen before and I wonder to myself if it was just something I was overlooking.

"Elizabeth…" I say but get lost in the emotions and can't finish my sentence.

Slowly, I climb off the bed and head to the bathroom. Out of the corner of my eye, I see her covering herself up with the blanket.

"Don't," I say as I look back at her. "I want to see you, I just need to clean the both of us up."

She seems to understand what I am trying to convey and lays there waiting.

I walk into the bathroom and grab a cloth from the basin on the sink. I wash myself up with some warm water then toss it into the laundry bin. I grab another cloth and wet it and walk back into the bedroom to clean up my wife.

When I walk back in, she's still laying there looking beautiful and freshly fucked. My cock tries to jump to attention again, but then I see the envelope that started this all on the floor by the bed. My heart starts to beat a rapid rhythm and I feel like I'm ruining this moment between us.

"Come here, Carter," Elizabeth says as she follows my gaze to the offending papers. "Let's do this together." She reaches down and grabs the envelope from the floor.

I make my way to the bed and clean my wife up like I originally intended and then grab the envelope out of her hands.

"No matter what, we're in this together," she whispers as I pull the paper with my fate on it out and read the results.

CHAPTER TWENTY-FOUR
CARTER

OUR DAY IN COURT

IT'S BEEN six weeks since our lives were turned upside down. I thought I'd had everything I wanted and needed but then a boulder was dropped at our feet. Our world, as we knew it was beginning to change.

Elizabeth and I have found our way together and haven't left each other's sides and our girls are happier than ever.

Today, however, so much can change. Today, we will face that beast that birthed them and the man who claims to be their biological father.

To me, it doesn't matter what the DNA results say, those girls are mine and always will be. I will fight to the death for them and now I know, so will my wife.

We walk hand in hand into the courthouse knowing a lot of things can change today. We don't know what the judge will do, but we know that we can't lose our girls.

When we walk into the courtroom, Maggie and Andrew are

already there. When I look to Andrew's left, I see a little boy who can't be older than two sitting there. Looking at him, I swear if I didn't know better, you'd think he and my sweet Sofia were twins. Isabella and Felicia have always looked like twins with Sofia as their younger sister. She was always so much smaller than the other girls and this little boy could easily pass as her twin.

In a way, this tears at my heartstrings just a little more.

Elizabeth gasps as she looks up and sees the situation in front of us. I know she just deduced the same thing I did when she looks at the innocent little boy sitting there. Her eyes go wide, and she looks from the boy to me a few times before she puts her head on my shoulder and begins to cry.

She's been crying a lot lately, but usually she does it in private. I haven't seen her cry in front of anyone before, and I wonder if she thinks that the worst will happen today instead of us settling this custody issue once and for all.

"I'm sorry," she says as she wipes her eyes and looks up at me. My heart is breaking seeing the pain in her eyes, but I can't let that show. I have been the strong one for my family for years; I can't let that cunt that is sitting across from us break me again. The last time I saw her I swore I'd never let her have any power over my feelings ever again.

Up in front of the courtroom, I see Robert standing there. He's the attorney that originally helped me get custody of my girls and has the paperwork that will show the court that Maggie gave up her rights to my girls and has no claim to them. Hopefully, once we present these papers to the judge, we'll be done with this whole mess and be able to move on with our lives. I want to give Elizabeth all the love and attention she deserves and my girls need to know that she'll always be their mother and never have to question who this despicable woman sitting across from us is.

I grab ahold of Elizabeth's hand once again and walk up to the front.

"Robert," I begin, "this is my wife Elizabeth. Please give us some good news."

Robert reaches out his hand to shake mine then my wife's and gives me a look that tells me I may not like what he has to say.

"Carter, I'm sorry, but I don't know if this is going to be as easy as we thought it would be," Robert tells me as he reaches down and grabs the folder that was already set up on the table. "It seems we may have missed a step when we made Maggie sign these papers. We had her sign over custody to you, and we asked her to sign over her parental rights, but we never filed those papers with the court. I'm hoping that they overlooked that on her side, but I don't think they would think they even had a case if they did. We may have a little bit of a fight on our hands, but I'm ready to fight. She hasn't been a part of their lives since they were born and I don't think any judge will look kindly on that. Plus, I need you and Elizabeth to sign these papers. I've backdated it, but don't bring attention to that. It's paperwork stating that Elizabeth was trying to adopt your girls as her own. If the court sees these papers were done before Maggie brought this lawsuit on, it may help us even more."

I want to hit something right now. I know that I can't, but I really want to. I really can't blame Robert for this mistake as none of us thought that Maggie would ever come back into our lives, but her showing up again is a possibility we should have thought of and done all those years ago. I'm so mad right now, but I can't show my feelings. I have to let it go, until I can't.

"Robert," I tell him, "I know this isn't your fault. I get it. But she can't take my girls. You have to make sure that never happens."

Years ago, when the fight over my girls first happened, I used to have panic attacks. I hadn't had one in years until Maggie showed back up in our lives. I have to get this back under control because if the judge and apposing attorney see me lose it, it could be detrimental to my case.

"We've got this," Elizabeth whispers in my ear. And just like that, my heart rate begins to slow back down to normal and I know she'll be the one to help me maintain my cool.

"Everyone rise," the bailiff says as he walks into the room. "The Honorable Judge McCauliff will now hear this case."

"Please be seated," the judge states as he makes a motion with his hands at the same time. "This is a preliminary custody hearing for the children, Isabella Lynn Montgomery, Sofia Marie Montgomery and Felicia Haley Montgomery. The plaintiff in the case, Mr. Andrew Anthony, has petitioned the court for custody of the children claiming he is the biological father of the girls. The petitioner's wife, Mrs. Magdalene Anthony has stated that at the time of the original custody agreement she had with Mr. Montgomery, she was unaware of the biological father's want to be a part of their lives and signed over custody to Mr. Montgomery believing that he would raise the girls as his own. The petitioner has requested that custody be transferred to him and his wife to raise the girls as they are biologically tied to them and not to Mr. Montgomery. While I don't believe children should be removed from the homes they were raised in, I also believe that children should be with their biological families unless there is a reason for them not to be. At this time, I want it to be clear, I will not remove the children from the only home they've known. But I will hear the case and make any judgements I see as being in the best interest of all parties concerned. Mr. Montgomery, I have your counterclaim that you believe you are the biological father of the children and would like to enter into evidence a DNA test that you had taken when Mrs. Anthony left you with the children after they were born. I also have received into evidence that your wife, Mrs. Elizabeth Montgomery is petitioning the court to adopt the three girls and that you have paper where Mrs. Anthony signed away her parental rights but they were never filed with the court. I understand you would like to file those papers now and have them validated in order to go against Mrs. Anthony's claim. Mr. Montgomery, unless there is a valid reason for this request, I will let you know right from the beginning that, that request will be denied.

"Mr. Cross, you may begin," the judge says as he looks to Andrew and Maggie's lawyer.

"Your honor, I have, in good faith, a belief that the DNA test Mr. Montgomery has is fake. Both of my clients have assured me that they are the biological parents of the girls and that Mr. Montgomery is not being honest about the results he received on the girls' DNA."

"Is this true, Mr. Montgomery?" the judge asks.

"Your honor," Robert says as he stands, "I have a sworn affidavit from the company we used when we had this test taken more than three years ago, that states Mr. Montgomery is indeed the biological father of the three children. This is an outrageous claim against my client's morals."

"Mr. Cross, what proof do you have that the DNA test is not correct?" the judge asks.

"Your honor, if you will. Here we have Mr. and Mrs. Anthony's young son. If you look at the pictures of the three girls, you will see that all three children are practically identical. As a matter of fact, the youngest of the triplets could be passed off as twins with their youngest child. If that doesn't show you enough that these children share the same parentage, then you must be blind."

"Enough," the judge barks. "How dare you have such an accusation against me. What kind of attorney are you? You're not going to win your clients' case by insulting either me or the other party."

"I apologize your honor," Mr. Cross says. "I was simply trying to make a statement and it came across incorrectly, please forgive me." He doesn't look like he's sorry at all, he actually looks kind of smug. Where the hell did Maggie find an attorney like that?

"Jeff has always been that way, he's a smug asshole," Elizabeth chuckles in my ear. "He and Andrew have been friends a long time and this has always been his way."

Well, that's a little bit of knowledge that I lean over and whisper into my attorney's ear. He looks back at me and smiles. He, too, knows that this could potentially work in our favor.

"Your honor, if you will," Robert says as he slowly approaches the bench. "Here is a copy of the original DNA test that was taken. As you can see, the blood tests show that Mr. Montgomery is indeed the biological father of the triplets. There's no reason for the Anthony's to have a claim to them at all."

The judge looks over the paperwork and then looks into my eyes.

"Mr. Montgomery," he addresses me directly. "When you took this test, were you aware that the children may not have been yours?"

"Your honor," I begin, "I never had a doubt that the children were mine. My attorney believed it would be for the best if we had the test done once Maggie, I'm sorry, Mrs. Anthony, started making claims that they were not. Until recently, I never even opened the envelope. I, too, was stunned when we walked into the courtroom and saw their child. He does look like my youngest of the triplets, Sofia, but Sofia also looks very much like her biological mother, so there's a good reason for that. I don't believe that the test is a lie, but if it pleases the court, I will submit to additional tests to prove my paternity."

This seems to make the judge happy. He looks down at the file in front of him and flips through some pages.

"Mr. Montgomery, thank you for your answer, it helps me with my preliminary decision. And please know," he says as he looks over at Maggie and Andrew, "this is *only* preliminary. I am ordering a new DNA test be done with all parties involved except for Mrs. Montgomery. All parties, including the minor son of the petitioners, will submit their DNA for testing so we can determine the true paternity of the children. I am requesting the young child for DNA also because it will let us know the exact relationship of the child to the other children. As for custody, Mrs. Anthony, I will not allow you to suddenly change your mind years after they have solely been in the custody of Mr. Montgomery. If you wanted to be a mother, you would have been there this whole time. However, I will allow you limited visitation with the girls until we get the DNA tests back.

"Mr. Montgomery," he continues, and I know my heart is already starting to break. I don't know how much more of this I can take, but he keeps on, "You are to take the girls to meet their mother one day a week. She will be allowed to be with them for 24 hours, unsupervised, until such a time that they develop a relationship with her. After the DNA tests are done, I will probably grant Mrs. Anthony more time with the girls if she can prove to have a healthy relationship with them."

"No," I gasp. "Please your honor, don't do this."

"I'm sorry Mr. Montgomery, but this is my decision." He hits his gavel on the podium and gets up and walks out.

CHAPTER TWENTY-FIVE
ELIZABETH

MAKING THINGS WORK

MY HEART BREAKS for my husband and my girls as the judge makes his decision then walks from the room. I want to grab him and run out of here, but I know we can't. There are papers to sign and DNA tests to conduct. I can't believe after all of these years, we are going to have to share the girls with cuntasaurus rex over there.

Yes, that's her official name to me, though I know I'm going to have to try and not say it out loud in front of the girls.

"Those girls will be mine," Maggie snickers at Carter. "I told you, you'd rue the day you fucked with me Carter. I just had to bide my time and wait until you least expected it. Did you think selling my home from underneath me would just happen? That there wouldn't be any consequences? No, I waited until I knew I could hit the hardest. See my husband over there, he's kind of ruthless. I knew I hit the jackpot with him. He'd do anything for me. Unlike you. Wait until you see what else we can do. This is only the beginning."

"Listen, bitch," I start to say as I make my way to her. Arms grab me from behind and I know it's Carter. He knows I'm on the warpath. The relationship we've built since we finally consummated our marriage has been nothing short of amazing.

"Not now, babe," Carter whispers in my ear. "She's trying to get us to react to prove we're unfit for the girls. Don't let her push your buttons. We'll handle this the right way."

It's crazy how he's the calm one after everything that creature did to him. I was actually very surprised that he held it together during the judge's entire diatribe. I expected him to snap a few times, but I guess that's what happens when you are the consummate professional and I'm the get down and dirty mechanic. I react faster than I think whereas he thinks before he acts.

"Fine," I say, looking *it* directly in the eye. "She's nothing but a piece of shit who doesn't deserve my time anyway."

Well, yeah, I really can't be trusted not to react. I turn on my heel and head out of the courtroom. When I get outside, I notice that Angela and Mikael are waiting for us. I knew my best friend would be here to support me, and I should have known Mikael would be here as well.

"Let's get a drink," Angela says. "It looks like you two could use one. My parents have the kids and I know they'd be upset if we picked them up too early."

I have to agree with Angie. Her parents have really taken to the girls. They treat them just like they belong to them. The girls also love them. They've never had grandparents and just love their Gigi and PopPop. Really, I can't blame them. They are really great parents and grandparents.

"Carter," I say as I turn in his arms. "Come on babe, we can all talk this out together. Let's get a drink and relax with Angie and Mikael while we figure out what to do next."

"Sounds good," Carter agrees, "but I have to sign paperwork and go down to the lab for them to take my blood first. Then, we have to bring the girls here to have them tested as well. I know we need to relax, but the sooner we get them tested and get the results, the sooner all this bullshit will be over. There's more than one way to skin a cat, and with Maggie's little confession in there, I think I know how to get her to back off."

He's right. I completely pushed it out of my mind that we need to take the girls in to have their blood drawn for this test. I turn around and look at my best friend and apologize that we can't go out with them.

"Don't worry," Angie answers. "We can still make this work. I'll call Mom and Dad and have them bring everyone down here. You can do what you need to do then they can take them back home. We'll all have a family dinner and together, as the *family* we are, we'll figure out how to get these fuckernutters out of our lives. You guys don't deserve this."

My best friend, she always has the answer. Mikael just looks at her, shakes his head and walks away. Hmm, I wonder if there could be something between those two.

"Elizabeth," Carter calls. I didn't realize he had walked away while I was talking to Angie.

"Call them," I tell Angie as I walk to where Carter is standing with our attorney.

"Angie is going to have her parents bring the kids down here, so we don't have to go get them. Let's go get your paperwork done while we wait."

"Okay," Carter says to me, then turns back to Robert. "Thank you for today. I hope we can get this done quickly. I don't blame you for anything, so stop worrying. We all should have known that one day she was going to start some shit."

Carter grabs my hand and we walk over to the clerk's office. When we get there, we see Mr. and Mrs. Trying-to-take-our-kids-away, so we wait outside, to avoid any more conflict. We don't speak. There are way too many emotions going through the both of us right now and we both understand that we need time to process.

"Mr. Montgomery, you can come in now," the clerk says from inside the office.

When we walk inside, I take notice that the assholes are no longer in sight. I look to Carter and he shrugs his shoulders. We must've both been really lost in our thoughts not to notice them leave. Good riddance.

"Because the last DNA tests were only done by swabs, we'll do a blood test for this one. You will need to head downstairs to the MedCorp office for them to draw the blood. The children will have finger pricks done, as they are young, and we don't need as much from them. We're going to try to make this as painless as possible, but they will feel a little prick. I'm so sorry you have to go through this, but we really want to ensure there are no questions after this round of tests are done. I will need you to fill out these papers and then you can go down. Mr. and Mrs. Anthony already headed downstairs with their son, Oliver. By the time you're done with your paperwork, they should be finished so you don't have to see them until they pick up the girls. The visitation day is set up for this Saturday with pickup at eight am and drop off on Sunday at the same time. Please don't be in violation of this visitation as it will reflect poorly on your character and the judge won't take that lightly. This visitation will happen every week until we appear back in court four weeks from today. Do you understand?" The clerk then hands the paperwork to Carter and tells him he can sit and fill it all out.

I didn't realize visitation would happen so fast. Saturday is only two days away and we'll have to prep the girls for this. I don't know how they are going to handle being away from their father for that long. As far as I know, they've never been away from him for more than a few hours at a time.

"Thank you," Carter says absentmindedly as he grabs the papers and takes a seat. I can see in his eyes and the way he is acting right now that his heart is breaking. Mine is too, to be honest.

"Please tell Angela we'll have to do this another day," Carter says without looking at me. "I need my girls and only have two days with them. I can't share them tonight, or tomorrow, with anyone."

Now my heart is breaking even more. I know he doesn't realize what he is saying right now. He didn't even include me in spending time with the girls. He just wants to be alone with them. I guess I can understand that, but I thought we were building a family and him shutting me out isn't conducive to our relationship.

I walk out of the room and tell Angie the new plans. She doesn't argue and says she understands. As we talk, her parents arrive with the girls and they come running right into my arms.

"Momma Elizabeth," Felicia says. She started calling me that just a few days ago and it melts my heart every time she does. I don't think she realizes what a gift her and her sisters are to me.

"We missed you and Daddy today," Felicia tells me.

"Gigi and PopPop gave us so much love today," states Isabella.

"They are fantastic grandparents, aren't they?" I ask, looking each girl in the eye.

"Yes," they all exclaim, happily.

I love that Angie's parents love these girls so much. It really means so much to me that they've adopted them into their hearts the way they have.

"Girls," I hear Carter say with so much emotion from behind me. I didn't even hear him come out of the clerk's office.

"Daddy," the three screech at the same time. Yes, it was absolutely a screech and all of us adults are trying to clear our ears out after that one. All three girls run and almost tackle Carter to the ground. It's as if it's been years instead of hours since they've seen him.

How the judge made his decision without even seeing this man and his kids together is beyond me. It's something I'm going to have to ask Robert about. If he doesn't have the answer, I know that he's not the right person for us now, though Carter may have thought he was years ago. What happened to a home study? We never had one of those. Isn't that what is typically done in a custody case? Or will that come next? Yeah, there are definitely a lot of questions that need answers. I make a mental note to do some more research on all of this.

While I was sitting here, lost in my own thoughts, Carter was telling his girls that they have to have tests done and turns to head downstairs with them. I'm so lost to myself and to him right now and my heart continues to break some more.

I don't think he even realizes that he didn't ask or wait for me to go with them. I guess after so many years of it just being the four of them, he totally forgot I was here.

"What about Elizabeth?" I hear Isabella whisper to Felicia and Sofia. It seems like she can tell her father is lost in another world and is trying not to let him hear her. That's the thing about young girls, though they think they are whispering, you can hear them from a mile away. If the situation wasn't such a somber one, I'd laugh at her trying to be quiet.

"Elizabeth." Carter suddenly turns around, shoulders slumped. "Please, come with us."

I know it wasn't his original thought but I go with him anyway, head held high. I came into this relationship with the sole purpose of Carter not losing his girls, even if the way he's acting right now is breaking my heart, I will see this through.

CHAPTER TWENTY-SIX
CARTER

THE SATURDAY THAT NEVER ENDS

THE LAST TWO days have been very stressful in our home. After explaining to the girls that they had to spend the night with Maggie, Isabella had a temper tantrum and Felicia purposely locked herself in the bathroom saying she'd never go. Sofia attached herself to Elizabeth and refused to leave her side, saying she already has a mommy and doesn't need another one.

I happen to agree. Elizabeth has been an amazing mother to my girls the short time she has known them. If you didn't know any better, you'd never know she wasn't their real mother. Wait, I meant biological mother. Because in reality, Elizabeth is more of a mother to these girls than I know Maggie could ever be to them.

Mine and Elizabeth's relationship has taken a step backwards. I know I made a huge mistake in the courthouse the other day when I said I wanted to be alone with my girls. I know I should've said and acted differently but I didn't. I was an asshole to my wife and I hope that while we're alone for the next twenty-four hours, I can find a way to make her forgive me.

I've been back to sleeping on the couch in our bedroom and I don't like it one bit. I loved holding my wife in my arms every night when we went to bed. I loved sinking so deep inside her that I didn't know where I ended, and she began.

It's my fault she's pulled away, but I intend to make it right again.

That is, if I can get over losing my girls for the night to that vile woman I thought I once loved.

Today is the day that Maggie will come get the girls and they will spend the night with her and Andrew. I'm not okay with this, but I know it's something I must do to stay on the good side of the judge. It will be good for the girls to get to know their little brother, but I really don't want them to get attached. I know it's selfish of me, but I think I've earned that right after everything Maggie did and how she just walked away without even looking back.

"Daddy," Isabella calls softly up to me, "I don't want to go. Why do I have to go?"

My poor baby, I try to calm her the best I can but there's nothing I can really do for them.

"Izzy, baby, it's only for one night," I tell her. "I promise Elizabeth and I will be here waiting for you tomorrow morning. It will be an exciting adventure."

I have been trying to convince the girls this will be fun for them, though I think they see right through me.

I jump when I hear the doorbell ring and look over at the clock. Seven forty-five, they are early. Shit. I was hoping they would be late, or better yet, not even show.

Elizabeth walks in the room holding both Sofia and Felicia in her arms. From the look on the girls' faces, I can see they have been crying.

Fuck, how am I supposed to do this to them?

"It's okay," Elizabeth whispers. "I calmed them down. They're ready. Right girls?"

"Yes, Mommy Elizabeth," both girls answer.

I don't know when Felicia also started calling Elizabeth mommy, but this breaks my heart even more.

The doorbell rings again and I realize that neither one of us wants to answer it.

Sighing to myself, I walk over and open it.

It's Andrew that's at the door and not Maggie. This, I am really not okay with. They've met Maggie before but never him. I can't send my girls off with a stranger, that will make them flip out more than they already have.

"Where's Maggie?" I ask as calmly as I can without letting the girls in on my irritation.

"She's home with Oliver," he states, matter of fact. "These are my children; I wanted to pick them up."

"No," I state. He's not taking my girls alone. I've decided to change his plans. "I will follow you to your house with them. You're early and they don't know you. I'm not sending them off with you on a whim. At least they've met Maggie once, and I'm not traumatizing them more than they already are. And before you think of arguing with me in front of them and making this worse, I advise you to go back to your car and wait while we get them ready."

Andrew doesn't say anything else and turns around and walks back to his car. I guess he may have a single decent bone in his body after all.

I walk back in the house and together Elizabeth and I get the girls ready to leave.

"Please come with us," I say and look over at my wife. "We need you."

Sure, I'm playing low ball here, but I do need my wife and I'm sure the girls really do need her to.

"I'll come for the girls," she answers and grabs two small hands and walks out the door.

I'm left alone in the house with Felicia and she tugs on my pant leg.

"Daddy," she whispers, "Mommy Elizabeth is going to need you to take care of her while we're gone. She's sick. Promise me you'll take care of her."

How did I not know my wife was sick? Man, I've been an asshole. More than I already thought I was. I really do need to fix things with her.

"I'll take care of her, I promise," I tell my daughter. "You need to promise me you'll take care of your sisters."

"I will Daddy," she promises. "I love you."

"I love you too, Licia girl."

We get into the car and I follow Andrew over to their house. It's actually not very far from where Elizabeth and I live, and I'm surprised I've never run into them before.

When we arrive, Elizabeth and I get out of the car to help the girls out. When we get out of the car, the girls look over at me with sad faces. I can't believe I'm leaving my children here with virtual strangers. It's going to break me more than I thought it would, but I know deep down in my heart this is what I need to do to keep the judge happy and to work on winning this case.

Maggie walks out the front of her house with her son in tow and it still shocks me how much he looks like the girls, Sofia especially. It's quite uncanny to tell you the truth. It makes me question the validity of the paternity test I had done years ago. If I didn't know any better, I would swear these children do share the same paternity, but Maggie never let me touch her after she got pregnant with the girls so there's no way they can be full siblings.

Elizabeth and I both kneel down and hug the girls.

"You be good girls," Elizabeth whispers to them. I see she's trying to hold back tears and all I really want to do is just snatch up my family and run away from here.

"We love you so much," I say, as I hold all four of my ladies in my arms. "We will see you tomorrow, I promise."

We all walk up the stairs, because God forbid Maggie come down to get the girls.

Maggie greets the girls, coldly, and turns to walk inside the house with them. It takes everything in me not to run inside after them, but instead I get in the car and just stare at the house for a moment.

Elizabeth reaches over and squeezes my hand. She's feeling this as much as I am, and I know now is the time I stop neglecting my wife's feelings and make things right.

"Do you want to go home?" I ask. "Or would you like to go out somewhere?"

Personally, I'd like to go home and get lost in my wife, but I know that there's more I need to do before that happens, like apologize for my behavior these last few days.

"I'd like to go home," Elizabeth replies as she pulls her hand from mine. "I need to be where our girls are supposed to be. I need the house to be perfect for when they come home tomorrow."

I understand where she is coming from. I feel the same. Instead of continuing the conversation, I turn the car around and head home. Neither of us speak, both lost in our own thoughts the entire drive.

Elizabeth immediately exits the vehicle when I pull up to our house. Although that's not what I had planned, I let her go inside. It'll give both her and me a few moments to gather our thoughts. I know what I want from her and for our lives, but I've done a shit job conveying that in the last few days. Everything has happened so quickly, I completely neglected her and haven't shown her how much she means to me.

I pull my car into the garage and head into the house.

"I've fallen for you," I say to her as soon as I see her. She's sitting in the kitchen with a bottle of wine in her hand just staring at it. "I've fallen in love with you and didn't realize how much that was true until I saw how much I've hurt you. I'm sorry, Elizabeth, I really am. I didn't mean to shut you out the last few days and I should've made you a part of everything. This is hard for me, and I know it's hard for you too."

I don't know how to stop talking right now, and I see the tears falling down her face. I have to find a way to comfort her but I am lost. After everything I did for Maggie and how she threw it all back at me in the end, I'm not sure how to act right now.

"Carter," Elizabeth speaks, "I know this has been hard on you. Those girls are not mine by blood, yet I feel like my soul is being ripped from me. I don't blame you, but you need to realize that I'm in this for the long haul too. When you told me it was forever, I felt a part of myself come alive once again. I thought you had meant it. But, then, the last two days, you closed the door on us being a family and it completely tore me apart."

"I didn't mean to. I'm so sorry, Elizabeth. I never wanted to hurt you. I don't know how to do this. I thought I knew how to keep a relationship and you saw how that turned out. Please, understand and help me." I know I shouldn't compare my relationships, but it's all I've known.

"Haven't you realized by now, I'm nothing like her?" Elizabeth pleads, and I can see clearly the pain I've caused her by my words and actions.

"I know you're not, and that's why I didn't realize that what I was doing was hurting you so much." I walk over to my wife and put my arms around her. "Please tell me you can forgive me. Please. I can't live with you being mad at me."

I lift her face gently with my hand and place a kiss on her lips. The fact that she just let me kiss her makes me believe that she'll forgive me, and we'll be okay.

"Carter, of course I forgive you, but, please, let me in. Talk to me. I've fallen for you too and want this to work. Not only for us, but for those girls."

I hear her words and know with all my heart that I'll never intentionally hurt her again. I scoop her up in my arms without thinking twice about it and take her to our bedroom.

"Let me show you how much I love you," I tell her as I place her on our bed. I pull my shirt over my head and make my intentions clear.

"Oh, Carter," she starts. "I love you too." She sits up on the bed and slowly begins removing her clothing.

It's been two long days without my wife and that ends now. As soon as we both strip out of our clothes, our mouths are devouring each other. I'm going to take my time with my wife today and show her just how much I love her and how much I want her.

I lay her back down on the bed and climb in beside her. I'm going to savor my woman's body today like she's never been savored before. I begin kissing and licking her neck, the spot I know that gets her worked up the best. She's already starting to writhe on the bed, but she's got a long way to go before I get to where she wants to be.

I begin moving south down her body. Her body is luscious and full and perfect. She has curves in all the right places and I can't wait to taste each and every one. As I make my way lower, I grasp her breasts in my hands and begin kneading them. Her moans of pleasure are fighting with my resolve to take this slow.

"Carter, please," she moans.

"No, not yet," I reply. I have to keep with the pace I am aiming for. She needs to know and feel how much I cherish her.

I take one of her nipples in my mouth and sweet heaven, this is just what I needed. My wife's taste is like no other I've ever tasted. I feast on her breast for a moment and to me they feel a bit fuller than the last time we were together. It's probably just how much I missed her body. I lick my fingers and begin tweaking her other nipple. I don't want to leave any part of her untouched.

She grabs my head in her hands and I know she's close to coming. Elizabeth's nipples are so sensitive, I know she can come just by me playing with them. Today, though, I'll give her a little extra.

I move over to begin suckling on her other nipple and move my hand down. I find her pussy wet underneath my hand and groan in anticipation. My cock is rock hard, and I know he's feeling neglected but this isn't about him right now. This is about giving my wife all she deserves and more.

I pump first one, then two fingers into her pussy while sucking on her nipple. She begins moaning loudly and this time I know I don't need to quiet her down. It's just us in the house, so she can scream all she wants, and I plan on making her scream all day and night.

As I pump into her pussy and suck on her nipple, I feel her start to tighten around my fingers. Oh, not yet sweet beautiful woman of mine. I remove my fingers from her pussy for just a moment and bring them to my lips. Tasting her on my hand makes me moan in pleasure right along with her.

"Taste," I tell her and bring my hand up to her mouth. She opens willingly and moans around my fingers.

I remove my fingers from her mouth and push them back into her sweetness, only this time, I take my pinky and move it to her ass. I gently rub around her hole as I pump in and out of her pussy and suck on her breasts. I wonder briefly, if she's ever enjoyed this before, but then stop myself from those thoughts. I don't care what she's done in her past, this is about us. Here and now.

As I breach her tight ass with my pinky, she screams out in pleasure. I almost come on the spot just from the noises she's making. Slowly, I begin pumping into both her pussy and her ass, still feasting on her tits and she comes unglued. She's clenching so hard with her hands on my head and her pussy around my fingers, I think she may break them.

Slowly, I pull my fingers out of her as she drifts down from her first orgasm of the day. She's well sated right now, but we've only just begun.

"Carter," she moans, "I need you inside me, right now."

Who am I to deny this beautiful woman below me?

I position myself over her body and in one swift motion, my

cock is seated deep inside her. This feeling, I don't think I'll ever get over. Feeling her pussy still coming down from the aftershocks of her orgasm is making me want to blow my load immediately.

I just lay there for a moment, trying to calm myself down. I need this to last. I'm not a one-pump chump, but right now I'm feeling like that's all it's going to take.

I wrap my arms around Elizabeth's head and begin kissing her. She kisses me back with a ferocity that tells me she wants more.

I slowly begin to pump into her and her moans grow louder.

Man, if I knew my wife was a screamer, I would've sound-proofed our room. I'd love to hear her scream like this all the time, but it would wake the girls and how would we explain that?

We build a steady rhythm, both of us working together to reach the same goal. This feeling, it's the most amazing feeling in the world. I know now, I never felt like this with Maggie; what I had with her was never love. Knowing now what loving someone really feels like, I was such a fool.

I pull out of my wife and flip her over. I have to feel what it's like to fuck her from behind. I immediately fill her back up with my cock and the sensation is amazing. I start bucking into her harder and a bit wilder. She's not complaining. By the sounds she's making, I can tell she's enjoying this as much as I am.

"More," she yells back at me.

"Anything for you," I tell her and start fucking her harder. I take my hand and start rubbing her asshole as I fuck her and she's pushing back into me. I take my finger, stick it in my mouth, to use my saliva as a lubricant, and breech her tight ass once again. I can feel myself within her and it's hard to hold back and not come.

She's pushing back into me even harder now, so I know she's enjoying what I'm doing. As I fuck her harder, I insert another finger into her ass and she comes immediately. The feeling of my fingers in her ass and her pussy gripping me like a vice make me come right along with her. I come so hard, I let out a roar. I feel like a beast and this woman is definitely my beauty.

Elizabeth collapses on the bed and I collapse on top of her.

"That was the best fucking sex of my life," I tell her. "I love you so much, Elizabeth. Just being with you makes everything so much better." She has to know she's everything to me.

"Mhmm," is all she manages. I want to laugh but I know the feeling.

"I need a nap," she states, and I can't help but agree.

I roll her over, and pull her on top of me, and that's the last thing I remember before we both fall into a fitful slumber.

CHAPTER TWENTY-SEVEN
ELIZABETH

HELPING MY FAMILY

IT'S Sunday morning and the girls will be home soon. Carter and I spent so much time loving each other yesterday and it feels so good to know he loves me as much as I love him. I now feel that we can make this all work and we will be much stronger together. We're going to do everything we can to keep our family together. We're not going to fight dirty, we're going to fight legally.

Carter's arms begin to tighten around me, so I know he's awake. I've been awake for a little while but have been enjoying how tight he's holding me to him. It's like he's afraid to let go. With all we're going through at the moment, I understand.

"Good morning, wife," he whispers in my ear. He rubs up against me and I can tell he's ready to go again. This man amazes me with his stamina, but I'm not going to complain.

"Good morning, husband," I whisper-moan back. Yeah, I could get used to this.

An hour later, we're in the kitchen preparing breakfast waiting for the girls to arrive home. Maggie called and said she was bringing them herself. I guess she knew Carter was upset with how things went yesterday.

The doorbell rings and both of us jump. We both walk over to answer the door because neither of us wants to be without the girls for another moment.

My heart breaks immediately when we open the door. Our girls look so sad and defeated. I've never seen them look like this. They don't even say hello to us. They just walk right in.

"Bye, girls, I'll see you next weekend," Maggie yells into the house. "They will learn not to be so damn spoiled."

Spoiled? The girls are anything but spoiled. What the fuck is she talking about? Before I can say anything to defend the girls, Carter shuts the door in her face and walks to the back of the house.

I follow him back through the house looking for the girls. Isabella is in the playroom, so I head in there.

"Good morning Isabella," I start as I sit on the couch next to her. She doesn't respond, just keeps her hands in her lap looking down at them. My heart hurts so much right now, I want to cry, but this isn't about me. This is about fixing my girls. "Do you want some breakfast? Daddy and I cooked your favorites for you this morning."

"No, thank you, ma'am," she answers in a quiet voice.

Ma'am? What the fuck?

"Isabella," I state a little firmer than I realized, "look at me and tell me what's wrong, please."

"Mother said you're not our mom and that we needed to call you ma'am and nothing else. She said that's she's our mother and we're to call her that. She yells a lot and Sofia cried all the time. I didn't like it. Felicia tried to protect Sofia and got in a lot of trouble and was told she couldn't have breakfast. So, I'm not going to eat if my sister can't eat."

"Carter," I yell. I'm fuming right now. How dare they deny my children food? Who the fuck do they think they are?

Carter walks into the room carrying Sofia in his arms. His face has rage written all over it. I'm going to assume he heard the same story I did, or something similar or maybe even worse. He looks around the room seeming a bit confused.

"Where's Felicia?" he asks, still looking around as if she'll appear out of nowhere.

"I thought she was with you," I reply and quickly pick Isabella up and walk out of the room.

Together, each of us holding the girls safely in our arms, we start to look around the house for Felicia. We find her in her bed, just lying there staring out into nowhere. My poor girls.

We both sit down on the bed and Sofia and Isabella climb out of our arms and lay next to their sister. These girls share a bond stronger than their DNA and you can see the love they have for one another.

"Felicia," both Carter and I say at the same time. I'll let him go first, since he's their father, but he looks to me and gives me a hand motion to continue. This is a huge step for him, I know, but it touches my heart how he trusts me to take care of his girls.

"Felicia, baby, look at me." When she doesn't do as I ask, I lie next to her and look right into her face. "Baby girl, I'm sorry your mother wasn't very nice to you. Daddy and I would never deny you anything you needed. We're going to do everything we can to make sure you're not yelled at or punished like that again. Come here and let us hold you. Daddy and I made your favorite breakfast, let's go eat as a family, please."

When I stop talking, Felicia breaks down into sobs. I grab her to me and hold her tight. I can't believe that vile woman hurt these babies so much. I want to do everything I can to keep them away from her. This solidifies my resolve to get answers to the questions I had the other day in the courthouse, on why and how this all transpired without the proper steps taken. Everything I'd read before the trial told me so much more was to happen before the judge would make any decisions. Like home visits, and the DNA tests.

Slowly, I lift Felicia into my arms and Carter does the same with Isabella and Sofia. We walk into the kitchen and set the girls down so they can eat. I go to the oven to get breakfast out when Felicia pats me on the leg. Felicia likes to cook, so I assume that she's wanting to help me. I don't ask any questions, just reach over to the drawer that has her tiny oven mitts Carter had made for her and hand them to her. She puts them on while I grab the tray from the oven. I hand her the tray and she walks it over to the table.

This is what the girls need. They need our normal routine, I see it clearly. As long as we keep things normal here at home, maybe we can reverse the effects those assholes caused.

We all sit down to eat as a family and the girls start coming back to themselves. This makes me smile, but I know Carter and I will have a lot of work to do so this doesn't happen again.

As the week goes on, our family starts to feel normal again. We laugh and play with the girls and keep to our routine as much as possible. They're going to need the stability and to know this is what they will come home to after their visit with those vile creatures this coming Saturday.

I wish with everything in me we did not have to let them go with them, but we have to do as the court has ordered. We have to try to prove that these people being in the girls' lives are not in their best interests.

Carter and I have decided privately to hire a child therapist to speak to the girls. We're hoping that if we bring a professional to court with us, we'll be able to prove that these people should not be around children.

We saw their son, he looked okay, but I'm wondering if that poor child is treated as poorly as our girls were. No child should have to endure their way of parenting and I'm hoping, for that little boy's sake, that they did this to try to drive a wedge between us and our girls.

THE WEEK HAS COME and gone, and the girls are coming home today after their second weekend with the people who are trying to take them from us. I'm hoping that everything we instilled in the girls this week stuck, and that they don't come back the same way they did last week.

Carter and I wait on the front steps for the girls this time. We want the girls to see we are waiting for them and they are wanted at home. That there's no reason for them to have to knock on the door or ring the bell when they arrive back to the only home they've ever known. We're hoping this will help with any damage those two may have caused in the last twenty-four hours.

When we see the car pull into the driveway, we both walk down the stairs to greet them. They pop open their doors as soon as the car stops and come running into our arms. This feels so good and hopefully shows that monster how children are supposed to treat their parents.

They are not withdrawn this time and it makes me so happy.

We don't even greet the people in the car and turn to walk into the house. We have no need to talk to them and it appears they don't wish to talk to us either. They just turn the car around and leave. Fine with me.

"How was your weekend?" Carter asks, not addressing anyone in particular so they know any and all of them can answer.

"It sucked," Sofia states plainly. I want to say something about her language, but Carter gives a little shake of his head to tell me to let it go. This time I will, but I plan to have a talk with them and let them know what's acceptable and what's not.

"Oliver can do whatever he wants and never gets in trouble, but we're not allowed to do anything but sit in the room. I don't like it there, Daddy," Isabella states.

Well, that answers my question as to how that little boy is treated. At least it's good to know he isn't treated poorly, but my girls deserve much better.

"Only a couple more weeks, girls, then hopefully this will all be over," Carter tells them. Man, I hope he's right. I don't think I could do this for the long haul.

We walk into the house and straight to the kitchen. After last week, we learned that they don't cook for the kids. They order out and that's not healthy. Carter hasn't raised the girls to eat fast food, and I intend to keep that up. It's so much better for them.

They also don't eat before ten a.m. The girls got in trouble last week because they wanted to eat when they got up. That's what caused Felicia to get into so much trouble when Sofia started crying that she was hungry. My baby girl was told she was fat and didn't need to eat anyway. They were limited on their food intake and that is not acceptable.

When Felicia walks into the kitchen, she squeals. She sees that I've set everything up to make pancakes instead of cooking them before they got home. I know how much my girlie likes to help cook, so I made sure to have everything ready for her this morning.

"Thank you, Momma Elizabeth," she whispers. I want to cry because it's been over a week since she's called me that and I feel then and there, that we're going to be okay again.

"Let's get started, shall we?" I tell her. She nods her head and goes to the sink to wash her hands. Goodness, I love this little girl.

Carter grabs Isabella and Sofia and tells me to holler for them when we're ready. He's going to take them to the playroom and show Isabella what he had done for her.

While the girls were away yesterday, we had a contractor come in and set up a little dance studio for Isabella. She's our tiny dancer and we know she's really going to excel at her craft. We want to show her how much we support her and her dreams. Even if she's only four years old.

Felicia and I set out to get breakfast done when we hear Isabella scream in excitement. I just smile to myself knowing we are making these girls happy. Instead of getting breakfast started, I grab Felicia's hand and lead her down the hall, so she can see what has her sister so happy.

When we walk into the room, Isabella is twirling around with Sofia. It's such a beautiful site to see, their smiles taking up their entire faces. I look down to Felicia, who hugs my leg and see she's smiling just as big as the other two.

"You did good, Momma Elizabeth," she whispers. It's amazing how she tells me I did good and doesn't say it to her dad. She gives me all the credit and doesn't think twice about it. I love the bond her and I have developed. She's a Momma's girl these days instead of a Daddy's girl like Isabella and Sofia.

"Mommy Elizabeth," Sofia yells, excitedly, "look at what Daddy gave Isabella, isn't it beautiful?" She's twirling around clumsily, unlike Isabella who is a natural.

"I see, pretty girl," I tell her.

"Shall we go finish breakfast or would you like to stay with your sisters?" I look down and ask Felicia.

"I want to cook," she answers.

I take her hand and we head back into the kitchen to get breakfast done.

CHAPTER TWENTY-EIGHT
ELIZABETH

ON THE RUN

A WEEK HAS GONE by and Carter and I are again waiting for the girls to come home. This is the last Saturday they will have with them until our court date on Thursday.

Hopefully, with everything I have gathered and the testimony of the counselor we've hired for the girls, this will be the very last time they have our girls.

We've done so much to work on their spirits since that first weekend. I've completely neglected my business because the girls needed me home with them. I have employees I trust, so I'm not worried about things at the shop. Angie has been around a lot when she's not working. Alfie has made it his mission to protect the girls as much as he can. He's more like a big brother to them, trying not to let anything hurt them. It melts my heart so much to see how my family has come together.

I'm not feeling very well this morning, so only Carter is waiting outside for the girls. I'm lying on the couch with some tea that Carter made me so that the girls will see me here when they get home. I hope they don't think me not being outside is because I don't want to see them, but it's been difficult for me to do anything today. I think I'm coming down with the flu and I am trying to do everything I can so I can get well quickly. I don't want to be sick when we go back to court and I'm still waiting on some things to come through to help us prove that the Anthonys are unfit to be with our children.

I look over to the clock and notice it's well after nine am. I wonder if I fell asleep for a little bit and didn't notice Carter come in with the girls. He's been so kind trying to take care of me and didn't even want me to get out of bed this morning.

I get up off the couch and have to get my bearings. I'm still feeling a bit dizzy, but I am feeling a lot better than I did when we first woke up this morning. I head straight to the playroom, thinking Carter must've gone there with the girls and is keeping them quietly playing. I don't see them in the room and I am growing a little concerned.

"Fuck." I hear Carter whisper yell. It seems he's in his office instead of with the girls. But, where are the girls, I wonder?

"Carter," I begin from his office doorway, "where are the girls? Did I miss them coming home?"

The look he gives me looks like one of anguish. I can't understand what is going on but I am now starting to worry.

"I don't know," he answers.

"What do you mean you don't know? What happened when they got home? Why didn't you wake me?"

"They didn't come home, Elizabeth," he states as calmly as he can. "I've been trying to reach Maggie for over an hour to see what the holdup is and can't get in touch with her. I want to drive over to their house, but I didn't want to leave you when you were sick. Mikael sent someone over there but there doesn't seem to be anyone home. I don't know why they are running so late. I've called the hospitals and police and there doesn't seem to be any accidents or anything."

My concern starts to turn to panic. I don't want to think the worst, but my gut is telling me that this is really bad.

"Come on," I tell him. "We're going over there now, we're going to get our girls. This is bullshit."

He looks like he wants to protest but then strides over to me with purpose.

We get into the car and make the short drive over to their house. Like Mikael said, there doesn't seem to be anyone home. We decide to go to the door and look in the windows to see if maybe they are home and just have their car somewhere else. What we see when we look inside has us both panicking.

Carter immediately goes for the door and tries to open it. It opens immediately, and he goes inside. I follow him and just about want to die when I see what he sees.

The place is empty. Not just empty of Andrew, Maggie and the kids, but the place is empty to the point there's not a chair, a table or even a speck of fucking dust. They're gone. They're all gone and there's nothing to even show they've ever been here.

Where are my kids? I need to know where my girls are. This can't be happening.

Suddenly, I feel sick again and extremely dizzy. I can't comprehend what's going on around me. Carter yells for me but it's like I'm underwater, I can't really hear him. Everything is muffled. I think I answer but I can't be sure. I try to back up to the wall, but suddenly, everything goes black....

I don't know how long I was out, but I come to lying in Carter's arms. He has the most worried expression on his face, and I don't know if it's for me or if it's because our girls are missing.

There are police everywhere at this point, walking through the empty house. I'm not sure they are going to find anything, it doesn't look like even a speck of dust was left behind.

"Thank God you're okay," Carter says as he sweeps my hair off my face. "I know you're worried about the girls, but we need to take you to the hospital to get checked out."

"No," I answer. My throat feels like sandpaper right now. "I just need some water and then we need to find the girls."

I know I'm being stubborn. I've been sick for a while but it's not about me right now. There are three beautiful, precious little girls who are somewhere they shouldn't be. They should be home with us, not on the run with people they barely even know.

"I thought you had this place under surveillance," Carter yells.

I look up and see Mikael walking into the house. Shit, this isn't going to be good. Carter depended on Mikael to help keep the girls safe and with them missing, he's going to blame anyone he can.

"It's not his fault," I say, trying to calm Carter down.

"Carter," Mikael begins, "I've had this place under surveillance twenty-four seven. My guys were knocked out with tranqs last night. They just came to a few moments ago when the police sirens came up the road. I'm sorry, man. You know I would never let anything happen to those girls. I love them like they're my own."

"I know," Carter sighs. "I'm sorry, brother. I know you've been going above and beyond but I need to know where my girls are."

Tears are running down Carter's face and I only remember one time ever seeing my husband cry. It was the night he begged me to marry him because he thought his ex was going to steal his girls. With that thought, now I feel like I'm responsible. I thought I was helping him. I gave into his request, but look, it was my ex who helped make this happen.

"Elizabeth, I'm taking you to the hospital. I need to at least know you're okay right now. Please give me this. I don't want to argue."

I give in to Carter's request. I know he needs to know that at least I'm okay because he doesn't have any answers when it comes to our children.

"Okay," I answer, "but, can we please go in the car? I don't want to go in the ambulance."

"Yeah."

"I'll get with the detectives and try to get you guys some

answers," Mikael tells us. "I'm so sorry. I failed you and the girls. I'll find them, I promise."

"It's not your fault," I try once again to reassure him, but he just turns on his heel and walks away.

Carter grabs my hand and helps me get up. This isn't going to be fun, but I guess we do need to find out why I've been so sick lately. It's been a few weeks and this bug just won't go away. For the most part, I have been able to hide it from Carter, but today, it just all came on so suddenly.

We get to the hospital and are seen rather quickly. This isn't normal for me, I'm used to waiting for hours on end in the waiting area, not rushed right in. I wonder, not for the first time, if this is because of who Carter is and the vast amount he is worth. I'm not complaining, though. Because the faster I'm seen, the sooner we can get back out there to look for the children.

"Hello, Mrs. Montgomery," a kind, blonde haired doctor says to me. "I'm Dr. Mitchell, I'm going to help figure out why you've been feeling under the weather lately."

"Thank you," I reply. "It's really no big deal. Just a little dizzy today—"

"No," Carter says as he cuts me off. "She tries to hide it, but she's been sick for a few weeks now. She thinks she hides it from me in the mornings, but I notice. We have three little girls at home so it's understandable that illnesses get passed around. None of the girls have been sick, though, so I'm concerned why Elizabeth isn't getting better."

I guess I wasn't as good at hiding being sick as I had originally thought.

"I'm going to do a quick exam and then have the nurse come draw some blood," Dr. Mitchell tells me. "I need for you to lie back on the table and I'm going to check you out, is that okay?"

"Yes, that's fine," I answer as I lie back on the bed.

The doctor first checks my heart and lungs, and then pokes around my abdomen a few times. She then takes her stethoscope and listens to different parts. When she's done, she takes off her gloves and writes a few things down on her notepad.

"Well, Mrs. Montgomery," the doctor starts, "I don't believe we need as many tests as I first thought. I believe with just one blood test, we'll know exactly why you aren't feeling so well lately, and I have a feeling, you'll be feeling better soon enough."

"What's wrong?" Carter asks immediately.

"Oh, I don't think anything is wrong, per se," the doctor answers. "I think the two of you are about to expand your family."

What? She can't be saying what I think she is.

"That can't be," I tell her. My heart is getting ready to break again, having to explain this. "I can't have children," I choke out. "I was told a few years back that there was no way I'd ever be able to have children. You see, I thought I was pregnant once."

At my declaration, Carter's eyes shoot to me. We've never had this discussion. Yeah, we've never used protection or had the birth control talk, but we weren't supposed to be a real husband and wife like we are now. Since we've consummated our marriage, I never thought to tell him about this. Looks like there's no time like the present.

"I once thought I was pregnant," I start again. "I was so happy. I told the father and he told me that there was no way. That he had a vasectomy. Since then, I learned he lied and that to prevent me from ever getting pregnant, he'd mix birth control in my juice in the mornings. When I went to get checked out why I wasn't getting a period, the doctor told me that it was near impossible for me to have children. It seemed that my uterus was unstable and even if I did get pregnant, I wouldn't be able to carry a child to term. In order to make sure I'd never have to go through the heartbreak of a miscarriage, she did an endometrial ablation. Between that and continuing to taking birth control, I never had to worry about getting pregnant again."

Carter seems a bit crushed by my news. Would he have been happy to have more children? I mean, now is not the time to even think about it with our three currently missing but would he have wanted more children in the future. Again, this is something we never discussed. I guess neither one of us thought this thing between us would last longer than it would take for him to get permanent custody of the girls.

"Mrs. Montgomery, I'm afraid to tell you ablations only last a couple of years and we all know birth control is not one hundred percent effective. When was the last time you had one?"

"About three years ago. I haven't had a period since, so I didn't think it was necessary to have another one yet."

"Well, why don't we get an ultrasound machine in here and take a look. If we don't see anything on an external exam, we'll run bloodwork. If the blood is positive, we'll do an internal exam. I don't want to be invasive if we don't have to be."

I agree with the doctor and she leaves the room so I can get changed.

Carter comes to me immediately and wraps me in his arms. Not the reaction I was expecting from him.

"It's okay," he whispers. "We can always adopt if you want more children."

Wow, this man amazes me more every day. Instead of being upset and thinking I can't give him children, he's trying to make me feel better.

I quickly undress and put on the ugly hospital robe I was given. I hate these things. I swear, the person who invented them had to be blind when they came up with the design and pattern. No one in their right mind would ever voluntarily put something like this on. What ever happened to privacy? All my bits are hanging out.

After I dress, I sit back up on the bed. Carter sits on the bed with me instead of sitting in the chair. His look is one I can't decipher at the moment. His eyes are a bit watery and it looks like he's trying to keep from crying.

"Are you ready, Mrs. Montgomery?" the doctor asks from

outside the room. Yes, room. We were put in a private room instead of a curtained area. Another thing I guess money can buy.

"Yes, please come in," I answer.

Carter gets off the bed and stands next to me holding my hand. He doesn't let go as the doctor walks in pushing an ultrasound machine. I thought we'd have a little more time while we waited for a tech, but it looks like this doctor just wants to get this done. I like that. I hate waiting.

"Okay, Mrs. Montgomery, let's check you out," she says as she sits on the stool by the edge of the bed.

She lifts my robe and then puts some gel on the wand and places it on my belly. It's a bit cold at first but then I don't notice a thing as I hear a thump thump thump sound.

"Oh. My. God," I cry. I can't believe what I'm seeing. I know what that is on the screen. How? I don't know how to react.

"Elizabeth," Carter whispers. I look up at the man and see tears in his eyes once again. "I can't believe I'm going to be a father again."

He has an awe to his voice. This man truly loves his children and by the sound of his voice, he already loves this one too.

"Well, congratulations, Mr. and Mrs. Montgomery," the doctor says. "Looks like we have a baby in here. And by the looks of things in this preliminary view, it doesn't look like we have anything to worry about. The uterus looks healthy as does the placenta and the sac. It looks like a miracle if you ask me. From the measurements I've done so far, it looks like you're about ten weeks along. Although there are still a few more weeks left in your first trimester, I would go out on a limb and say you're in the safe zone. Most miscarriages happen within the first twelve weeks, and with the diagnosis you received from your previous doctor, I think you would've spontaneously aborted the fetus by now."

The doctor herself looks like she's happy. She moves the wand around on my belly a bit more, but I think I'm lost in everything surrounding me. All I can do is look at the screen and see that while my life may be a nightmare at the moment, one of my greatest dreams is about to come true.

"Congratulations you two and I hope they find the rest of your children quickly. We were watching the news at the nurse's station and I'm so sorry this is happening at what should be a happy time for you. Only a monster would rip their children out of their parents' lives. I'm sorry, it may be unprofessional, but I can't stand women who use their children against their fathers."

With those words, the doctor leaves the room. Carter and I sit there, just staring at the screen where the doctor left the picture of our baby up for us to see.

We need to find our children. They need to be here with us and enjoy their little brother or sister. I vow, right then, that I will give it everything I have to find out how and why the judge granted them visitation so quickly and allowed this all to happen.

CHAPTER TWENTY-NINE
CARTER

HOLDING ONTO HOPE

SIX MONTHS LATER

THE WHIRLWIND of emotions Elizabeth and I have felt in these last months are indescribable. We've been happy, we've been sad, but the one thing we haven't done is give up hope. It's been so hard on the both of us, trying to celebrate our expanding family when there are three of us still missing.

The police have all but given up hope on finding our girls. The FBI has been involved but I don't think they have our case as an active case right now. I think they've given up hope on ever finding our girls, as well.

It's been six long months of hoping and praying. Following lead after lead, following tips given by strangers. It's all come back to being bad information and us not finding our children.

I've put out rewards for information leading to their whereabouts. We've gone on local and national news begging and pleading for just someone to know or have seen our children and those douchebags who took them from us.

After we left the hospital the day our girls went missing, Elizabeth made it her mission to find out how they were even able to get a hold of them in the first place. I spoke with Robert about this on many occasions and Mikael looked into it all, as well. No one understood how they were able to get any type of custody of my children without child services, psychologists and home studies done.

It turned out, the judge had a gambling problem. Andrew had his own investigation done in order to get what he wanted. He blackmailed the judge into making this all go in his and Maggie's favor. He was making payments to the judge to help him get out of debt, the last payment which the judge could've finally happily retired on was set for the day we were due in court for the revealing of all the paternity tests.

The tests. Those, too, were rigged. The lab the court was using was the one Maggie's friend Felicia worked at. The results of the DNA tests were rigged to show Andrew as the father. Since Maggie left without Felicia, and Felicia was up the proverbial shit's creek for her hand in all this, she sung like a canary when questioned by the FBI. Guess those girls were really only loyal to the money and not to each other. Felicia will spend some time behind bars, but she did get a lighter sentence for cooperating with the police.

The judge has been behind bars since this all went down. Though Felicia's trial was quick, the judge isn't getting off as easy. You can't be a sitting judge and compromise yourself in so many ways. We've been led to believe that the judge will never see a day of freedom again for the rest of his natural life. I'm not upset about that, to say the least. Someone has to pay, and I don't think the time any of these assholes spend behind bars will be long enough.

There are many questions, however, with Oliver's paternity. That poor kid, I do feel sorry for him. He's going to hurt as much as my girls are probably hurting right now. He'll likely never see the only parents he's ever known, and that, there, my friends, is the kicker.

Oliver's paternity test came back as me being his biological father, which we all know is damn near impossible. Maggie and I had never been intimate since she found out she was pregnant with the girls. Hell, I hadn't even seen her since the girls were just a few months old. We still don't have the answer to that one.

Elizabeth and I talked in depth about what will happen with Oliver. We don't want him to spend his life in the system, so we are going to adopt him. I'm hoping that he'll be able to adjust to us being his new family. I would hope that in all these months of him being with his sisters, at least he'll feel comfortable enough with them and it won't be a shock to him.

We've already hired psychologists for the children, for when they finally make it back home to us. I have no doubt that I will get my children back, I just hope it's before our new baby is born.

Elizabeth has been having a difficult time as of late. Angela has been here helping almost every day while Mikael and I have been trying to follow every lead that comes our way. She's been a Godsend and I'm hoping that she and Mikael can one day see what Elizabeth and I have been witnessing since the beginning. They both deserve happiness after all they've been through in life, and we think they'll find that happiness in each other.

Mikael has been blaming himself for so long, but really, it's not his fault. Who knew that Andrew and Maggie could be this evil and devious? I never, in a million years, would have even thought Maggie would go to these extremes. Kidnapping our children just to get revenge was never warranted. I didn't do anything to that woman, ever. I gave her the world and in turn, she gave me her ass to kiss.

Sitting here at my desk in the house, I click through the new list of suspected places Maggie and Andrew may be with the children. Elizabeth is finally asleep after she and Angie spent the entire day painting the nursery.

I watched them for a while.

At first, they were laughing, joking about the colors and saying that if the doctors were wrong, they'd have to repaint the room. I didn't see anything wrong with a girl living in a blue room, but they thought differently.

Suddenly, seemingly out of nowhere, Elizabeth fell to the floor and started sobbing.

"How can I be happy, Angie?" she asked her best friend. "My girls are missing out on so much. Carter is miserable but tries to hide it, but he's so loving and happy for our son at the same time. My heart is a wreck. I don't know how to do this. What if they are being mistreated? Or worse."

I watched her sob in Angie's arms and wanted to tell her it would be okay, but I can't. I can't lie to my wife.

She's absolutely right.

I have been happy, and sad, and elated and miserable. I have done my best not to show her this, but apparently, I've been doing a shit job at it.

"I just want my girls' home," she said as she choked back a sob. "None of this feels right without them, Ange. I don't know how to be happy when I feel so sad. And that poor boy, he's going to be so lost. How will I be able to comfort him and be the mother he needs with a newborn? Will the girls hate us? Have they brainwashed them?"

I wanted them home too, my beautiful wife. It took everything in me not to go into the room and snatch my wife up in my arms and tell her that it will all be okay. She's just conveyed every feeling I have in a few sentences.

"Oh, Elizabeth," I heard Angie choking back a sob herself. "Let's celebrate the love you found and the life you've created. It will all work out in the end, you'll see. God is not cruel. Look how things worked out for me. I have the utmost faith it will all work out for you, too. That man of yours will never let those girls go. He will make sure Oliver feels just as much love as he gives the girls. He will bring them home and you will be a happy family again."

Instead of interrupting their moment, I walked away. I had to keep that promise Angela just made to Elizabeth. I had to fix my family. I had to find my children and bring them home. All four of them.

Coming out of my memory, I feel the wetness on my cheeks. I wipe it away quickly. I don't want Elizabeth to see me this way. She's been through enough already.

Her concern about Oliver makes me think. That poor little boy doesn't even know I'm his dad. Hell, I didn't even know I was his father. How that bitch pulled that off is something I will make her answer for. How dare she keep one of my children away from me! She knows how much family means to me.

I pick up my cell and dial Mikael. This is our normal routine. We call each other every few hours, getting updates. Right now, he's following a lead in Colorado. I don't want to sound negative, but I have a feeling that this is another dead end.

"Nothing," Mikael says as he answers the phone. No greeting, no pretenses. It's not needed between us.

"Fuck!" I can't believe this. Why are people making false claims? Don't they understand how much it takes out of us every time we hit a dead end? Don't they know I won't pay the ransom unless the tip they call in is a viable one?

"Yeah," Mikael sighs. "I get it dude. I don't know how much more I can take of this bullshit."

This is affecting Mikael almost as much as it affects us. I can hear the weariness in his voice.

"Elizabeth broke down again today," I tell him. "I don't know how much more she can take. This can't be good for her or the baby. She doesn't need this stress."

"I get it brother. I wish I could have found them by now. I don't know what else to do."

He's done so much more than I would've ever expected of him, but I don't voice that to him. I tried once, and I swear the man wanted to choke me out for it.

"Hold on," Mikael suddenly says. There's an inflection in his voice that wasn't there before. One I haven't heard in a long fucking time

"What is it?" I question, immediately on alert.

"Get here, now," Mikael says. "I found them. Get here, get on a fucking plane! Come get your family! Before they ghost us again."

"Elizabeth," I scream. I don't even care about anything else right now.

I drop the phone and go running to find her. She needs this good news now more than ever.

"Elizabeth," I call again when I don't find her in our bed.

"In here." I hear her reply from the nursery.

When I walk in, she's sitting on the floor again. This time, she's holding her stomach and a picture of our girls. Tears are running down her face, and hopefully, now they'll be happy tears and not sad ones.

"Mikael thinks he found them," I whisper. I can't get my emotions under control and by the look on Elizabeth's face, she can't either.

"Are you sure?" she whispers back. She's scared to be happy. I'm scared too. There have been too many leads that didn't pan out but if Mikael said he actually found them, I have to believe him. He wouldn't ever say something if it weren't fact.

"Yes," I reply. "I was on the phone with Mikael when suddenly he told me to get there. I have to go to Colorado. I know you can't travel. But, I have to go get them."

"Go," she says. Doesn't even have to think about it. "Bring our children home. Get them here before he arrives." She finishes that sentence while cradling her stomach where our unborn son rests.

It's so difficult for me to leave her. She's been having Braxton Hicks' contractions a lot lately and the doctor told her she needs to take it easy. Things haven't been easy at all for us, so I know with me having to go meet Mikael and retrieve our girls is hard for Elizabeth. I don't know if I'm doing the right thing by leaving her here, but I'm sure if she wasn't feeling well, she'd tell me.

It's important that I'm the one to bring our family home but if it was going to harm Elizabeth or the baby, I'd trust Mikael to bring them.

She told me to go get them and I'm not going to let her down. I'm going to bring our children home for her.

"I love you, Elizabeth. Our family is finally going to be whole again."

"I love you, too, Carter. Now get the hell out of here and go get my kids. Make sure you bring home our new addition while I take care of this one."

I run out of the room and grab my duffle bag. It's always packed. There's nothing for me to do but call my pilot and head to the airstrip. I grab the court order we obtained giving me full custody of Oliver, along with my girls. I've finally put my money to use and have everything I need so that I won't have to wait for another court to let me have them when it comes to rescuing my children and bringing all of them home once and for all. Oliver will know love just as the rest of my children do.

Three hours later, we touch down in Colorado. Mikael is on the runway waiting for me.

"They're on the move," he tells me. "Let's go, we're running out of time before they disappear again."

I quickly get into the car and we're off.

"Did you see them? Did they look healthy?" I ask. I have a ton of questions, but these are the most important ones. I don't need the answers to the others immediately, but I need these.

"Yes, I saw them on a closed-circuit camera. I couldn't tell you anything, only that it's definitely them. The picture was grainy as shit, but I know my girls and they were definitely my girls. The little boy was with them, too. Did you bring the court orders? We'll need them for the local police once we get there. They won't just hand the kids over to us. They'll take them to the hospital for evaluation, and then you'll be able to see them. I need you to try and be a little patient. I know it's hard, but I don't need you causing a ruckus and fucking this up more than it is. Can you do that? Or should I take you to the hotel until the authorities move in and take them?"

I don't answer him, I just nod my head. I know what he's saying is true. It'll be hard to keep my composure, but I'll do anything I have to do to ensure my children are safely returned to me. I can't wait to bring them home. For the first time in I don't know how long, my heart feels full.

CHAPTER THIRTY
ELIZABETH

MY FAMILY

I COULDN'T TELL Carter how I was feeling when he walked in the room. I didn't want him to put me first when his priority needs to be the girls, and that's what he would've done.

I need him to go get our children and bring them home. Our lives have been so empty without them. I need the girls here to be a part of all this. I need them here when their new little brother enters the world.

I can't say first brother, because as we recently found out, he's not. They have more blood ties to the brother they are on the run with than the one I am carrying, but, they'll never know the difference if I have anything to say about it.

I was having more contractions when Carter left, but I knew if I told him, he would've stayed behind.

It's been three days since my husband left to bring our girls home. He called while they were gone and told me it felt like they were chasing shadows. I wanted to cry, but I had to be strong for him. He's there, in the thick of things and needs strength. He doesn't need to worry about me and the baby right now when he has four other children to worry about.

Wow. That thought just floors me.

Less than a year ago, I was resigned to the fact that I'd never be a mother, and, yet, here I am, about to be a mother of five. How crazy is that?

There it goes, another contraction.

I look at the clock. It's been about seven minutes since my last one. I decide it's time to call in the reinforcements.

"Angie," I say on a gasp. Of course, as soon as she finally answers the phone, another contraction hits. "I need you. I have to go to the hospital, now."

"I'm on my way," she answers. She knew when Carter left what was happening. She argued with me that I should've told him that the contractions weren't another false alarm, but then she understood that I needed him to be there for the girls.

I gather all the things I need for the hospital. Carter was adamant we had a go bag all packed just in case, and I've never been more glad that he did. I don't think I could pack anything in the state I'm in now.

Now, it's time to call my husband. He answers on the second ring.

"Carter," I try to say calmly. "I'm going to the hospital now."

"What do you mean?" he answers. I can hear the panic in his voice. This is exactly what I didn't want.

"The baby is coming," I tell him as calmly as I can. I need him to be there, finding our girls, not worried about me.

"What do you mean he's coming?" he all but yells. "He's not supposed to be here for a few more weeks! I'm here and not there. Oh, my God, Elizabeth. I can't get there right now. The Feds have them surrounded; I should be able to get to the girls soon!"

I hear the panic in his voice and want to reassure him. At the same time, I hear the excitement that he's just about to have our girls back. I have to calm him, somehow.

"Carter," I breathe. "Listen to me. I need you to bring our family home. I've got this. Angie is on her way. I'll do my best to wait for you. I know it's early. Maybe they can stop the contractions. Get our girls. They will need you. I'm okay, I promise."

I don't know if what I'm saying is the truth, but I do know that I need him to have a clear head on his shoulders right now. One wrong thing said or done and he will flip. It may be detrimental to getting our girls back as soon as possible.

"I love you, Carter, you're doing the right thing for our family" I try to reassure him. "Bring me home our girls and I'll be sure this little one is okay."

It's the best I can do under the circumstances.

"I love you, Elizabeth." Carter sighs. "I'm so sorry I'm not there right now. It is my job to take care of my family and I'm failing you right now."

"No, Carter," I say. "You're not failing me. You're giving me my family back."

"Elizabeth." I hear so much emotion in just that one word, my name. I know this is killing him. But at the same time, I know I made the right decision when it came to not telling him how I felt when he left. He definitely would've stayed behind, and I couldn't let him do that.

"We'll be okay," I answer the question he can't ask. "I promise. Get our family; we'll be waiting on you when you return."

With that, I hang up the phone and go out front to wait for my best friend.

IT'S BEEN the longest eighteen hours of my life, but, looking down at the bundle I'm holding in my arms, it was well worth it.

Kaleb Michael Montgomery was born at seven-fifteen am,

weighing in at seven pounds, fourteen ounces. He's perfect. Absolutely perfect.

I don't think I understood the love you feel when you hold your baby in your arms. He's every bit of everything I ever wanted. He has a head of black hair and a haze of blue surrounding his eyes that the doctors tell me will go away in a few weeks. I don't know what color his eyes will be, but I can already tell you he's the spitting image of his father.

My labor wasn't easy. I wound up having to have a C-section after all was said and done. I'll be here for a few more days, but that's okay. It'll give me time to heal and a little extra time to adjust to being a mother to a newborn.

Angie was by my side throughout the entire endeavor. She's been a champ. From me trying to break her hand, to her crying right along with me when my baby was placed in my arms.

I'm sorry Carter missed all of this, but I know I did the right thing. I just hope he'll understand.

I haven't heard from my husband in two days. I don't know what's going on, and with a newborn baby and the privacy, or the lack thereof, the hospital affords you, I'm too exhausted to be upset. The nurses are in and out of the room constantly and I really wish I were home already. I know if he hasn't reached out there has to be a reason. He wouldn't just go days without talking to me. It's so not like him.

"I can't wait for you to meet your daddy," I coo to my little man lying in my arms. He's got a full belly after I nursed him and is quickly falling back asleep.

He didn't have any trouble latching on and milking me for all I'm worth, that's for sure. When I decided to nurse, the nurses told me it could take some time for a newborn to adapt. Not my son. No, the boy feasted on me like he knew exactly what he wanted. He'd make his father real damn proud, I'm sure.

"You look so much like him. I'm sorry he's not here yet, but I'm sure they'll be here soon. They're all going to love you. Your sisters are amazing. Sofia is probably going to think you're her baby. Felicia is going to try to cook for you all the time thinking you can eat just like her, and Isabella will try to turn you into a male ballerina. I can't wait for our family to be whole again."

I'm talking to my son like he understands what I'm saying. It's all hope, I know this, but I need to keep on or I'll go to a place I don't ever want to go. I have to believe my family is okay and will be here soon.

"I just know your father and your brother and sisters are going to love you," I tell my boy.

I don't hide the tears streaming down my face. No need to, no one else is here.

I sent Angie home to be with Alfie, so I'm all alone.

Right at that moment, the door opens.

I can't believe my eyes.

"Is that ours?" I hear my sweet little Isabella whisper. I want to tell her to yell, for once, as the sound of her voice is like music to my ears.

I can't believe my girls are finally home.

"Mommy!" That's my Felicia, and her scream makes my heart soar.

This is what I've been dreaming of. For them to be home when their brother arrived. They might not have been here exactly when he was born, but they're here to help us bring him home. We'll all go home together as a family.

I look up and the face of the man who had made all my dreams come true has tears running down his cheeks. He's holding Sofia and Oliver in his arms and both of them have their heads hidden in his shoulder.

"Sofia," I start. "Do you want to come meet your baby brother?" I don't know why she hasn't said anything yet, or even looked at me. It starts to worry me.

When she doesn't answer, I look into Carter's eyes again and he slightly shakes his head. We'll have to talk about this later; I'm not going to push.

"Come on girls, climb on up here," I tell them. "You, too, Oliver." It's going to take a little time to adjust to having Oliver be a part of our family, but I will try my hardest.

At my mention of his name, he turns his head to look my way. The sadness that's there is too much.

"Carter," I direct to my husband, "come and meet our son, and bring me yours so I can meet him, too."

I'm hoping by switching off, I'll be able to give Oliver a little reassurance that this is where he belongs, and my husband hasn't even met our son yet, he needs this just as much.

"I'm so sorry I wasn't here, Elizabeth," Carter says as he walks over to the bed. "I tried my hardest. The authorities weren't releasing the children to me until they contacted the courts. I tried, I promise."

So, that's why he hasn't come all the way to me yet. He thinks I'm upset he wasn't here, but that's not it at all. He was doing what he needed to do for our family and I'll never be upset about that.

"Carter," I say. "No. I'm not upset, my love. I've never been happier. You brought our children home and I brought our baby into the world. Nothing can make me happier than you all being here, right now. Please, come meet our son."

I lift Kaleb higher in my arms, as an offer to my husband to take him.

Finally, he walks over to the bed. When he places Oliver down, I gently pull him over to me. He snuggles right into my side and starts crying. Oh, poor boy, I hope you won't shed too many more tears. I can't say this out loud though, I know he just needs this.

When Carter tries to put Sofia down, she latches on to him and refuses to let go. Tears immediately come to my eyes seeing her refuse me. I can't imagine what my poor girl went through, but I won't push her.

"Sofia," Carter says lightly. "Can you please sit with Mommy Elizabeth, so I can get your baby brother?"

"I don't want to," she whispers back to him.

"Sofia, baby," I try. "I've missed you so much. Can I please give you a hug?

"No," she replies and digs deeper into Carter's shoulder.

I can't push her, I know, but goodness, my heart is shattering all over again. I decide to go a different direction.

"Isabella, Felicia, do you want to come up here and sit with me?" I ask the other two girls.

"Yes," they both scream and run up to the bed. Carter reaches down and gently lifts each girl and they immediately snuggle up to me. I see the struggle he has only being able to use one arm, but my amazing husband makes it happen.

"I've missed you all," I say as I kiss each one of their heads.

"We missed you, Mommy," Isabella replies as Felicia just starts crying.

I'm trying to hold my girls as tight as possible but being in a hospital bed and having Isabella, Felicia and Oliver surrounding me, it's not easy. Never mind the tenderness I'm still feeling from having my stomach cut open.

Oliver stopped crying, but still hasn't moved from his spot by my side. That's fine with me. He's going to need so much from all of us.

Sofia pops her head up and looks at the picture in front of her. I see the struggle in her innocent eyes. She looks like she wants to be a part of the snuggles but is still leery.

"Is that why you didn't want us?" Sofia asks as she points to Kaleb.

"Sweet girl," I tell her, "I've always wanted you. I've always wanted all of you."

Now I understand her hesitation. They were obviously led to believe we didn't want them. That's the farthest thing from the truth.

"My heart hurt every day you girls weren't here with us, I love you."

"We love you too, Mommy," Felicia says and snuggles in closer. "I knewed you didn't give us away. I told you so!" The last part she yells in Sofia's direction.

"Oh, my baby girl," I say as I look at Sofia again. "I love you so much and would never want you anywhere but with us. I'm so sorry this happened."

At that, Sofia dives out of Carters arms and lands directly on my chest and starts sobbing. Thank goodness Carter was fast enough to grab Kaleb as he must've sensed her actions coming. I don't let out the pain I feel in my body from her diving onto to me because the pain she's been feeling in her little heart is so much more important.

"I love you, Mommy," she cries harder. "I'm sorry I wasn't gooder. I promise to be better."

"Oh, my sweet girls," I cry as I hold all three of them to me the best I can. "You've always been the best things that came into my life, I'm so happy you're home."

"He's perfect," Carter whispers in awe at his newborn son. "You're perfect," he says as he looks up from our son's face and into my eyes.

"We're all perfect," I say as I look at my family, whole again with a bonus child to love and cherish.

EPILOGUE

CARTER

SIX MONTHS LATER

IT'S BEEN A GRUELING six months for our family. Elizabeth has had her hands full with Kaleb, and Oliver attached himself to her side immediately. You can clearly see Oliver was just as desperate to have a real mother as my girls had been.

All four of the children have been seeing psychologists since the day they came home. We knew they would need it, desperately. It appears it's helping them, but there are still days that are a bit rough.

It seems Andrew and Maggie tried to convince the girls that we no longer wanted them. My children were denied food and a decent place to sleep until they started to believe that we didn't want them anymore. They were also put on 'diets' as Maggie told them they were too fat to be her children. My children were never heavy but with her telling them that for so long, it took a while to get them back into a routine and being happy with themselves when it came to eating.

We also found out that Maggie never really took care of any of the children. Andrew was the only caregiver, if you could even call him that, and when I say the children, I'm also including Oliver.

Poor Oliver, we found out, was conceived through IVF. Maggie had been saving old condoms from when we were together as it had been her plan to trap me into giving her all my worth from the day she met me. She and Haley were the ones who had devised this scheme and recruited Felicia into their mix when they needed a lab to get their dirty work done. They'd been freezing my sperm in hopes of one day getting one of them knocked up.

When Maggie found Andrew as newly single after I sold her apartment, she put her plan into motion. Andrew fell for her lies, hook, line and sinker. I would feel bad for him, but he's been as much the villain as she was. When I found out the things he did to my wife, and then him running away with my children, any sympathy I would have felt for him went right out the window.

Haley was with the duo and our children when we finally caught up with all of them in Colorado. They've all since been extradited back here to New Jersey to stand trial for kidnapping our children.

Yesterday was that trial. We made sure to be there, front and center in the courtroom to watch them all get their dues.

When Felicia turned state's evidence, it was clear the trial was going to go faster than either Andrew or Maggie thought it would. Seeing the look on their faces when Maggie's supposed best friend took the stand was priceless. Felicia is the only one who seemed at all sorry for the hand she had in all of this. She never realized how truly sick and demented her friend was. It was because she had grown a conscience that Andrew and Maggie had run with the kids in the first place. She was tired of Maggie's games and was going to let everyone in on the truth at our custody hearing. She's tried to contact us to apologize for her actions, but we're not ready to hear it. I have a belief that one day she'll be able to turn her life around. She'll be doing some time, but not as much as the others.

She'll be able to start her life over on the outside in just a few years.

Haley's sentence was much worse. She was convicted of three charges of aiding and abetting in a kidnapping and will serve life in prison. She tried everything she could to get out of it, even going so far as to claim that Andrew and Maggie had kidnapped her, but the courts weren't hearing any of it.

Andrew and Maggie were both charged with three counts of first-degree kidnapping and will serve three consecutive life sentences. They'll likely never see the outside world again, and believe me when I say, the world is much better for it.

They also had all parental rights stripped from them and will never be allowed to see any of the children again. That is, unless, the children want to see them when they reach the age of majority. Honestly, I don't see that happening. I do plan to tell the four of them the truth when they are old enough to be able to handle it. I have collected all the articles and transcripts for them to read through when they are ready. I don't ever want them to think that I would make anything up., I want them to have the truth and the evidence behind it.

Today was the day we went to court to have Elizabeth officially become the legal mother of my oldest four children. She's always been their mother at heart since the day she met each one of them, but today she was made their mother by law.

At the same time, Oliver's birth records were corrected and I'm now legally his father. Without knowing, I was always his biological father, but now he'll share my last name, too.

We have a celebration planned for today with our friends and family to finally welcome our children home and to celebrate us all legally being a family.

With everything that transpired in the last year, we need this for all of us.

Mikael still hasn't forgiven himself for losing my girls though we've tried so many times to convince him it was never his fault in the first place. He's been having a very rough time with things and I need my best friend back as the carefree man I've always known him to be.

Angela will also be here with her parents and her son, Alfie. Alfie is an amazing child with a talent that I can't wait to see mature. Angie has been here all the time, helping Elizabeth with our children. Angie's parents have been the best grandparents we could ask for.

I started this journey, holding on to hope that one day I'd have everything I've ever dreamed of, and with hope and patience, I have more than I ever expected.

My family may not be perfect, but it's the perfect family for me. I never plan to ever let them go, I'll always be holding on.

ACKNOWLEDGMENTS

First and foremost, to my family for believing in me, for staying by my side, for helping me through when I was struggling, thank you. I couldn't have done this without you.

Felicia, you pushed me to follow my dream. You encouraged, yeah I use encourage loosely, more like threatened, me to finish this book and make it all a reality. Really, I don't know how people make it through life without you in it. I am a better person because of you.

Harper, I know it's difficult time right now, but you were the person who inspired me to do this. Your love, strength and perseverance is what made Carter become a stronger man. Keep rocking, woman, you've got this.

Melissa, thank you for basically dropping everything you were doing and working to help me make this all work. You flipping rock and I can't wait for you to get your groove back.

Michelle, thank you for being a voice I didn't know I needed. You knew how to make things better when I thought they were just okay.

Maggie, my editor, sorry for making you want to change your name. But it was worth it!

Andrew, Heather, and Samantha, thank you for keeping me

liquored up through some difficult writing scenes. And for keeping my corner of the bar empty on Friday nights so I can continue to rock out the words.

My pre-readers, you ladies all rock! Your excitement and encouragement kept me stronger. Sorry you had to wait so long for the last few chapters.... nah, I'm not.

An epic thanks goes out to my son for putting up with my shit. I know I spent many a cranky day trying to work out this plot and without you, I couldn't have done it. You are my world and I couldn't be the person I am without you!

ABOUT THE AUTHOR

KiKi Malone has dreamed of writing for many years. Through many challenges, she's finally decided to put everything aside and make her dreams a reality. She's been an active part of the reading community for years and finally had the courage to bring her own stories to life.

With the help and support of her family and friends, she strives to bring you the best of herself and her fictional worlds.

When KiKi isn't dreaming and writing, she's working her day job scrambling numbers together, creating elaborate spreadsheets and reports.

She loves reading, relaxing, her cats, and the winter. There's nothing better in her world that cuddling up in the corner of the couch with a hot cup of coffee, her blanket, her cats, and a good book.

KiKi likes to mix it up, writing both romance and drama. Sometimes she'll mix it all up together and sometimes, she'll just give you one or the other.

Some of KiKi's works are written from vivid dreams of things that never happened, yet others have some real life mixed in to bring some reality to her stories.

KiKi is a mother and it's been the best and most rewarding job title she's ever held.

KiKi's first book, Holding On, brought something out of her she could only dream of. And that was to finally finish something she started.